The acolyte reached for Kane's right wrist

Kane drew back his arm before the man could touch him; his Sin Eater was hidden there, the blaster disguised by the folds of his jacket.

"It is right to feel fear on first sacrifice, but no harm will come to you," the acolyte said gently.

"Sorry." Kane shook his head. "Just have a thing about needles." He held out his left arm—the one without the hidden blaster—pulling back the sleeve. "Go ahead."

The acolyte brought the cup and needle down close to Kane's wrist and instructed him to chant a prayer to the stone god. Kane recited the words he'd heard at the congregation a few days before, when he and Brigid had enlisted in this ragtag pilgrimage.

Kane hated the chant, but he couldn't draw attention to himself—not until he and Brigid had found out exactly what was going on here.

Other titles in this series:

Armageddon Axis	Skull Throne
Wreath of Fire	Satan's Seed
Shadow Scourge	Dark Goddess
Hell Rising	Grailstone Gambit
Doom Dynasty	Ghostwalk
Tigers of Heaven	Pantheon of Vengeance
Purgatory Road	Death Cry
Sargasso Plunder	Serpent's Tooth
Tomb of Time	Shadow Box
Prodigal Chalice	Janus Trap
Devil in the Moon	Warlord of the Pit
Dragoneye	Reality Echo
Far Empire	Infinity Breach
Equinox Zero	Oblivion Stone
Talon and Fang	Distortion Offensive
Sea of Plague	Cradle of Destiny
Awakening	Scarlet Dream
Mad God's Wrath	Truth Engine
Sun Lord	Infestation Cubed
Mask of the Sphinx	Planet Hate
Uluru Destiny	Dragon City
Evil Abyss	God War
Children of the Serpent	Genesis Sinister
Successors	Savage Dawn
Cerberus Storm	Sorrow Space
Refuge	Immortal Twilight
Rim of the World	Cosmic Rift
Lords of the Deep	Necropolis
Hydra's Ring	Shadow Born
Closing the Cosmic Eye	Judgment Plague

James Axler
Outlanders®

390750477723538

ERMINAL WHITE

A GOLD EAGLE BOOK FROM
W⊕RLDWIDE®

TORONTO • NEW YORK • LONDON
AMSTERDAM • PARIS • SYDNEY • HAMBURG
STOCKHOLM • ATHENS • TOKYO • MILAN
MADRID • WARSAW • BUDAPEST • AUCKLAND

Recycling programs
for this product may
not exist in your area.

First edition February 2015

ISBN-13: 978-0-373-63885-7

Terminal White

Copyright © 2015 by Worldwide Library

Special thanks to Rik Hoskin for his contribution to this work.

By indirections find directions out.
>   —William Shakespeare,
>   *Hamlet*, 1564–1616

The Road to Outlands—
From Secret Government Files to the Future

Almost two hundred years after the global holocaust, Kane, a former Magistrate of Cobaltville, often thought the world had been lucky to survive at all after a nuclear device detonated in the Russian embassy in Washington, DC. The aftermath—forever known as skydark—reshaped continents and turned civilization into ashes.

Nearly depopulated, America became the Deathlands— poisoned by radiation, home to chaos and mutated life forms. Feudal rule reappeared in the form of baronies, while remote outposts clung to a brutish existence.

What eventually helped shape this wasteland were the redoubts, the secret preholocaust military installations with stores of weapons, and the home of gateways, the locational matter-transfer facilities. Some of the redoubts hid clues that had once fed wild theories of government cover-ups and alien visitations.

Rearmed from redoubt stockpiles, the barons consolidated their power and reclaimed technology for the villes. Their power, supported by some invisible authority, extended beyond their fortified walls to what was now called the Outlands. It was here that the rootstock of humanity survived, living with hellzones and chemical storms, hounded by Magistrates.

In the villes, rigid laws were enforced—to atone for the sins of the past and prepare the way for a better future. That was the barons' public credo and their right-to-rule.

Kane, along with friend and fellow Magistrate Grant, had upheld that claim until a fateful Outlands expedition. A displaced piece of technology…a question to a keeper of the archives…a vague clue about alien masters—and their world shifted radically. Suddenly, Brigid Baptiste, the archivist, faced summary execution, and Grant a quick termination. For Kane there was forgiveness if he pledged his unquestioning allegiance to Baron Cobalt and his unknown masters and abandoned his friends.

But that allegiance would make him support a mysterious and alien power and deny loyalty and friends. Then what else was there?

Kane had been brought up solely to serve the ville. Brigid's only link with her family was her mother's red-gold hair, green eyes and supple form. Grant's clues to his lineage were his ebony skin and powerful physique. But Domi, she of the white hair, was an Outlander pressed into sexual servitude in Cobaltville. She at least knew her roots and was a reminder to the exiles that the outcasts belonged in the human family.

Parents, friends, community—the very rootedness of humanity was denied. With no continuity, there was no forward momentum to the future. And that was the crux—when Kane began to wonder if there was a future.

For Kane, it wouldn't do. So the only way was out—way, way out.

After their escape, they found shelter at the forgotten Cerberus redoubt headed by Lakesh, a scientist, Cobaltville's head archivist, and secret opponent of the barons.

With their past turned into a lie, their future threatened, only one thing was left to give meaning to the outcasts. The hunger for freedom, the will to resist the hostile influences. And perhaps, by opposing, end them.

Designated Task #012: Sex.

All residents of Ioville are expected to engage in sexual congress four times a month. Partners are selected by strict rotation to increase the chances of pregnancy. Partners are provided blind each session, and while the subject is given no choice over whom, the longevity of the operation and health of the participants are constantly assessed.

Like all functions in Ioville, the sex act is methodical and devoid of emotional resonance. It is a means to an end: the creation of children to people the ville in subsequent years. The birthrate is high, due to the strict methods employed.

My ovulation rhythms have not been fully recorded yet, which means I have yet to be slotted into the rotation. Here in Ioville no act is wasted.

Grand nurseries have been created to house the youngest of the newborns while their parents continue to perform their designated tasks. The nurseries look after the well-being and education of the children through to age eleven, at which point the young are redesignated as adults and are welcomed into the workforce, where they will be assigned their tasks. With this redesignation they are expected to engage in Designated Task #012.

—*From the journal of Citizen 619F.*

Chapter 1

The bastard child of a thousand deluded devotees hurtled toward Kane across the flame-lit temple, an unearthly howl issuing from its gaping wound of a mouth.

Kane's Sin Eater appeared in his hand, the hidden handblaster materializing from its forearm holster. The former Magistrate began blasting a stream of 9 mm titanium-shelled bullets at the eight-foot-tall monster as it charged across the slate floor at him. Its composite arms reached out and batted the bullets aside like a tumble of dislodged shale flickering through the air, lines of blood rippling between each loose stone. And then the creature reached for Kane as the horrified pilgrims watched, its stony arm distending and parting as it grasped for Kane's weapon.

How do I get myself into these jams? Kane wondered as that inhuman arm reached for the barrel of his blaster.

Eighty-six minutes earlier.

THE TOWER COULD be seen from miles away, its red eye shining even through the pouring rain that darkened the skies.

"The last time I was here," Brigid Baptiste explained, "this whole place was just a field of beets."

Kane pushed apart the canvas covers of the transport wag with his hands and peered out at the road. The

canvas was heavy from the rain, and Kane felt a wash
of rainwater run over his hand and down his arm as he
adjusted the flaps to see.

They were bumping along a gravel road that was perfectly straight and was bordered on either side by a line
of carefully matched stones placed at roughly twelve-
foot intervals. Carved from slate, each stone was disc-
like and flat like a roof tile, and each measured eight feet
in height, its base sunken into the ground. The gray slate
had turned black with the rainwater, and the curtain of
rain continued to fall, drenching the road, the wag, the
standing stones and everything else in its chilling torrent. Beyond those stones were meadows of wildflowers,
their colors vibrant even now, seen through the morning shower. To Kane, a trained Magistrate, the stones
looked like sentries, guarding the pathway up to their
destination, the red-eyed tower.

"Never much liked beets," Kane muttered as the rugged transport jounced along the road, the shushing noise
of the gravel and the rain mingling to a roar as loud as
a waterfall.

Kane was a clean-shaven, muscular man in his early
thirties, with steel-gray eyes and short dark hair. He
stood an inch over six feet tall and there was something
of the wolf about him, not only because of his build but
also because of the way his eyes took in everything
and the way he always seemed to be alone no matter
the company he was in. He was both a pack leader and
a loner, just like the strongest wolf.

Kane's eyes were restlessly observant, drinking in
every detail of the journey and his fellow passengers—
thirty-one in all, including himself and Brigid, crammed
into the bus-like back of the wagon. Kane had once been
a Magistrate for Cobaltville, a type of law-enforcer who

followed the baron's dictates, until he became disillusioned with the regime and embroiled in a conspiracy that had led to his expulsion from the ville. Since then, Kane had hooked up with Cerberus, an organization dedicated to the protection of humankind from outside forces. It was another kind of law enforcement, to be sure, but one predicated on a more noble foundation. It was as a Cerberus exile that Kane had faced rogue gods and deranged aliens—and sometimes both at once—and had traveled across the globe and beyond to protect his fellow man. Right now, that role had brought Kane to the arable farmlands of the north, where he was riding in the back of the scratch-built transport wagon along with his partner, Brigid Baptiste, and twenty-nine other pilgrims, heading for one of the most sacred sites in North America.

Kane knew where he was going, even if he had not visited before. It was a temple, which—in Kane's experience—boiled down to being another way for someone to control someone else for their own personal gain. He had enforced that system when he had been a Magistrate, enforced the iron will of Baron Cobalt, turning a blind eye to the inequalities and cruelties that that system reinforced. But now the nine barons were gone and their baronies were crumbling, struggling to continue without them, the rot slowly but surely eating them up from within. In time, Kane thought, the whole system would fall by the wayside—and he considered it his job to make sure that what came next wasn't simply more of the same.

Brigid sat on the bench seat beside Kane, watching the road and the sights beyond as the wag continued its slow journey along the recently laid track. She was a slim, beautiful woman in her late twenties, with pale skin and a mane of red-gold hair like dancing flames. Her eyes were the bewitching green of cut emeralds. She had a high forehead that suggested intelligence, and full lips that promised a more passionate aspect. In reality, Brigid had both of these qualities and many more besides. But she had one quality that was as rare as it was useful—an eidetic memory, the ability to perfectly remember anything she had seen, even just for an instant. She too had been raised in Cobaltville, working as an archivist in the Historical Division until she had stumbled upon the same conspiracy as Kane, a conspiracy at the heart of which was the intention of alien beings to subjugate humankind and destroy all independence and free will. Like Kane, Brigid had been expelled from the ville and declared an Outlander by its ruling baron, a human-alien hybrid called Baron Cobalt. Along with Kane's Magistrate partner Grant, Brigid had subsequently been recruited into the Cerberus organization.

Like the other adherents on the transport, Brigid and Kane were dressed in ordinary clothes that suggested a farming background. Kane wore a beaten brown leather jacket, patched at the elbows, over a checkered shirt, with dark pants and scuffed work boots that had seen better days. Brigid wore a leather jacket in a lighter shade of brown, an oversize man's shirt and sleeveless T-shirt, with combat pants and hard-wearing boots. Beneath both of their outfits, the two Cerberus warriors wore shadow suits—skintight environment suits that regulated the wearer's temperature as well as providing protection from blunt trauma and environmental threats. The shadow suits were perfectly hidden under their ragged clothes; no one on the transport would suspect they were in the presence of two highly efficient warriors.

The other people in the transport looked to be mostly rural types. Several, however, had dressed in what were obviously their finest clothes; two men wearing dark wool suits, a woman in a rose-pink floor-length dress with a matching wide-brimmed hat resting on her lap where she sat near the open rear of the wagon. Brigid guessed that those three saw this pilgrimage a little like attending church way back before the nukecaust, the way parishioners would wear their "Sunday finest" to show their respect for the Lord.

"I miss my George so much," the woman with the hat was telling her bench mate in a low voice. "He walked into that storm out west two years ago and never returned."

"That storm has taken a lot of people," her companion sympathized. "'Cause of the nukecaust, they say it might never blow itself out."

There were several other figures inside the bus-like transport, too, and all were dressed in matching robes that looked similar to a monk's habit. The robes were made from a rough, fustian material and featured a hood that could be drawn down over the head to hang low over the face, along with a crimson shield-like insignia sewn over the right breast. The shield insignia haunted Kane—it was eerily similar to the shield he had worn when he had been a Magistrate for Cobaltville, years before. Two similarly dressed adherents were sitting up front, one of them working the driving controls while the other had used a map to give directions until they'd reached this stone-lined road that led solely to their final destination. Kane and Brigid had met these people before—firewalkers, Brigid had dubbed them, because of their seeming invulnerability when under a self-imposed trancelike state of meditation. Whether the firewalkers could still perform such superhuman feats now, with their leader—an alien prince called Ullikummis—dead, was unknown to the Cerberus teammates at this moment. As Kane might have said in his lighter moments, that only added to the fun.

Something big was happening, the Cerberus teammates knew. Excited rumors had been buzzing in the shadowy community of stone adherents that was strung across the continent in patches. There was talk that Ullikummis walked again.

They were in a place that the old maps called Saskatchewan in a country called Canada. If it had a new name, Kane had never bothered to learn it—his journeys across the globe on behalf of the Cerberus organization left him with little time to learn local customs or enjoy the sights. Rather, he and his Cerberus allies seemed to spend most of their time running headlong into danger, as arrows, bullets and honest-to-goodness death rays blasted all about them. Somehow, no matter the odds, the field personnel had always survived, thanks in part to their own phenomenal skills and in part to their backup, based in the redoubt in the Bitterroot Mountains in Montana.

There was a palpable air of excitement in the pilgrims' rugged transport now. The passengers had been gathered from a specified pickup point where they had been instructed to wait after being recruited at one of the numerous public sermons given by the stone adherents.

The wag was twenty feet long, with a wire frame over which strips of canvas had been laid to protect the travelers from the icy torrent that fell from the skies. The vehicle was unpainted, leaving the metallic frame gleaming darkly, and it featured seven wheels including a rear-mounted steering assist to tackle the rougher ground around the worship site. In the two hundred years since the nukecaust, the paved roads had fallen into disrepair, and sites like the one this wag was heading toward were poorly served by existing communications links. As Brigid had pointed out, the last time she had been here it had been a farmer's field—and that had been less than eighteen months ago.

Brakes groaned as the transport pulled to a halt. Up ahead, Kane could see that the gravel road became wider, the standing stones funneling outward to leave a broad, circular expanse of gravel in the center of which was the towering structure with the red eye. The tower was roughly three or four stories—or thirty-five feet—high and built with straight, slightly rounded sides as if some baton had been shoved into the soil. It was phallic, Kane thought, but that didn't come as any surprise—he had seen plenty of temples to the gods, and the phallus was a recurring theme. The baton-like structure was carved from dark stone like the standing stones, while dotted along its sides were streaks of polished redorange glass. A single red glass circle had been placed close to the tower's pinnacle, like a mighty eye staring down on the people below. This "eye" faced into the sun, drawing its rays inside the structure itself.

Kane recognized that design, too—it drew from the familiar pattern used in the nine baronies, the red circle atop the Administration Monolith that gave the citizens the impression that they were being watched at all times. One of the more insidious ways in which the stone adherents of Ullikummis operated was to take the familiar iconography of the baronies and twist it to their own ends—hence the cycloptic eye in the tower and the use of the breast badge that was familiar to anyone who had seen a Magistrate uniform.

"Somebody's gone to a lot of trouble to make this place seem special," Kane muttered to Brigid as he let the gap in the canvas slip closed again.

At the same time, one of the robed adherents addressed the group from the rear of the wag, close to the open gate at which passengers embarked and debarked, speaking in a bold voice. "Chosen of stone, we walk from here," he explained, "to truly appreciate the majesty of his birthplace, as is the will of the infinite lord."

"Will, my ass," Kane muttered from the side of his mouth as he and Brigid joined the other passengers, filing toward the open rear of the stopped vehicle.

A moment later, the first of the pilgrims stepped from the transport, dropping down to the rain-wet gravel a few feet below. In less than a minute, everyone had disembarked from the wagon, and they clustered on the gravel in the lee of the baton-like tower, Kane and Brigid among them. The group were excited but they adopted a reverential silence as they strode across the ground before the grand structure, staring up at it in awe. To them, this was a place of incredible religious significance— the birthplace of Ullikummis, their savior, their god.

To all, that is, except for Kane and Brigid, of course; they were here to scope out the site and see whether something dangerous was building here, well out of sight of the crumbling baronies that had split North America into nine territories of harsh and subtle control. They had faced Ullikummis before—fought him and stopped him before he could take over the world.

A little over a year ago, a large meteor had crash-landed here. From within that meteor had emerged Ullikummis, a member of an alien race of creatures called the Annunaki who had posed as gods several millennia ago, and deceived humankind into worshipping them.

Ullikummis had been an outcast of his own people, imprisoned in the meteor and flung into space, only to return five thousand years later and rain havoc on the world in his fury at what had been done to him. When he reappeared, Ullikummis had sown the seeds of a new religion, one dedicated to his worship and that granted its users incredible—almost supernatural—control of their physical bodies. But he had been opposed by the brave warriors of Cerberus, who had seen the worst that the Annunaki race was capable of, and realized the wicked intentions at the heart of the stone god's plans. In retaliation, Ullikummis had almost destroyed the Cerberus organization, infiltrating their headquarters and brainwashing several of their number, including Brigid Baptiste. However, the monster had finally been destroyed by Kane, thrown into the sun using a teleportational rig.

Although Ullikummis had been defeated, his worshippers continued to blindly follow his teachings, creating a new and growing cult in his name. Kane and Brigid had initially been dispatched to check the site of the fallen meteor prison, but on discovering it was now an impenetrable and highly guarded temple dedicated to Ullikummis the stone god, they had gone undercover, infiltrating the congregation at a mass in his name before joining this pilgrimage to the site itself.

"Roundabout way to see a hunk of space rock," Kane grumbled to Brigid as they joined the others on the walk to the temple's entry itself.

"It's not as if we had anything better to do," Brigid replied, wiping aside a sodden curl of flame-red hair.

Kane had no answer to that. He just tried to resist the urge to check that he was still armed.

More adherents waited at the doors, dressed in the familiar robes of coarse fabric, red shield on the breast, hoods up against the chill and rain. Beyond them, a tall archway led into the tower itself, open but set deep into the structure so that the punishing rain would not go straight inside. There were other pilgrims, too, another smaller group just entering the grand archway, their own transport parked up to the side of the gravel pen. Several of the group stopped before the archway and knelt, bowing so that they touched their foreheads to the ground in a gesture of absolute supplication.

Kane and Brigid were ushered along with the rest of their party, making their way toward the arch. "Think we ought to bow?" Kane asked, whispering the question from the side of his mouth.

Brigid didn't reply, but instead dropped to her knees in the wet gravel and began pleading to the stone god to help her and the world he so loved. Kane was impressed—if he didn't know better, he'd be convinced she was buying into this stone cult nonsense, hook, line and sinker.

They passed through the archway and entered a lobby-like area, which opened out into the main chamber of the tower. The lobby was eight paces end to end, but ran entirely around the base of the tower in a complete circuit. It was divided from the main chamber by thick stone pillars, rough-surfaced and tightly packed so that only a sliver of the main room could be seen through them. The pillars were so closely spaced that only one or two people could pass between them into the main chamber at any one time, which meant that the lobby momentarily became a bottleneck as the group of thirty-one passed through.

Within, the tower felt warm after the icy rain, and Kane took a moment just to breathe in the air. It had a scent to it, a trace of burning, like toast left too long under the grill.

It was darker inside, too, even after the dullness of the overcast day. The tower had no formal windows, only ragged lines cut into the external walls. Each of these lines had been filled with red-orange glass, giving a kind of fiery half-light to the interior. It felt a little like stepping into a volcano. Kane jolted, recognizing the quality of that light: when Ullikummis had penetrated Cerberus's defences and taken control of their headquarters, he had reshaped it into something he had dubbed Life Camp Zero, a cross between a prison and a reeducation center. The walls of the Cerberus redoubt had been masked by living rock, the light fixtures replaced with bubbles of volcanic fire, casting everything in a hot orange glow. This place—this *temple*—had that same glow. It disoriented Kane for a moment—he had been a prisoner in Life Camp Zero, had suffered terribly at the hands of his jailers before ultimately turning the tables and killing them. He didn't think much about that period of his life—when he had absorbed an obedience stone into his body and momentarily sacrificed his independence to Ullikummis so that he could escape.

Brigid, too, had sacrificed her independence to Ullikummis, though for her it was involuntary. Ullikummis had held her in a cell in a sea fortress called Bensalem, where he had twisted her thought processes, brainwashing her into seeing things in a new and inhuman way—the way of the Annunaki. Brigid's senses had been overwhelmed with the psychic onslaught and she had finally given up, hiding her real personality in a higher plane of consciousness and letting her body be possessed by her wicked Annunaki self—an abomination called Brigid Haight. The evil she had committed as Haight still haunted her, even though she had had no control of her actions.

"Kane, you've stopped," Brigid said quietly, pushing her hand gently against her partner's back.

Kane shook his head. "Sorry, I was miles away," he admitted. "The light kind of…brings it all back."

Brigid nodded once in understanding. "The stone lord is still with us," she said, raising her voice so that the people around her could hear. No matter how disconcerting this experience was, she and Kane had to remember that they were here undercover; that for all intents and purposes, they were just two more pilgrims hoping to find salvation in the wisdom of the stone god.

A moment later, the Cerberus warriors had moved past the pillars and into the depths of the temple. The fiery glow was brighter here, the light shimmering a little as if it were alive—an illusion from the passing clouds and the rain on the slivers of red glass.

The interior chamber was circular and of moderate but impressive size, like a midsize conference room or a small theater, able to hold perhaps eighty people before it felt crowded. Just now, Kane estimated, there were fifty pilgrims here, plus a half-dozen acolytes, easily identifiable by their robes and red insignias. However, the room's proportions seemed more impressive because it stretched all the way up through to the height of the tower, rising thirty-five feet into the air in a grand column, where the giant red eye glared outward and in, casting a red oval disc across a spot on the floor. That red spot highlighted a huge brown rock standing in the very center of the chamber. The rock was almost circular but it had split down the middle to reveal a hollow interior, the two sides pulled apart by incredible force. The rock was as large as a Sherman tank, and where

Kane could see the interior he saw that the walls were thick, despite its hollow center. This had been the prison cell of Ullikummis, launched into space millennia ago, returning to Earth less than two years ago and bringing its sole prisoner back home. The rock was surrounded by a circle of hard-packed earth, beyond which the floor had been paved with large slabs of slate.

Across to one side stood a caldron pit, blistering with flames, their heat emanating throughout the room.

There was one other item in this central chamber besides the caldron and the rock, and it transfixed Brigid Baptiste from the moment she walked through the gap in the pillars. It was an exquisitely carved alabaster statue of a woman, a third again life-size, standing with arms outstretched as though to welcome someone into a hug. The woman was slim and tall, with long legs and a cloak over her shoulders that draped down past her knees. She wore a skintight catsuit that, in reality, would have hugged every curve of her svelte, athletic form. The catsuit had been painted in a glossy black, like a beetle's wing. The face had been left unpainted, the white alabaster shining pink in the glow from the fire windows, but the lion's mane of hair had been daubed with color— a rich red-gold like a halo of living flames.

Brigid gasped as she saw the statue. "Kane, look!" she said.

Kane turned, eyeing the statue in admiration.

"It's Haight," Brigid whispered. "It's…me."

Designated Task #004: Manufacturing.

Like all villes, manufacturing is performed here at Epsilon Level. I have been assigned to a work crew of twenty people who perform the repetitive tasks of sorting, assembling and checking the parts necessary for the construction of the Sandcats. The Sandcats are sprayed white, better to camouflage them in the snow, and their tracks are rigorously tested to ensure they have sufficient grip for the treacherous icy conditions that exist beyond the ville walls.

Each Sandcat is armed with the standard array of twin USMG-73 heavy machine guns set in a blister turret above the blocky body of the vehicle itself. These guns are automated, with a linked positronic brain connecting engine to guns—this way, the engine may steer in a direction advantageous to combat as well as pursuit or retreat.

The workshop itself is noisy with the sounds of construction, welding, sifting and hammering that make up the assembling of the vehicles. No chatter is permitted from the shop floor, so I know my fellow workers only by sight rather than by name. We share occasional nods when our eyes meet, but most citizens are diligent in their work and have no cause to look up except during the brief transition periods when their shift begins and ends. At these moments, I observe my fellow workers with quiet admiration, proud of what we have achieved in a given shift.

Each shift is nine hours in total with three designated breaks. Breaks are staggered across the workforce so that the production line never ceases, and no two members of the production line are assigned a break at the same time. The three breaks are fifteen, twenty and fifteen minutes, the two shorter breaks arranged during the top and tail of the day. In these breaks, workers are provided with nutrition and water, and are allowed a comfort break of no more than four minutes. Self-decontamination is expected after any comfort break.

The rest area is slight, a small "room" shielded from the main floor of the factory by low barricades, effectively penning the worker in from the shop floor. The noise of the factory is immense in these moments, when one is trying to relax and imbibe sufficient nutrients to continue the important task.

Citizens travel to and from the factory via trolleybus or on foot, depending on the location of their residence and on the location of their designated activities before or after their shift. For two evenings of each week I am assigned to Designated Task #011—cleaning duties— after my shift, which take an additional 3.7 hours. This is for the good of the ville. Post-shift on other days, I have a rota of tasks to attend to, including Designated Tasks #008, #012 and #013.

—From the journal of Citizen 619F.

Chapter 2

From warrior to traitor to legend—Brigid could barely process the path her life had taken. To find her effigy here, standing beside the rock that had brought these people's god to Earth, was unsettling. She had worked for Ullikummis, acting as his "hand in the darkness" while he made a power grab to revive his mother, Ninlil, and gain control of the Annunaki pantheon. Brigid had kidnapped the hybrid child Quav, within whom the genetic template for Ninlil resided, betraying and almost killing her trusted friends in the process. She had even shot Kane, and only his shadow suit coupled with a rejuvenating pool called the Chalice of Rebirth had ensured his survival. It had been a dark time for Brigid, darker than she could bear. Her essence, her personality—even the thing that some religions might call her soul—had hidden away from the whole debacle, and had only been released when a trigger had been engaged—a trigger that had acted almost as a rebirth for Brigid Baptiste herself. So to find her dark aspect, the creature called Brigid Haight, worshipped here as some kind of—what?—demigoddess, was unnerving.

Brigid felt the tug of Kane's hand on her arm, turned to see his stern face. "Come on, Baptiste," he encouraged in a low voice, "people'll notice if you're not careful."

"People will notice," Brigid repeated, barely mouthing the words. What a turn of events that would be—for all these believers to suddenly learn that their demigoddess, the dark hand of the stone god himself, was walking among them.

Brigid turned away from the statue, away from its idealized representation of her own stunning appearance.

Ahead, the devotees were being encouraged to walk past the broken meteor—"the cradle of the stone god," as the acolytes called it—and show reverence and appreciation for his mighty works and promised utopia. Everyone who passed reached out to touch the rock, some trembling and weeping as they did so. Kane found the displays of emotion disturbing—he had fought Ullikummis, knew him to be nothing but an inhuman monster subjugating mankind to use for his own whims. And yet, his message had somehow taken root in the public imagination, was growing even now, many months on from the death of the monster himself. The people craved something—release from the fear that the fall of the baronies had brought, fear that the world could devolve once more into the post-nukecaust chaos that had become known as the Deathlands era. Then, survival was everything, and the strong preyed on the weak, humans turned into little more than animals—predatory, vicious animals. The Program of Unification had changed all that, a design for living that had fostered new openness and trust between people, that had created the safe havens of the nine villes that had dominated and controlled North America. The barons had brought control, often crushing and dictatorial, but a control that people desired and needed to function and to advance after those dark years. When the barons had resigned, leaving their baronies to assume their true forms as Annunaki space gods, they had left a power vacuum that was proving hard to fill. People were scared—and this, this broken rock prison with all its connotations of evil and subjugation, appealed to that fear, quelled it in a way Kane could barely comprehend.

Kane and Brigid were next to be ushered past the rock, waiting a moment as the preceding pilgrim—a woman with tangled blond hair and a baby bump—wailed at its hollow chamber, the place where Ullikummis had waited five thousand years in cramped imprisonment. "Save us," she cried. "Show us the glory of your utopia."

Kane bit his tongue in disgust. Then he and Brigid stepped up to the meteor, their expressions fixed and solemn. There were two ideograms carved high on the surface of the boulder. Together they read Son Of Enlil. Enlil was the cruellest of the Annunaki royal family, and his rebirth in modern times had caused Kane and his Cerberus teammates untold hours of grief. That he had a son who'd returned to challenge him for his throne had been like a never-ending nightmare that only got worse and worse.

Kane placed his hand against the stone and bowed his head. He thought of how he had ultimately thrown Ullikummis into the sun, watched as his stone body hurtled toward the fiery ball in space, drawn by the sun's gravity, burned up forever. "Warm our hearts, stone god," Kane said aloud, and around him the acolytes and other pilgrims nodded and smiled in agreement at the seemingly innocuous sentiment. And burn in hell, Kane added in his mind.

Brigid took Kane's place a moment later, staring at the rock. She had seen it before, over a year ago, shortly after it had landed here. Back then, this area had been an arable farmer's field, surrounded by more of the same. The fields had been mostly root vegetables, with a simple farmhouse located amid them, close to the lone road. The house was destroyed now, the fields turned over to wildflowers, and this site—this abomination—had sprung up in place of the fallen meteor in the field. It sickened her—this failing by man to need leadership, to almost desire subjugation. Maybe the barons had been right all along.

Brigid stepped away, and her place was taken by two more pilgrims who pawed lovingly at the rock, this cradle of their stone god.

After conversing with the rock, each pilgrim was led to an enclosed space behind it. Kane and Brigid entered this area, not knowing what to expect. Two robed acolytes spoke to them in soft tones as they led them through a drawn curtain colored black like the wet slate. Behind this sat several simple desks and chairs, each of which was sectioned off by another short curtain that hung down only as low as a man's waist. They were a little like the voting booths found in many twenty-first-century democracies. Kane was ushered behind one of the curtains with the acolyte while Brigid was directed to the desk next to it.

Once there, the robed acolyte—a young man with wide-set eyes and a shaven head—sat before Kane and addressed him in a calming, quiet tone. "Now you are expected to give life to god," he said, reeling off the words as if they were entirely normal. "Have you been made aware of what this entails?"

Kane shook his head. "I must've missed that sermon."

"No matter," the robed man said gently. "It is a very simple matter." He opened a small box located on the table—roughly the size of a travel sewing kit—and drew out an eight-inch-long needle along with something that reminded Kane of a shot glass. "We take a few drops of your blood—three or four is enough—which is your sacrifice to the stone god."

Kane eyed the needle warily. "Is that thing clean?" he asked.

"We sterilize the sacrificial lances after each use," the stone acolyte confirmed. "For the stone is clean and thus cleanliness is a sign of god."

Kane nodded. "Okay. What do you need me to do?"

The acolyte drew the curtain across the little chamber for their privacy, then reached for Kane's right wrist. Kane drew back his arm before the man could touch him; his Sin Eater was hidden there, disguised by the folds of the jacket.

"It is right to feel fear on first sacrifice, but no harm will come to you," the acolyte soothed gently.

"Sorry," Kane said, shaking his head. "Just have a thing about needles." He held out his left arm—the one without the hidden blaster—pulling back the sleeve. "Go ahead."

The acolyte brought the cup and needle down close to Kane's wrist and instructed him to chant a prayer to the stone god. Kane recited the words he had heard at the congregation a few days before, when he and Brigid had enlisted in this ragtag pilgrimage.

"Ullikummis, lord of stone, grant me the presence of mind to recognize your works, and to embrace utopia when it descends upon us, healing all of mankind and washing away the sins of the past."

The acolyte pricked Kane's thumb with the needle and squeezed four droplets of blood from it.

"The bedrock of the world has slipped, but it can

be corrected in time. Love shared, blessings shared, stone laid."

Kane hated the chant but he couldn't draw attention to himself—not until he and Brigid had found out exactly what was going on here.

IN THE BOOTH beside Kane's, Brigid was going through an identical ritual, giving three drops of blood as she recited the prayer to Ullikummis.

Another visitor entered the third curtained booth, performing the same rite under the direction of another acolyte, and that same rite was repeated for every visitor, forty-seven people giving just a few drops of blood to show their devotion to their lord.

This blood was then removed and each little sample was added to a large chalice carved of stone that had been left rough around its edges. By the time Kane and Brigid emerged from the booths, the chalice was almost full to the brim, topped up no doubt by blood from the acolytes themselves. Three robed acolytes stood behind the stone chalice while the others manning the sacrifice booths stepped out to add their contents to the mix.

"Any idea where this is going?" Kane whispered to Brigid as they walked out of the booths and made their way toward the caldron pit where the other pilgrims were amassing.

Brigid put a hand up to disguise her mouth as she replied. "Probably just mumbo-jumbo," she whispered back.

Kane didn't like that "probably"—it rankled on him like a bad tooth.

The last pilgrim's blood was added to the chalice, and then the lead acolyte, a man Kane thought of as their leader, held the chalice aloft and began to speak in a loud, portentous tone. "Witness," he said. "You have all given of your lives so that the stone god may rise again. Everyone who has visited this sacred place, the cradle where god was born—everyone has given of themselves and their blood, a thousand devotees who would shed their own blood to make the world a better place. You have all given of yourselves to fuel his self. You have all given your love that his love might walk here among us today."

Beside the leader, two of the robed acolytes began using shovels to sift through a pile of pebbles behind them. Kane had not noticed that before, hidden as it was behind the flaming pit, and for a moment he mistook it for coal or a similar fuel that might be used to stoke the fire. But then he realized—with a sinking feeling—what those stones were. While he was on Earth, Ullikummis had budded "stone seeds" from his own body—hundreds, perhaps thousands of the things had gone into circulation. The stones had different properties but they each connected the user to Ullikummis in some way. For many, the stones were simply used to generate obedience, lodging under their skin and driving away all thoughts but those that Ullikummis himself planted within a victim's mind. For others, the ones whom Brigid had dubbed firewalkers, the stones granted limited periods of invulnerability, turning their own flesh into the stone hide of their master.

The strange stones were a tie to Ullikummis, and Cerberus scientists had learned that they were powered—brought to life, if you will—by the iron content in a person's blood. However, the stones had lost their influence once Ullikummis had been dispatched from the Earth, and the Cerberus personnel had speculated that they may work on a proximity basis as well as needing the ferrous content to fuel them.

Suddenly, Kane saw where this oddball ceremony was leading—and his stomach twisted in knots as the realization dawned. Surely they could not revive Ullikummis through his depowered stones. That could not be done—could it?

Kane and Brigid watched as two great heaps of stones were shoveled into the caldron pit, spitting out sparks as the flames touched them. As one, the crowd of pilgrims stepped back, watching in awe as the flames lit the sacred temple, turning the walls a richer shade of orange.

Then the senior acolyte stepped forward, his arms straight, holding the chalice aloft in both hands. "Our love is rock," he chanted, "and rock never breaks." Then he tipped the scarlet contents of the chalice into the flaming pit, moving the stone cup in a circular motion, draining it of its blood. The flames were doused in places as the liquid struck, and a hissing sound echoed through the temple as steam billowed from the caldron pit.

For a moment nothing happened; the flames kept burning, igniting higher as they recovered from the dousing that they had received. The acolytes stepped back from the caldron pit, watching it through the haze of smoke.

And then Kane saw it—something moving amid the flames. It looked like a man, head rising, shoulders, chest and arms slowly emerging from the fire.

The other people in the room saw it, too, and they stood transfixed as the imperfect figure seemed to pull itself from the flames.

It's some kind of illusion, Kane told himself. Gotta be.

But it wasn't. The manlike figure drew itself higher,

lifting its torso out of the fire. It was rough, unfinished, its skin—if it was skin—lumpy and incomplete. There were gaps between parts of its flesh—open gaps through which the flames of the caldron could be seen. And something else became clear as it drew itself out of those flames: it was big; bigger than a man, broad-shouldered and towering to nine feet in height. That was the exact same height as Ullikummis when he had first walked the Earth, before his legs had been hobbled by Enki's sword, leaving him a full foot shorter.

A deathly hush filled the room as the figure emerged from the fire. Kane and Brigid watched with the others as the figure took its first unsteady step out of the fire. It was made of stones, malformed and lumpy. It looked like someone had spilled pebbles into the shape of a man, a lumbering pile of shale staggering slowly across the temple. Its face was just an impression, deep, lifeless sockets for eyes, a gaping maw for a mouth.

"Our love is rock," the acolyte leading the ceremony chanted, "and rock never breaks." Around him, the other acolytes took up the chant, and so did the pilgrims.

The stone man took another lumbering step away from the flame pit, its footfall like a landslide smashing against the slate. Then it raised its right arm and reached for the closest pilgrim—the well-dressed woman with the hat, blond hair cut in a bob.

"Me?" the well-dressed woman gasped. "My lord, what am I to you?"

The answer wasn't an answer; it was an action—swift, sudden and deadly. The stone figure's arm seemed to extend, breaking apart, the gaps between each pebble-like component becoming wider, and its fingers rammed through the woman's face, smashing through her skull in the blink of an eye. The woman let out a bleat, then her flailing body was dangling from those weirdly extended fingers, dancing like a string puppet.

A mutual gasp fluttered through the room as the pilgrims watched, and Kane and Brigid took a surreptitious step back, adopting ready poses.

The woman's body seemed to dangle for a moment before stiffening again as the spine arched, thrusting the woman's breasts forward while her feet slipped backward on the temple floor on pointed toes. A whimper seemed to emanate from her throat, and Kane saw blood rushing along the shaft of stones that now crossed the temple chamber, leading from the woman to the stone monstrosity that had emerged from the caldron. The woman shivered, shook and dropped, unleashing one last gasp of pain as she crumpled to the deck.

Across the room, the stone figure seemed to become fuller somehow, more substantial, sinews forming between its broken body of stones.

"Take me next!" cried one of the pilgrims to Kane's left, stepping forward.

"No, take me!" a man demanded from Kane's right. "I lost my wife to the west snows!"

Beside him, a woman stepped forward, ripping open her cotton blouse. "No, me. My children were taken by the snows. Let my unquenched love for them power you, oh lord," she implored.

"This is getting out of hand," Kane muttered as more of the pilgrims offered themselves to the stone monster.

The stone figure thrust its arms forward again, and those limbs broke apart into tendril-like appendages as they sought their next victims. The Cerberus people had seen the individual stones do this before, under lab conditions, but never anything on this scale. One of those snaking, tendril-like arms reached toward Brigid Baptiste, cutting the air like a handful of tossed stones held in freeze-frame. Kane saw it coming, shoved her back protectively with a swift jab of his arm. Brigid fell to the floor and the arm hurried on, touching the pilgrim behind her, burrowing into the poor deluded fool's face even as he screamed in pleasure.

"Take me, oh lord," the man cried, tears of joy and pain pouring from his eyes like an overworked storm drain. "Let me live in y— Argh!"

The man and another pilgrim stumbled back, giving themselves willingly to the artificial man. Their legs buckled, knees folded, and they sunk to the floor as their blood and life was sucked from their joyful frames, feeding into the patchwork body of the stone creature who had emerged from the fire.

Then the stone monster tilted its head back, blood rushing visibly between the mass of stones, and it cried out, an eerie, inhuman howl—the first cry after birth.

"The lord lives," the senior acolyte cried joyously. "He lives in all of us, in all of you."

"Not for much longer he doesn't," Kane muttered, powering his hidden Sin Eater pistol into the palm of his right hand from its hidden wrist holster. He had had enough of this.

The Sin Eater's holster was activated by a specific flinch movement of Kane's wrist tendons, powering the weapon into his hand. The weapon itself was a compact hand blaster, roughly fourteen inches in length but able to fold in on itself for storage in the hidden holster. The Sin Eater was the official sidearm of the Magistrate Division, and his carrying it dated back to when Kane had still been a hard-contact Mag. The blaster was armed with 9 mm rounds. The trigger had no guard, as the necessity had never been foreseen that any kind of safety features for the weapon would ever be required. Thus, if the user's index finger was crooked at the time the weapon reached his hand, the pistol would begin firing automatically.

Beside Kane, Brigid was sprawled on the floor, her head spinning where it had struck the hard slate there, trying to shake the muzziness that occluded her thoughts. Wake up, she told herself. Wake up and act. If her body understood the words, then it didn't seem inclined to play along.

All around Kane, people were dropping as the life force was sucked out of them by the stone abomination. Pregnant woman; bald man; teen with acne and dyed hair; overweight farmhand with a beard that touched his belly—all of them fell as the stone monster touched them with its distended fingers, exchanging their lives and strength for its own. The stone thing was buoyed with every touch, rising taller, each step more determined, and all the while its gaping wound of a mouth shrieked its hideous ululation.

"Time to put this stone wannabe out to pasture," Kane grumbled as he stroked the trigger of the Sin Eater and sent a stream of bullets at the rough-hewn abomination.

Designated Task #009: Food Harvesting.

Food is grown in massive hydroponics labs located in the west and north corners of Delta Level. Vast artificial fields have been sown with seeds which grow various crops—tomatoes, potatoes, lettuce, carrots, etc.—in uniform lines. The crop is tested thoroughly throughout its lifespan to ensure it is growing in the correct manner: size, shape, color. Any imperfect crop is removed and recycled as feed for the animals in one of the other areas of Delta Level.

Picking the crops is partially automated, but the amount of moisture coupled with the gentle touch required means that humans are considered superior and more efficient with much of the menial work. As such, I have been assigned to work here two days a week as a rest from the construction of war machines on Epsilon Level. My first assignment is to tend to the pears which grow with resilience from a line of trees in room D41977. The crop is hard-skinned and tasteless, but it holds nutrients enough to sustain life. Most of it will be turned to pulp which is then added to the daily meal ration each citizen is allocated, wherein its lack of a distinctive taste will be rendered irrelevant.

My crop picking is slow because I am still new to the task and have yet to get used to the automated ladders used by the pickers. These ladders stand at a thirty-degree angle with a wheeled base, and they follow the instructions of a computer brain. The brain analyzes the optimum speed for fruit picking based on a scan of each tree and its crop, then follows that calculation to provide a window within which the tree must be stripped of its bounty. The speed seems fast to me, and it becomes inevitable that many of the crop which I pick are bruised. The supervisors show no concern for the bruised fruit, and merely chastise me for my inadequacy in stripping every pear tree in my designated batch.

"Your deficiency will be taken out of your food allowance next week," a supervisor informs me without looking up from her tally sheets. I stare at the gray peaked cap she wears for a long moment, wondering if she might meet my eyes and perhaps explain how I am to increase productivity, but she never looks up.

The conclusion of my shift is accompanied by a very real sense of disappointment, the knowledge that I have failed to live up to the expectations that the barons have in me as a citizen of Ioville. My back aches from stretching, my arms, too, from constantly reaching above me. I vow to try harder tomorrow.

—From the journal of Citizen 619F.

Chapter 3

A stream of 9 mm bullets zipped across the temple at the wretched stone monster that had emerged from the fire. Kane watched as the bullets trailed from his Sin Eater, while around him two dozen of the faithful who had joined him on this pilgrimage looked horrified at the sudden turn of events. They believed they were there to give of themselves whatever their god required, even if it was their lives. But Kane didn't believe—he knew better. He knew that this stone monstrosity was nothing more than a trick. The iron content in the blood it was being fed combined with the trigger inside those stone seeds, bringing it to nothing more than a cruel imitation of life. At least that's what Kane guessed was happening as he squeezed the Sin Eater's trigger.

Bullets hurtled toward the stone menace. The first bullets struck its rocky, mismatched hide and the creature let loose a surprised shriek, its distended fingers pulling free from two more sacrifices—a dark-skinned woman with a mop of braided hair and one of the robed acolytes who was ministering the proceedings. The stone monster's fingers rattled back into the hands, the wrists pulling back and the overlong limbs retracting to a more normal length, returning to the stone figure's shoulders. In their wake, its two victims sagged to the floor, visibly shaking, neither fully awake nor truly asleep.

Kane's bullets sparked as they struck the creature's rough hide, sounding like cymbals being clashed together with every rebound. But the monster only turned, fixing Kane with its dark, shadowy glare.

"You recognize me?" Kane challenged the creature as around him pilgrims ducked out of the way of the fight.

The stone creature tilted its head in the semblance of a nod.

"Yeah, I think you do," Kane snarled. "I'm the guy who killed your daddy."

The bastard child of a thousand deluded devotees hurtled toward Kane then, charging across the flame-lit temple floor, screaming an unearthly howl from its gaping wound of a mouth.

Kane's Sin Eater pistol blasted again, a stream of 9 mm titanium-shelled bullets catching in the light of the flames like fireflies in the dusk.

The monster's composite arms reached out and batted Kane's bullets aside, like twin landslides waving impossibly through the air, lines of warm blood rippling between each loose stone.

Kane leaped back but he was too late. The creature grabbed him, shooting one of its extending arms toward him and snagging his Sin Eater out of his hand.

How do I get myself into these jams? Kane wondered as that inhuman arm flicked the Sin Eater aside.

But there was no time to think—only to act. As the stone monster hurtled closer, charging for all the world like a runaway steam train, Kane began running at it. The two figures met in a crash of breaking shale amid the firelit chamber, and suddenly Kane was running up the monster's body, using its rocky crags as steps before driving his booted foot into the abomination's face.

The monster wavered in place, great chunks of its

still-forming body spilling to the floor like so much thrown sand.

All around the temple, the pilgrims were reacting with horror, calling for it to stop, asking who this man was who would dare violate their god. Kane ignored them as he leaped from the stone edifice that walked like a man, ducking and rolling to the slate floor even as the nightmare figure reached for him with one of its extending, pendulous arms. He recognized it—kind of. It was a pale imitation of Ullikummis, a memory only half-remembered, the details blurry, forgotten.

How do you break a thing that's already broken? Kane wondered as a lashing arm came sailing toward his head in a flurry of stones and blood.

Kane dropped out of the way of that swinging extendable arm, slid on his buttocks across the slate floor to where his blaster had dropped, snatched it up as he rolled.

A half-dozen pilgrims surrounded Kane as he recovered, their outraged faces glaring at him. Two men took the lead and kicked Kane while he lay on the ground, booting him in the sides. Kane groaned as he felt the first foot strike him on the ribs, followed an instant later by a second kick in the gut, forcing him to double over and expel the breath he held.

Kane could not shoot them. They were victims. Stupid, yes, but victims all the same.

Another foot sailed at Kane's face and he reacted instinctively, left arm snapping up to block it, then grabbing his attacker's ankle and twisting. The pilgrim shrieked as a sudden stab of pain tore through his ligaments, and then he crashed to the floor beside Kane, grasping in agony at his twisted ankle.

From across the chamber, the hulking form of the

stone monstrosity stalked through the flame-lit darkness, seeking out its next victim and the blood it desperately craved.

"Stop!" It was a woman's voice, loud enough to penetrate the rabble of panic and confusion, and it was accompanied by a brilliant flash of light and clap of thunder.

Everyone in the chamber turned, all except for an elderly man who walked with a stick who was even now having his blood drained from him by the stone thing that had come to life.

Across the chamber, Brigid Baptiste was standing before the statue of her other self, of Brigid Haight. She had stripped off her jacket and the loose shirt she had worn, revealing the tight black bodysuit she wore beneath—the shadow suit. The shadow suits had been discovered in Redoubt Yankee and were so named because they absorbed light, reducing the profile and visibility of the wearer. However, in the flickering light of the temple, the shadow suit's similarity to the sleek black leathers, which Brigid had worn while possessed by Haight, "wrapping her body in the dead" as she had termed it then, was impossible to miss. With her grim expression and wild halo of red-gold hair, she looked for all the world like the hateful thing she had been before—Ullikummis's hand in darkness.

"Stop this, all of you," Brigid shouted, her narrowed eyes scanning across every face in the room.

For a moment there was silence—shocked silence at this vision of the woman whose statue dominated one wall of the temple chamber. Then, the leader of the robed acolytes cried, "The demigoddess has returned!" He dropped to his knees, arms outthrust in praise.

Beside him, two more acolytes fell immediately to

their knees, bending low until they touched the floor with their foreheads, muttering confused praises for the glorious return they were blessed to witness. In a few moments, it seemed that everyone in the temple had fallen to their knees to worship Brigid—all except for Kane, who lay sprawled and bloodied on the floor, and the stone monster that loomed over its latest victim.

Still surrounded, Kane peered between the kneeling bodies of his attackers, and his brow furrowed. "Baptiste?" he muttered incredulously. "Don't tell me this has all got to you."

"Hear me now and hear me well," Brigid announced, pitching her voice in a low timbre of command. "This monster—" she pointed to the stone creature that had been brought to life in the flaming pit "—is a false god. He is not the great one. He is nothing but simple puppetry, brought to life to test your faith."

A stunned buzz burbled through the worshippers, and one pilgrim loudly cried, "We've been tricked!"

"Yes, you have been tricked," Brigid assured the crowd, striding toward them on her booted heels. "I walk among you now because such heresy cannot be allowed to flourish."

As she passed Kane, Brigid caught his eye and he detected just the slightest wink of one narrowed eye. Relief sang through him, bolstering his tired limbs and aching body.

"B-but what should we...?" an elderly woman asked, confused by the direction her pilgrimage had turned.

"Leave this place," Brigid told her, addressing everyone in the room. "Feed not this false idol. Let it wither and die, struck from your very minds in disgust."

"Oh, brother," Kane muttered. "Laying it on a bit thick, aren't we?" But no one heard him.

The pilgrims and the acolytes were stunned, and for a moment they all just knelt there, watching the demigoddess Brigid Haight walk among them, a vision from legend come back to life.

"Go now!" Brigid commanded. "Swiftly. While I deal with this pretender!" And she stomped with a determined swagger toward the stone monster that loomed by the fire pit.

There came a mass exodus from the temple then, pilgrims and acolytes hurrying out into the rain. Kane joined the crowd, slipping behind a pillar as sixty-something people hurried from the temple, which was alive with more flashes and bright bangs, as if a thunderstorm were occurring within its hallowed walls. Kane knew it wasn't a thunderstorm, of course, or any other kind of godly, supernatural show. No, he had recognized the thing Brigid had used when she had made her first dramatic reappearance as "Brigid Haight." She had employed a man-made device called a flashbang, similar in shape and size to a palm-sized ball bearing and designed as a nonlethal part of the standard Cerberus field mission arsenal. Once triggered, the flashbang brought an almighty flash of light and noise. It was similar to an explosive being set off, only the flashbang did no damage, as such. Instead, it was used by the Cerberus personnel to confuse and disorient opponents—and, just once, to pose as demigods, it seemed.

Once the temple was clear, Kane made his way across to Brigid, who was standing a good distance away from the other standing figure in the room—the stone monster—watching it warily as they slowly circled one another. Around them, the fallen bodies of almost a dozen pilgrims and one robed acolyte lay, their skin pale where the blood had been drained.

"So, what do we do now," Kane asked, "your goddess-ness?"

Brigid shot him a look. "Worked, didn't it?"

"I had things in hand," Kane assured her.

"You were getting your ass handed to you by three hick farmers and an old woman who walked with a stick," Brigid shot back.

Kane shrugged, knowing that now was not the time to argue. "Plan?"

Brigid eyed the stalking stone figure across the temple. It was moving slowly, its limbs breaking apart, chips of stone trailing behind the main body.

"It needs blood," Brigid said. "Its body is made up of stone seeds—the obedience stones Ullikummis generated from his body."

"Yeah, he's a regular chip off the old block," Kane agreed, as the stone monster lunged at him and Brigid.

The two Cerberus warriors danced out of the way—which was far easier now that the temple wasn't crowded with other people—and they sprinted across the empty room until they were behind the fallen meteor, placing it between them and the monster.

"Those stone seeds require the iron content in human blood to power them, remember?" Brigid told Kane. "Without blood, they revert to a dormant state."

"But Junior there just got a big feast of blood," Kane reminded Brigid. "Enough to bring him to life."

"Yes, enough to bring him to life," Brigid agreed, "but not enough to sustain him. That's why he needs to absorb the blood from his victims."

The stone monster emerged from behind the meteor rock, unleashing a gurgled cry as it reached for Kane and Brigid. Brigid spun out of its reach while Kane dropped back and blasted a burst of fire from his Sin

Eater. The monster swayed in place, recoiling from the impact of 9 mm bullets peppering its disjointed stone body.

"How long do you estimate before the kid needs his next feed?" Kane asked Brigid in a breathless voice as he hurried across the temple to join her.

"Hard to say," Brigid answered, "but I think he's moving slower than he was. Don't you?"

Kane watched the stalking figure emerge from behind the rock prison. It was moving slower; Brigid was right. It seemed to lurch more now, and barely remained upright as it searched for the two Cerberus warriors—the only sources of blood left in the temple chamber.

"So, what—we keep out of that thing's way until it burns through its energy source?"

"Where's the fun in that?" Brigid said with a smile. Kane looked down and saw what she held in her open hand. It was a metal sphere, similar to the flashbangs she had used to shock and awe the pilgrims in the temple—only this one was primed with a full explosive load.

The stone monster charged at them again, but this time Brigid was ready. As it came within a dozen feet of the Cerberus duo, she primed and tossed the explosive, then she and Kane ducked and turned away. A moment later, an explosion rocked the temple, and tiny chips of stone hurtled across the room as the monster's body was split into a thousand pieces.

"I thought you came on this mission unarmed?" Kane challenged Brigid as they drew themselves up from the slate floor.

"No blaster," Brigid agreed, "but I still sneaked a few things into my pockets. Just in case."

"You sweet, sweet demigoddess," Kane replied with a smirk. "No wonder your people love you so."

Designated Task #015: Fitness.

Twice a week, I have been assigned to a training facility on Cappa Level where I am instructed in basic protection. "A ville is only as safe as its weakest member," we are told, and so each member is rigorously trained to remain in the peak of physical health.

The training is threefold. Emphasis is placed on the basic strengthening of the body—something I have been informed is unnecessary in my case as I entered Ioville in prime physical condition.

When this entry occurred I cannot say. However I have been led to understand it was recently.

The second task is combat, which takes the form of hand-to-hand defence along with instructions on how to initiate a successful attack. Once again, it appears that I am competent at these tasks, despite having no specific memory of training for them.

The third task involves the familiarity, usage and maintenance of weapons including firearms. Most of this training concentrates on the use of small arms. However, I have also been shown how to operate the USMG-73 heavy machine guns which arm the Sandcats I build in the workshop at Designated Task #004, the standard weapons arrays on Deathbird helicopters, and have been shown how to use and sharpen a combat knife.

Fitness strikes me as a strange task, because it is the only place in the ville where one hears talking between the participants. The instructors are all Magistrates and it seems that they are determined to make the citizens as proficient as they are.

The older citizens of Ioville struggle with the tasks.

—*From the journal of Citizen 619F.*

Chapter 4

Kane and Brigid exited the temple shortly after, taking a few sample stones with them for full analysis back at Cerberus headquarters. Brigid pulled her jacket back on over her shadow suit, and used the shirt she had removed to tie her hair up like a scarf, wrapping her red-gold locks in the light cloth to disguise her most eye-catching feature and enable her to pass among pilgrims without comment. They left the temple amid another explosion from a flashbang, ensuring that no one saw them exit.

The acolytes and pilgrims were still waiting outside, close to the temple, kneeling and chanting as they listened to the ominous sounds of explosions and wondering what was occurring within. Brigid had had two more charges with her while Kane was carrying four of his own and so, setting timers on the devices, they had left them to continue exploding, putting on a show that ran for another ten minutes, with a new explosion every couple of minutes to stop the curious pilgrims from reentering their sacred place too soon.

"Our love is rock and rock never breaks," the devoted repeated as a mantra from where they knelt in the gravel outside the temple doors.

Kane shook his head in despair as he and Brigid emerged during a cacophonous explosion. "Poor deluded saps," he muttered, disgusted by their devotion.

Some of the pilgrims appeared terrified by what they

had witnessed, while a few bore tears of joy on their smiling faces as they praised the return of the demigoddess. The tears mixed with the relentless rain, washing from the heavens with disinterest.

Kane and Brigid joined the worshippers outside the temple, and when the next explosion rocked the sacred site they were ready. During the general confusion, Kane and Brigid slipped away, taking a route across the fields, staying low to the ground and hidden by the overgrown wildflowers from a casual glance. Behind them, the other pilgrims and the acolytes bowed their heads lower, imagining what must be going on inside the temple grounds. They were dumb, in Kane's opinion, but it wasn't their fault—the barons had kept people dumb, drummed out their curiosity. The barons hadn't wanted people—they had wanted devoted automatons who would worship and praise them. Here was their legacy.

Brigid and Kane walked in silence for a while, just creating as much distance from the site of the temple as they could. Finally, Kane turned to Brigid, worry creasing his brow.

"You know, for a moment back there I thought you'd turned sour," Kane admitted, the concern clear on his face.

Brigid shook her head. "Never. Never again," she promised.

It was all they needed to say, but they had needed to say it. Brigid had been changed once by Ullikummis, possessed by her dark self, the creature called Haight. She had turned on Kane and their allies, shot Kane in the chest while he was defenceless. The wound between them would always be there, but they worked every day to get past it, to erase its memory.

Kane and Brigid were *anam-charas*, soul friends, their destinies entwined throughout all of time. No matter what form they took, no matter what bodies their souls wore, they were destined to always find one another, watch over one another, protect one another. It wasn't love, not in a carnal way, anyway—it was something deeper and more transcendental than that. Their friend Domi had once asked Brigid if the *anam-chara* bond was like they were brother and sister, and Brigid had laughed. "If Kane were my brother he might listen to me once in a while," she had said. Beyond that, she had never been able to explain what the bond really was; she only knew it was theirs and that it was eternal.

They trekked for an hour before reporting in to Cerberus to request their ride back home. By that time they had reached a dirt track running between two vegetable fields, carrots to one side, potatoes to the other, a distant farmhouse looking out toward them.

"Grant, this is Kane," Kane said, activating his Commtact. The Commtact was a small radio communications device that was hidden beneath the skin of all Cerberus field personnel. Each subdermal device was a top-of-the-line communication unit, the designs for which had been discovered among the artifacts in Redoubt Yankee several years before by the Cerberus exiles. Commtacts featured sensor circuitry incorporating an analog-to-digital voice encoder that was subcutaneously embedded in a subject's mastoid bone. As well as radio communications, the Commtact could function as a translation device, operating in real time. Once the pintels made contact, transmissions were funnelled directly to the wearer's auditory canals through the skull casing, vibrating the ear canal to create sound, which had the additional effect that they could pick up and enhance any subvocalization made by the user. In theory, even if a user went completely deaf they would still be able to hear normally, in a fashion, courtesy of the Commtact device.

The radio link molded below Kane's ear spoke with the familiar voice of his partner. "Hey, Kane, how did it go?" Even over the Commtact relay, Grant's voice was deep as rumbling thunder.

"We bewildered and destroyed," Kane replied. "Just another day at the office."

Grant's laughter echoed through Kane's skull from the Commtact.

"Triangulate on our position and give us a ride," Kane said. "We're all set to go home."

The triangulation was easy. Kane, Brigid and all other Cerberus personnel had a biolink transponder injected into their bloodstream. The transponder used nanotechnology to relay a subject's position and detail their current state of health to a satellite pickup station, which then delivered that information to the Cerberus redoubt in the Montana mountains. This technology along with the Commtacts allowed Cerberus to remain in constant touch with its personnel while they were in the field, and it could be accessed by the operations staff to home in on an individual to deliver aid.

In this case, that aid came in the form of a Deathbird, a modified AH-64 Apache helicopter, that arrived over the field of potatoes, shaking their fluttering leaves in its passage. The Deathbird featured a turret-mounted chain gun, as well as missile armaments—and it had been on call in case the mission went sour.

Kane and Brigid watched as the Apache dropped down to the ground, landing gently on the dirt strip between fields, its rotor blades whirring in a blur. As soon as it was down, the two Cerberus rebels hurried toward it in a crouched run, keeping their heads and limbs well below the height of those rotating blades, even though they knew there was room to maneuver below them. Too many times, the drag created by the rotors had wrong-footed a man and created a shockingly swift accident as the fast-spinning rotors became like knives cutting the air.

Kane drew back the side door. Brigid tottered inside with Kane just a couple of steps behind her. As soon as Kane was in, Brigid shouted, "Clear!" and the helicopter ascended into the skies once more.

Piloting the craft was a large dark-skinned man in his late thirties, with a shaved head and gunslinger's mustache. He was wearing a shadow suit that matched those worn by his passengers. Though large, the man was all muscle—accentuated by the tight fit of the shadow suit—without an ounce of fat on his body. This was Grant, who had served as Kane's field partner all the way back to their days as Magistrates and with whom he had been partnered ever since. Grant was a proficient hand-to-hand combatant, as well as being trained in the use of most ballistic weapons. He was also a phenomenal pilot—Kane would argue he was the greatest pilot that Cerberus would ever know…excluding himself, of course.

"So, you guys pick up anything good while you were shopping?" Grant asked in his rumbling-thunder voice as Kane drew the side door closed.

Kane shrugged. "Trouble, a few stones. The usual."

"Stones," Grant muttered, shaking his head. "Like we've not had enough of *that* for one lifetime."

Kane and Brigid had to agree.

THE TRIO ARRIVED back at the Cerberus redoubt two hours later. The redoubt was built into one of the mountains in the Bitterroot range in Montana, where it was hidden from view. It occupied an ancient military base which had remained forgotten or ignored in the two centuries since the nukecaust of 2001. A peculiar mythology had grown up around the mountains in the years since that nuclear conflict, with their dark, mysterious forests and seemingly bottomless ravines. Now, the wilderness surrounding the redoubt was virtually unpopulated. The nearest settlement could be found in the flatlands some miles away and consisted of a small band of Indians, Sioux and Cheyenne, led by a shaman named Sky Dog who had befriended the Cerberus exiles many years ago.

Inside, the redoubt featured state-of-the-art technology despite its rough exterior. The redoubt was manned by a full complement of staff, over fifty in total, many of whom were experts in their chosen field of scientific study. The staff relied on two orbiting satellites at their disposal—the Keyhole commsat and the Vela-class reconnaissance satellite—which provided much of the data for analysis in their ongoing mission to protect humankind. Gaining access to the satellites had taken long man-hours of intense trial-and-error work by many of the top scientists on hand at the mountain base. Concealed uplinks were tucked beneath camouflage netting around the redoubt, hidden away within the rocky clefts of the mountain range and chattering with the orbiting satellites. This arrangement gave the staff in residence a near-limitless stream of feed data surveying the surface of the Earth, as well as providing near-instantaneous communication with field teams across the globe, such as Kane's team, which was designated CAT Alpha.

They convened in the Cerberus meeting room, a rarely used lecture theater with several stepped rows of fixed seats. Kane and Brigid had showered and changed clothes, so Grant was already sitting when they entered, his massive frame almost too much for the regular-size seat. Three other people were in the room—Lakesh, Donald Bry and Reba DeFore—and all were dressed in the standard white duty uniform.

Mohandas Lakesh Singh was a physics and cybernetics expert who was the head of the Cerberus organization. A man of medium height, he appeared to be in his fifties, with a dusky complexion and vivid blue eyes that shone like sapphires when he addressed you. His black hair was slicked back away from his forehead, showing a few threads of gray, especially at the sides above the ears. Lakesh had an aquiline nose and a refined mouth, and his breadth of knowledge was second to none, except perhaps Brigid's. Though he was, for all intents, a man in his fifties, Lakesh was in fact far older than that— he had been born in the twentieth century, but thanks to cryogenics and organ replacement, he had lived past his two-hundred-and-fiftieth year and was still going strong. Amazingly, Lakesh had been one of the original scientists involved in the Cerberus facility based at this redoubt in the twentieth century, a research project developing and investigating the applications of a fixed-point teleportational device called the mat-trans. The mat-trans was still in operation all these years on, although it was only one of a number of transportation options that the Cerberus personnel employed.

Beside Lakesh stood Donald Bry, Lakesh's right-hand man and the unofficial second-in-command of the Cerberus operation. In his thirties, Donald had an unruly mop of ginger curls atop his head and a look of perpetual worry on his features. Donald's field of expertise was computers, but he was also knowledgeable about most of the general goings-on relating to Cerberus and its field operations, including communications and the intricacies of the biolink transponders.

The final person in the room was Reba DeFore, a stocky, bronze-skinned woman with ash-blond hair, which she had clipped back from her face in an elaborate French twist. DeFore was the redoubt's medical expert, and she had patched up Kane, Grant and Brigid more times than she cared to count.

"Grant tells me you ran into an old friend out in Saskatchewan," Lakesh began after welcoming Kane and Brigid. They had been gone for four days.

Kane nodded gravely. "Ullikummis. Not quite back, but his devotees are trying real hard to hasten the second coming."

"Wrong savior," Brigid corrected him. "They were using the old stone seeds," she elaborated, "that budded from his body, charging them with human blood."

"Sacrifices?" Lakesh asked, raising an eyebrow.

"No," Brigid said. "At least, none so far. The blood of pilgrims gave the thing life, but it seemed mindless—like it didn't have any purpose. It just stumbled around draining blood from anyone who stepped into its grasp."

"And we blew it up before it could get very far with that," Kane added.

Lakesh nodded solemnly. "A worrying development, dear friends," he said.

"Were any of you hurt?" DeFore asked as the room went silent.

"I took a few knocks," Kane admitted, "and Brigid took a few, too—"

"When you knocked me to the floor," Brigid pointed out.

"—but we're all good, I think," Kane finished.

DeFore proposed checking them over anyway and, using a portable medical kit, accessed their transponders for a full rundown on their current health. The shadow suit had protected Kane from most of the knocks he had taken at the hands of the deluded pilgrims, and other than a bruised arm, Brigid had got off scot-free.

While DeFore was sterilizing the few scrapes and grazes Kane had taken during the frenetic conflict, the group discussed their mission in detail. As they reached the wrap-up, Brigid recalled one thing that had stood out as possibly important.

"A few people have mentioned something about a storm out to the west over the past few days," she said. "Sounded vicious, like it's taken some lives." She shrugged.

Donald Bry brought up a map on the projector screen that dominated the wall behind the stage. Using the old designations, west of Saskatchewan was Alberta or British Columbia. "This is pretty much no-man's-land now," Bry stated as he indicated those areas.

"Well out of reach of the baronies," Kane pointed out as he eyed the map.

Lakesh looked at Kane querulously. "Something on your mind, Kane?" he asked.

"Not sure," Kane said. "People were speaking about this storm like it was a big deal. A big deal well away from the baronies, where there wouldn't likely be much in the way of organized help."

Lakesh took a slow breath as he looked at the map.

"We could send out a rescue party, see if anyone needed our assistance," he said.

"Helping people is what we do," Grant reminded everyone. "Can't always be fighting crazy aliens and nutty priests."

"It's a lot of territory," Bry argued. "Do you have any idea whereabouts this storm hit?"

Brigid's red-gold locks cascaded about her face as she shook her head. "We had more important concerns at the time."

"Would a satellite scan find evidence?" Kane suggested.

"It may," Lakesh confirmed. "It really depends on how much damage the storm created and whether there was any notable habitation there to begin with. If it's trashed, unpopulated territory we'd be hard-pushed to confirm it from the air."

Kane fixed Lakesh with his no-nonsense stare. "Look," he said.

Lakesh nodded once, accepting Kane's challenge. He had organized Cerberus to help people, and while a storm was not the kind of threat he had had in mind, helping those in danger or trouble was the operation's remit. They would use the satellites to scan the area to the west of the sacred temple of the stone god, and maybe—just maybe—find a place where help was needed.

Designated Task #016: Sleep.

Sleep has been prescribed for all citizens at an optimum 6.2 hours a day. Sleep occurs when a citizen is not on shift, and this may be in the day or night. After 6.2

hours an alarm alerts the citizen to wake, after which their routine begins again.

I note that the sleep patterns of my immediate neighbors in this residential block are different to my own, accounting for their own shifts at their designated tasks.

My bed is soft and uncomfortable, the padding inadequate and the base structure of the sofa which it converts from pushing against my body as I toss and turn. I have no one to report this to.

—From the journal of Citizen 619F.

Chapter 5

"Storm," Brewster Philboyd announced emotionlessly.

"Storm," Lakesh agreed.

The two of them were sitting in office chairs in the Cerberus operations room. The room was a vast space with high ceilings and pleasing indirect lighting. Two aisles of computer terminals faced a giant screen on which material could be flagged. A giant Mercator map dominated one wall, showing the world before the nuke-caust had reshaped the coastlines of North America and other locales. The map was peppered with glowing locator dots, which were joined to one another with dotted lines of diodes, creating an image reminiscent of the kind of flight maps that airlines had given to passengers in the twentieth century. The indicated routes were not flight paths, however, but rather they showed the locations and connections of the sprawling mat-trans network. Developed for the US military, the majority of the units were located within North America, but a few outposts could be seen farther afield.

A separate chamber was located in one corner of the room, far from the entry doors. This chamber had reinforced armaglass walls tinted a coffee-brown color. Within was contained the Cerberus installation's mat-trans unit, along with a small anteroom which could be sealed off if necessary.

Right now the mat-trans chamber was empty but the main ops room was buzzing with activity.

"Big one, too," Philboyd said as he enhanced the satellite image on his screen, giving a wider view of the storm over British Columbia. Philboyd was a tall, lanky man who seemed somehow hunched over whenever he sat in the standard office furniture of the ops room. His blond hair was swept back and slightly receding while the skin on his cheeks showed evidence of acne scarring from his youth. Philboyd wore round spectacles with dark frames and was a physicist of some good standing. Like many of the personnel who populated the Cerberus redoubt, Philboyd was a transplant from the twentieth century, part of a research project that had been located on the Manitius Moon Base. After the nukecaust had struck, the moon base had gone into lockdown, plunging its staff into cryogenic deep freeze and retaining that expertise for another generation. It had taken a Cerberus exploration party to discover and relocate them to the redoubt.

Lakesh looked at the monitor screen where the satellite feed was playing out. It showed a desolate area of the territory that had once been Canada, around the point where Alberta met British Columbia. The area was white with fallen snow, a few clumps of trees visible as dark shadows on the ground. There was no sign of human habitation; any roads or tracks cutting through the land had been painted white with snow. In the midst of this desolate wasteland was a whirling blur of cloud, feeding the land with ice crystals. It was a small, isolated shower but it still covered several miles. "I didn't expect the storm to still be raging," Lakesh muttered, shaking his head.

"No housing nearby," Philboyd observed, twiddling

the image control dial to pull out farther from the storm. "Closest settlement is approximately ninety miles away. If this is your storm, it's not affecting anyone other than the moose and squirrels."

Lakesh rubbed his forehead, deep in thought. "Storms move," he said. "Can we trace its path, backtrack to see if it has caused any devastation?"

Philboyd looked quizzically askance at Lakesh. "With respect, Doctor, I understood that what we were looking for was a past event. This storm is happening very much now."

"It is," Lakesh agreed, still thinking, "but hurricanes and tropical storms can rage for days, even weeks."

Philboyd widened his search area, scanned for signs of devastation. There was nothing obvious—if the storm had destroyed anything it was obscured by the clouds.

Lakesh was still thinking, working through the possibilities in his incisive, analytical mind. "What are those clouds hiding, Mr. Philboyd?" he pondered.

Philboyd didn't answer, but merely tapped a few commands into his computer keyboard and brought up a surveillance map showing the area. The map showed in a separate window on-screen and it was blank. "Nothing," he said. "Just wilderness."

Lakesh bent closer to the screen, studying the map. "Not wilderness," he decided. "It's too flat for that."

"Sir?"

"Brewster—can we backtrack this image twenty-four hours, say?" Lakesh asked. He knew that they could; the satellite would have made a sweep over this area one day before. He was already beginning to suspect something, although he couldn't put his finger on what.

Philboyd pulled up the records, ran the surveillance footage from one day before. Its time stamp glowed in the lower left corner as it played, moving slowly across the area which Lakesh and Philboyd were looking at now in a standard sweep. As it crossed the particular spot they had been observing, Philboyd let out a surprised laugh.

Lakesh did not laugh, however. What they were looking at, remarkable as it seemed, was what appeared to be the very same storm playing out in the very same spot.

"That's one persistent storm," Philboyd stated.

Lakesh pointed to the screen. "But not crossing here, or here," he said. "It's fixed to one location. Brewster—take us back another day."

A few taps of his keyboard and Philboyd had called up the older footage. Once again, the storm was in the exact same spot. They went back further over the next two hours, checking the records going back not just weeks but months. The surveillance satellite had monitored this point every day as part of its routine sweep pattern, and every day showed the same clouds in place. On some days, it would be sunny around the storm, while on others it would be so cloudy all around that they could not pick out the specific clouds that made up the storm. But over time, Lakesh and Philboyd reached the somewhat unsettling conclusion that here, on one single point on the planet, the same storm had been playing out for not just months but possibly years.

"A never-ending storm," Lakesh said with gravity. "Incredible."

"But not impossible," Philboyd stated. "The Great Red Spot on Jupiter is the eye of a gigantic storm—the largest in the solar system—and our records suggest it has run for centuries."

"But on Earth, with our wind patterns and atmospheric changes…?" Lakesh wondered.

"A holdover from the nukecaust?" Philboyd proposed. The nuclear holocaust had done dreadful things to the Earth's weather patterns. Holdovers were rare but they did occasionally happen, particularly in areas of high radiation.

Lakesh scratched his chin thoughtfully. "What else do we know about this area?" he asked aloud.

"Right now? Not a lot," Philboyd confirmed. "There has been no reason to pay it particular scrutiny—"

"There's your reason, Mr. Philboyd," Lakesh said, pointing at the storm cloud on his screen. "Get scrutinizing."

TWO DAYS LATER, the team regathered in the meeting room, where Lakesh and Bry brought them up to speed with what had been discovered.

"The first reference to the coordinates appears in a backup database from Ragnarville, in a file dating back three and a half years," Lakesh explained. "The reference is minor and the information attached to it encrypted—"

"The file encryption was a beast," Donald Bry said, taking up the story, "and we had a lot of trouble getting past it. So much so that I decided to run a search on one of the other databases. To my surprise, the same file with the same encryption appeared on the database of Baron Cobalt."

"Same encryption means no joy, I take it," Grant observed sourly.

"But," Lakesh said, "it meant something. If two barons were looking at the same data, it meant they were collaborating."

Kane shook his head. "Where is all this going, Lakesh? The barons are dead now."

"They are, but their legacy is still with us," Lakesh pointed out. "And what Donald here discovered may be a rather big part of that legacy."

"So pull the trigger already," Kane said impatiently.

Bry paused for a moment before replying. "Baron Cobalt's database was locked just like Ragnar's, so I tried checking through the other baronial databases. In the Snakefishville database—now Luilekkerville of course—I found the same coordinates attached to something called Terminal White."

"And who or what is Terminal White?" Brigid asked.

"That is a mystery," Donald admitted, "but a fascinating one. Once we had the Snakefish link I could backtrack into the Ragnarville and Cobalt databases and look for a link. The phrase 'Terminal White' appears in all of them, relating to an area to the north of their territories. It would appear to be a shared project involving all three barons—at least—working together toward some undefined goal."

"Three-way power grab, maybe?" Kane mused.

Brigid nodded warily. "Hmm, perhaps they were collaborating to take over the other baronies, then split them among themselves. And that all fell apart when the snake gods emerged, changing the stakes."

"Not just the stakes," Kane reminded her, "but the rules of the whole darn shooting match."

Kane turned back to Bry and Lakesh, a look of concern on his face. "So, did you find anything else?"

Bry shook his head regretfully. "We're still running checks, trying to burrow into the data. We've scanned the databases of each of the baronies, well, as much as we can access at this stage. We have the name or term, but everything else is encrypted like a ticking time bomb—if we push too hard we'll wipe the data entirely."

"And with a lot of that data already lost or ransacked after the fall of the baronies," Lakesh said, "much of Donald's information is already coming from old files that would be regarded as 'lost.'"

"The data is very high-level security," Bry added. "I suspect a lot of this information was carried person to person, baron to baron, and not stored on any database. What little we have uncovered is purely relating to the site, but the coordinates and the site match up both with each other and with the storm we've observed in satellite surveillance."

"The barons are gone," Kane said grimly. "Any research project they started should have shut down, too. Shouldn't it?"

Brigid shook her head. "Kane, you know we're going to have to look," she said. "Don't try to find a way out of it—that's beneath you."

Kane ground his teeth in irritation. "I want to protect people—not databases," he muttered.

"They'll come," Grant told him. "They always do."

Designated Task #011: Cleaning.

Each resident of Ioville is expected to exhibit a professional level of cleanliness at all times. The cleanliness of the ville is paramount and is the responsibility of every citizen.

After my manufacturing shift—nine hours with three designated breaks—I am assigned ville cleaning duties with another citizen, named Citizen 058F—a woman like me.

Our duties involve checking the factories and walkways of Epsilon Level, cleaning and sterilizing all walls and floors, checking and sterilizing the stairwells and elevators in the west tower, checking and sterilizing the linking walkways between west and north towers, cleaning and maintaining fire safety equipment, collecting and labeling any debris larger than a fingernail so that it may be retained and analyzed, and assisting in the cleaning of all personnel exiting manufactory 8.

Once our circuit is completed, another team takes our place to begin cleaning again while we are designated as off-shift. At this stage, we are stripped and sent through the personnel cleaning facility at factory 8 to ensure that we have not picked up any rogue dirt or dangerous debris. Once we are clean, we are expected to return to our residences. Citizen 058F resides in a block close to my own, and so we travel together via trolleybus. We do not discuss where she works during the day, preferring to sit in composed silence as the bus makes its circuit of the ville. She gets off one stop before me.

—*From the journal of Citizen 619F.*

Chapter 6

At dawn the next morning, two sleek bronze-hued aircraft cut across the skies over the former province of Alberta in the western part of Canada. The craft were known as Mantas, aircraft designed in ancient prehistory by an alien race and capable of phenomenal acceleration and other feats, including subspace travel. They had emerged from a hidden hangar in the Cerberus redoubt at a little before dawn, launching one after another and veering northward in perfect formation.

Identical in appearance, the Mantas were constructed from a bronze-hued metal whose liquid sheen glimmered in the early-morning sunlight. Their graceful designs consisted of flattened wedges with swooping wings curving out to either side of the body in mimicry of the seagoing manta, and it was this similarity that had spawned their popularised name of Manta Craft. Each Manta's wingspan was twenty yards and their body length was almost fifteen, but it was the beauty of their design that was breathtaking, an effortless combination of every principle of aerodynamics wrapped up in a gleaming, burned-gold finish. The entire surface of each craft was decorated with curious geometric designs; elaborate cuneiform markings, swirling glyphs and cup-and-spiral symbols. Each vehicle featured an elongated hump in the center of the body which provided the only indication of a cockpit.

Inside those cockpits sat three individuals. Piloting each craft were Kane and Grant, dressed in their shadow suits, their heads hidden behind the almost-spherical, bulb-like helmets that were built into the pilot seats of each vehicle. The interior was small and simple, with very few displays showing other than a few indicator lights. Rather, the dashboards existed in virtual space, projected onto the pilot's retina using the heads-up technology of the weird-looking helmets.

The third occupant of the Mantas was Brigid Baptiste, sitting in the backseat of Kane's vehicle, where she was using a portable tablet computer to analyze the local weather patterns and generally familiarize herself with the local climate and terrain. It wasn't necessary, of course—she had already gone through all of the material the night before and her eidetic memory ensured she would not forget so much as a single detail. And yet, nervousness or perhaps that human instinct that one might have missed something made Brigid check the material again while running through scenarios in her head.

"You okay back there, Baptiste?" Kane asked, raising his voice slightly over the low hum of the Manta's engine. The Manta utilised two different types of engines, depending on the specific flying that was required of it. One was a ramjet while the other was a solid fuel pulse detonation, which was useful for work outside the planet's atmosphere. Neither was especially noisy, however, and Kane raised his voice more out of habit and the weird feeling of his skull being encased and muffled by the helmet rather than any real need. "You've been awfully quiet."

"Just thinking," Brigid said as the Manta cut through the cold air high over Mount Robson in the Canadian Rockies.

"What do you think we're going to find?" Kane asked, making conversation. "Another baron?"

"I don't like to speculate," Brigid said.

"Go on, speculating's fun," Kane encouraged.

"I hope we find nothing," Brigid said. "Absolutely nothing."

"Yeah, that's the adventurous spirit we've all come to admire in you, Baptiste," Kane teased.

The two Mantas sped on, cutting through the cold air like knives through cloth.

THE SNOWSTORM LOOMED up ahead like an angry ghost. Dark clouds haunted the sky, thick as smoke from a fire, a thick sheet of white snow descending from them coupled with spits of razor-sharp ice. It was almost like a curtain draped across the landscape, a thick line that no one in their right mind would try to cross.

Leading to that ominous curtain was the desolate wilderness of Canada, ravines and sweeping plains, streaks of thick forest that thinned out as they approached the static storm. Down there, occasional animals could be seen flitting among the trees, birds taking wing.

Kane and Grant brought their sleek Manta aircraft toward the snow curtain on a low approach, observing the landscape carefully, searching for signs of life. Other than the occasional wolf or raccoon there was nothing but trees and scrub dappled with icy snow.

The Mantas could travel in subspace and under the sea, so neither pilot had any fear of entering the snowstorm. Their only concern was the lack of visibility it ensured, leaving them entirely reliant on their crafts' formidable scanning capabilities.

Grant's voice patched over their linked Commtacts. "Nothing happening so far," he stated. "Looks clear."

Watching his heads-up displays, Kane nodded. "Displays are clear," he confirmed.

And yet there was something eerily uncanny about the storm, seen from high up and this far out. It really was like a curtain, a thick line delineating one part of the terrain from another. If what Cerberus had discovered was true—that this spot had been encased in this storm for years—then it was anyone's guess what they might find within.

Kane sent more power to his engines, accelerating toward the thick white curtain of snow. A moment later the two bronze aircraft had disappeared within.

IT WAS MOMENTARILY STRANGE. Moving from light and normality into a world the only description of which was one word: *white*.

Snow fell, thick lines of it fluttering diagonally across the Mantas' windshields, painting everything the same shade of white. People wear black at funerals, thought Brigid, but white is more somber, more chilling. When seen like this, a great expanse of nothing but white and cold, that is the picture of death, the way it overwhelms and demolishes and rewrites.

The Mantas hurtled on, crossing the vast expanse of land hidden by the blizzard, their sensor displays showing the flat terrain stretching out before them.

"There's nothing here," Kane muttered, triggering his Commtact automatically.

"Nothing on my side, either," Grant confirmed. "Just snow."

The Mantas hurtled onward, crossing the dull white landscape, ice thrown against their wings and bodies. Below, the land seemed unchanging. Whatever it had once been was hidden beneath the blanket of masking white.

"Kane," Grant radioed, "I'm picking up a heat signature on our ten."

Kane had seen the same heat signature appear on his own heads-up display even as Grant began to speak. "I see it," he confirmed. "You want to give it a closer look?"

"You know I do," Grant replied.

"Yeah, anything to break the monotony," Kane agreed.

Without breaking formation, the two Mantas vectored toward the ten o'clock, chasing the mysterious heat signature amid the falling snow.

THE SOURCE OF the heat signature proved hard to pinpoint—not least because it was hidden by the curtain of falling snow. After a few sweeps across the general area of the source, Kane proposed landing and checking the area on foot to verify whatever it was that was pumping out warmth. His colleagues agreed and within a couple of minutes the Cerberus team had brought their sleek Mantas down in the vertical landings that the incredible vehicles were geared for, dropping out of the sky like stones.

Kane drew back the hatch of his Manta and took a breath of the cold air. The cold burned against the back of his throat as he breathed in, and he had to blink back tears. While the shadow suit would regulate his body temperature, there was only so much it could cover, and inhaling freezing-cold air is still inhaling freezing-cold air.

The snow was falling thickly, cutting vision down to just a few feet.

"Brisk day for a walk," Grant called as he strode across the snow from his own Manta toward Kane's. He materialized through the white curtain of snow like a shadow coming suddenly to life. He had dressed in a long leather-style coat over his shadow suit, with thick-soled combat boots to augment the shadow suit's built-in foot molds that were more like hard socks. The top of the boots could barely be seen, for the snow here was compact but deep. Grant's coat was made from a Kevlar/Nomex mix, making it both flame retardant and able to repel bullets. It didn't make Grant invulnerable, but it gave him an edge at least. The last item that Grant wore was a woollen hat to cover his shaved head. The hat was black, matching the rest of his outfit.

"Damn brisk," Kane agreed as he and Brigid exited the cockpit, sealing the hatch behind him.

Consulting the tablet's portable scanner, the three Cerberus warriors trudged through the snow toward the heat source. Brigid's hair fluttered wildly in the wind, as did the tails of Grant's duster. Kane had dressed in a shorter jacket over his shadow suit, its pockets giving him extra storage space, along with a belt, which contained a half-dozen pouches within which he had stored his usual armory of flashbangs and miniexplosives.

"Could be under the snow," Kane suggested as they looked around, mystified, for the heat source.

"No," Brigid said, checking the details on her scanner. "Whatever's emanating heat is moving…slowly, but it's moving."

Kane looked at the tablet screen, swiftly making sense of the icons. "There," he said, pointing a little way to their right.

Before Kane had lowered his hand, something large and white came barreling out of the snow curtain toward them from the right. It was like a curved wall, wider than a house, and was accompanied by the growl of a mighty engine.

Designated Task #007: Food Preparation.

I am assigned to Delta Level for two days every week once my shift at Designated Task #004 has finished. There, I am tasked to prepare meals for the ville, specifically for my tower. This involves cleaning, peeling and chopping vegetables and fruit before they are mulched together in a nutritious paste-like gruel. The gruel smells strongly during preparation. On my first occasion I waited forty minutes until my allocated break, at which point I left the room and vomited, the smell too much. I have trained myself to be better now, but it is all I can do to keep myself from vomiting while I wash and chop and peel, such is the sweet malodor of the mashed components.

The food is portioned into small trays, which are then distributed to the canteens around the ville. The serving of the food is a separate Designated Task, #008.

—*From the journal of Citizen 619F.*

Chapter 7

Twenty feet wide and painted white, the unit was perfectly camouflaged for the environment. The noise of the engine should have given the behemoth's approach away, but the thick snow had muffled it almost entirely until it had reached within a dozen feet of the Cerberus warriors.

Kane leaped one way, Grant and Brigid the other as the massive unit came barreling at them, accompanied by a churning engine noise that boomed like thunder in the mountains.

Kane rolled and brought himself back up as the vehicle passed, his Sin Eater appearing without conscious thought in the palm of his hand. He was tracking the monster machine as it trundled away, automatically activating his Commtact as he watched it disappear behind the camouflaging curtain of falling snow. "Check in—everyone okay?" he asked.

"ALIVE," GRANT WHUFFED, his voice coming in a breathless growl as he skittered across the snow. He was scrambling forward in a tumble of dislodged snow, out of control.

Grant was thirty feet away from Kane and still moving, having leaped in the opposite direction to his partner. There had been no time to plan the maneuver— Grant had simply leaped out of the behemoth's path.

When he did so, Grant had been surprised by breaking
ice and a dip in the snow and had suddenly found himself scrambling down a steep slope, not quite balanced or
in control of his descent. A dark copse of leafless trees
loomed up ahead like grave markers in the whiteness.
Grant felt his feet lift off the ground as he bumped over
something hidden by the snow, and for a moment he was
in the air. Then he crashed into the foremost tree with a
yelp of pain, and a shower of snow came tumbling over
him, dislodged from the tree's splayed branches.

Grant muttered something unintelligible as he sagged
to the ground, his descent curtailed in an instant.

BRIGID HAD BEEN more successful, diving out of the path
of the artificial monster, tucking and rolling as the thing
roared past. "Me, too," she chimed in, responding to
Kane's query from where she now lay sprawled on the
freezing white blanket of snow.

But she had become temporarily confused, lost on
the white blanket, snow-blind.

REASSURED BY HIS partners' responses, Kane watched the
vehicle lumber past him in a descending hum of growl-
ing engine. The noise was almost obliterated by the muf-
fling effect of the snow, and after barely a dozen feet it
had—incredibly—all but fallen into silence.

Kane pulled himself up from the ground and started
after the disappearing vehicle, the Sin Eater clenched in
his right hand. It was traveling slowly—Kane estimated
it was moving at no more than ten miles an hour—but
it was big and heavy and the environment had perfectly
masked its approach until almost too late.

It wasn't just wide—it was long, too; fifty feet of towering vehicle, like a double-stack train carriage bump-

ing over the alabaster environment like a skipping stone on a lake.

Twin funnels or chimneys were located on its roof, one on each end, wide as a Manta's wing and all but obscured by the falling snow. Kane could barely see them through the thick snow—thicker than before, in fact.

In a split-second decision, Kane sent the Sin Eater back to its hidden holster and began hurrying after the vehicle. "I'm going after it," Kane said into the Commtact pickup.

"Kane—wait!" Brigid urged, but Kane ignored her.

The thick snow slowed his movements—it was more like wading than running—but Kane was close enough that he should be able to reach the mysterious vehicle in a dozen paces at the speed it was traveling. Through the there-again-gone-again curtain of snow, he saw bars lining the back vertical and horizontal pipes that presumably carried some kind of warming fluid to keep the vehicle running in the extreme cold. Kane reached for one, kicking his legs high to pull himself over the thick snow. It was like hurdling, keeping up with the slow-moving machine through the dense carpet of snow, the blasted thing frustratingly just out of reach, like something chased in a dream.

Snow fell on his face, settled on his shoulders as he moved through the harsh environment.

Then he had it, right arm lunging forward and snagging one of those vertical pipes. Kane let out a gasp as he grabbed it, held tight and dragged himself forward, forcing his legs to high-jump over the thick snow.

For a moment, Kane's shoulder fired with pain, the stress of dragging himself forward onto the vehicle—slow-moving but moving all the same. Snow obscured his sight, the whiteness of the vehicle itself contributing to the confusion. Then his left hand grasped blindly at something sticking out from the rear, another line of pipe work that felt ice-cold to the touch, even with his gloves and the regulated temperature of the shadow suit. Kane snarled as he swung himself up onto the back plate, lifting himself up by the two pipes, drawing his legs and feet out of the snow.

It was a precarious position. The snowy ground bumped beneath him, inches from the soles of his Mag boots. Kane tensed both arms and pulled, drawing himself up onto the back of the mysterious vehicle in a proxy chin-up.

Kane's feet worked along the vehicle's side, scrabbling for purchase against the ice-cold metal. He kicked out, holding himself up by the twin pipes, and the toe of his left boot clipped against something—a ledge, hidden by a powdering of snow. The ledge ran around the bottom of the vehicle in a rim no wider than an inch, and it was thick with ice crystals.

Kane looked down, eyeballing the ledge as he brushed the snow aside with his toe. He could balance on it, feet sideways while still clinging to the pipes—it wasn't much but it was something, enough at least to take the pressure off his straining arms.

"I'm on board," Kane whispered into his Commtact.

"YOU'RE WHAT?" Brigid spat. "Kane, no!"

The snow was falling around her, thicker it seemed than it had been just a few moments ago. She stared into the whiteness, searching for the vehicular behemoth that Kane had chased, but it was already lost to the obscuring curtain of white.

She had been moving toward where Grant lay, a lone dark blotch on the white carpet. He hadn't spoken after his initial response to Kane's query, but Brigid had been alerted by the noise of breaking branches as he slammed into the copse of trees.

"Grant's not responding," Brigid explained, inwardly cursing her inability to see the vehicle that Kane had now boarded.

"SAY AGAIN?" KANE SHOT back in reply. Snow fell on him in a ceaseless torrent, turning his hair prematurely white. He could not hear Brigid over the sound of the vehicle's engine—and the way the moving vehicle shook his jaw was making it sound like someone was playing a drum solo through the Commtact.

"Grant's not responding," Brigid repeated, and this time Kane pieced together what she was saying.

"Check on him," Kane whispered, resisting the urge to shout over the roar of the vehicle. He didn't want to prematurely alert whoever was driving the thing that they had a stowaway in the form of this Cerberus warrior.

As he spoke, Kane was tilting his head this way and that, searching the rear of the vehicle through the obscuring snow for some way to get to a more secure position. Something was sticking out of the side, a jutting arrangement of pipes that ran in horizontal lines like a ladder. Kane shifted his precariously balanced body, reaching out the full extent of his left arm and clawing the corner of the vehicle until he had a solid grip on it. Then he pulled himself over, his booted feet scrambling along the tiny ledge at an awkward angle.

Kane drew himself to the edge, his face pressed hard against the chill metal. He reached again, blind now, his left hand running up and down and farther outward until he grabbed one of the line of pipes that ran up the vehicle's side. Then, with a mighty yank, Kane swung out and pulled himself around, whipping around the edge of the slow-moving vehicle until he was around the corner.

Around this side of the vehicle—a revelation. The pipes weren't pipes at all, they were a ladder, painted white and permanently affixed to the side of the strange vehicle, running up its side and to its roof. Kane grabbed ahold of one of the jutting bars of metal attached to its side, the metal ice-cold to the touch. Kane ignored the freezing temperature and clambered up the rungs.

"I'm secure," Kane explained over the shared Commtact frequency as he pulled himself up the side of the vehicle's metal frame.

He scrambled up the rungs of the ladder, drawing himself higher up the side of the mystery vehicle that had been generating the heat that they had detected when they entered the snowstorm. Kane didn't know what it was—not yet—but he was certain that the best way to find out was to get on board.

BRIGID WADED CAREFULLY down to where Grant lay unmoving among the little group of trees that formed a perfect circle. Grant was lying faceup in the snow, his breath coming from his open mouth in visible clouds of mist, hanging there like a slowly deflating balloon that refilled every time he breathed out. He didn't react to her, didn't move or look up.

As she came closer, Brigid called to her partner.

"Grant?"

The word sounded muffled in the denseness of the snow-filled air, almost as though the sound had to dodge between snow flurries to reach its target. The bigger man did not respond.

"Grant?" Brigid said again, breathing a little harder

as she reached the man. She put her hand against one of the trees for balance and a shower of snow tumbled from its upper branches. Brigid brushed the snow from her sleeve and crouched down, checking Grant's pulse.

The pulse was solid and she could see his breath—it was hard to miss even through the falling snow—but he didn't respond to her calling or stir when she touched him. There was blood on his forehead, too, she saw now, a thin line of it trickling down the left-hand side of his face like a crack in the shell of an egg.

"Grant?" Brigid said again, gazing around her for the first time since she had stopped moving.

There was no sign of the vehicle that Kane had leaped aboard, not even a whisper of engine noise carrying over the dull plains of whiteness. In fact, the only thing breaking up the white veil was the copse of trees, dark trunks and leafless branches clawing up into the gray-white sky like the hands of a skeleton.

Brigid glanced at the trees for a moment, then looked again, more closely, eyeing the tooling on the bark of the nearest one's trunk. The pattern repeated in three-foot intervals a little like wallpaper, complex but repeating just the same, in a way that nature doesn't. The pattern was repeated on the other trees, the same complex mix of whorls and indentations copied across each tree trunk. A normal person might not notice it straight away, but Brigid's eidetic memory picked up on the repetition almost as if someone had run a highlighter pen through it. There was only one possible conclusion: the trees were artificial.

Swiftly, Brigid checked over Grant to make sure his wound wasn't life-threatening. Then she pushed herself up from the ground and touched the nearest of the trees, running her hand up and down its trunk.

"What are you?" Brigid muttered to herself.

As she spoke, something appeared behind her, the whispered shuffle of moving feet alerting her sensitive hearing. She turned but saw only whiteness.

THE WINDS BLEW, buffeting Kane against the side of the colossal vehicle as he climbed the ladder, swirling snow into his eyes and nostrils. He kept his mouth shut, a thin line where his lips met, eyes narrowed against the assault.

He could not see the top of the vehicle. White on white and with the falling snow slapping against his face, it was hard to see anything at all. So he just kept climbing, gloved hands grasping the next rung, then the next, up and up until he finally found there were no more rungs left to climb.

Kane opened his eyes a little wider, looking above him. Snow was pouring vigorously toward him, more like a waterfall than a snow flurry. He let loose a grunt of frustration as the snow caught in his eyelashes, ice-cold against the surface of his left eye.

Up there, just above his hands, he could make out the line of gray where the sky met the whiteness of the vehicle. It was barely discernible but it *was* there. He could reach up, grab it—just had to be careful not to get thrown off his ride by the high winds.

Kane took a steadying breath through his nostrils, reached up and grabbed the edge of the vehicle with his left hand, then followed a second later with his right arm, lifting it up and outward until he had the forearm all the way over the side, scrabbling left and right until he found something to grab on to. That something was an indentation of some kind, deep enough to get the joints of his first two knuckles in to secure himself.

His feet swayed out for a moment as he struggled to get higher up the ladder, slipping momentarily on the ice-slick ladder rungs. Then he was over the side, up on the roof of the swaying, towering vehicle.

And what he saw there made him pause with astonishment.

IT TOOK A MOMENT for Brigid to see the figures moving toward her. They wore reflective suits, with full facemasks and hoods over their heads. The mirrored surfaces reflected the snow, creating almost perfect camouflage for the environment. She counted four of them—no five, six—dammit but they were hard to see in this snow.

"My friend's hurt," Brigid said, wary of the strangers.

The closest of the group raised a hand, and Brigid saw a weapon in it—a blaster, painted white so that it was all but hidden in the snow. The stranger said nothing.

"I don't mean to—" Brigid began, but even as she spoke, the stranger with the gun fired, sending a dart-like projectile toward her with a whuff of pressurized air.

Communiqué to Ioville Magistrate 620M:

Report for training, Cappa Level. Citizens are to be instructed in all forms of combat and fitness. You are to supervise and instruct, accompanied by Magistrate 265M. Session to last 180 minutes, with one break of eight minutes.

Message ends.

Chapter 8

"Target acquired," a man's voice came from one of the reflective suits.

Brigid ducked and rolled, years of training kicking in even as the blaster fired. The dart sailed past her, cutting the air three inches above her left shoulder before imbedding itself in a tree with a comical *sproing*.

"You missed," one of the white-clad figures exclaimed as Brigid rolled aside.

As she brought herself into an upright crouch, Brigid saw the other figures raise their arms—although this was difficult to distinguish with the reflective suits on the white background—and she realized that they were bringing more blasters into play.

A line of darts peppered the ground around her as Brigid leaped back, slipping between the artificial trees.

Brigid kept moving, her hand reaching down for the blaster she had strapped to her hip—the familiar TP-9 semiautomatic pistol. The TP-9 was a bulky hand pistol with a covered targeting scope across the top, finished in molded matte black. The grip was set just off-center beneath the barrel, creating a lopsided square in the user's hand, hand and wrist making the final side and corner.

The silver-clad figures followed Brigid into the copse of artificial trees, stepping past Grant's prone form. They were hard to spot clearly, and Brigid had to keep her wits about her to keep track of them; meanwhile, she must have stood out like a beacon with her flame-bright hair amid the stark whiteness. Only here, among the trees, did she have some semblance of cover and camouflage.

Another dart whipped by Brigid's face, the wind of its passage blowing her hair back. Close, she thought. Damn close.

Brigid raised her blaster to target her attackers. Leg shots would disable them—that's all she needed just now, until she could find out who they were and just what was going on.

"There!" one of the figures shouted, and Brigid ducked as another pair of darts thudded against the trunk of the closest tree, preceded only by the whisper of expelled air.

Brigid brought the TP-9 around and fired, sending a short burst of bullets through the trees at the group of strangers. The action was loud in the muffled snows-cape, the sounds of the shots carrying like a crack of thunder.

Two of Brigid's attackers fell with that first volley, slumping to the ground with yelps of pain as their legs were cut out from under them. Brigid barely saw the movements, white on white as they were; instead she intuited how many she had hit from the sounds of the falling bodies, two muffled thumps amid the tiny copse of trees.

"The stranger is armed," Brigid heard one of her attackers announce.

"Disarm her," another responded.

Saying and doing—two different things, Brigid thought as she weaved through the group of trees. Up close the trees were convincing, but there was a regularity to them that reminded Brigid of something else—

antenna uplinks, the kind used to pick up and broadcast radio signals across the globe. The trunk would house the power source, she realized, while the irregular splay of branches would funnel and boost the signal, sending and receiving radio communications as required. And with the radio comms could come something else, too—a tester signal used to monitor the environment.

No wonder the group of mirror-clad figures had come to find her so quickly—Grant must have tripped some kind of sensor alarm when he slammed into the antenna.

The cough of an air gun behind her alerted Brigid to a more immediate matter. She dipped her head low even as another dart whipped past overhead, missing her by a foot and a half.

Could be that these people were mad at her team for trespassing. If that was the case, then a little sit-down discussion should smooth things over. But they'd come out armed and they weren't discussing anything. Whatever was going on out here, hidden in the permanent snowstorm, Brigid's best chance to discover rested on getting these people on side. And that meant disarming them so they couldn't fight back.

ATOP THE VEHICLE, the noise was incredible.

Kane crouched on the roof of the mechanical behemoth, openmouthed as he stared at what waited there—a single gigantic chimney, of a size and diameter that rivaled anything seen in an industrial furnace. The chimney took up almost all of the surface of the vehicle's roof, its round edges touching the sides of the vehicle and leaving just a little room, top and bottom, for the roof itself.

Kane tried to estimate the thing's size. It towered high above the vehicle itself, adding perhaps half the height of the vehicle again, perhaps more than that—it was hard to tell with the white painted exterior against the snow-thick sky.

And the snow *was* thick. Really thick, like looking into the glass bowl of a popcorn maker, thicker by far than it had been at ground level. Kane realized with a start just why that was—the chimney was billowing a white plume of snow high above, blasting a chill jet into the air above the vehicle as it trundled along on its indefatigable path.

"It's making snow," Kane muttered, the words lost to the roiling roar of the mechanism before him.

He watched for a moment as the broad chimneylike structure continued to belch snow into the sky above him. The jet blasted high into the air like something at a fireworks display, and Kane realized that only a small offshoot of that snow jet was falling down on him—most of it was being channeled far higher into the atmosphere, generating a continuous stream of white flecks.

But why, Kane wondered, would anyone want to make snow?

It didn't make sense.

The answers, he realized, had to be below, inside the cab of this one-of-a-kind machine. Kane looked around him, searching for a way inside.

As he looked, the vehicle lurched over a bump in the ground, and Kane was thrown a half-dozen paces around the rooftop until he found himself scrambling for purchase, his legs dangling over the side. He clung there as the vehicle trundled on, reassuring himself that it had righted its path over whatever had got in its way.

Then he pulled himself back on board and scrambled across the snow-wet rooftop, keeping his head down and his body low. His breath came behind him in huffed clouds of vapor while Kane tracked around the chimney.

He figured there had to be a way in from up here— an access hatch for repairing the chimney itself. Sure enough, there was. A covered manhole lay at the front of the vehicle just beyond the edge of the chimney, painted white like everything else on the vehicle, with a bar-type handle secured beside it to assist anyone who climbed up here. Kane crept toward it.

HIDDEN AMONG THE tiny group of trees, Brigid spun as another dart whipped through the air before her. The dart glanced against her chest, but the strong weave of the shadow suit deflected it, butting it away so that it landed on the snowy ground, its energy spent.

Got to disarm them, Brigid told herself as she raised her blaster and located one of the hidden figures amid the whiteness. The TP-9 bucked in her hand as she fired, sending a single 9 mm bullet into the white-clad figure's leg with a sound like thunder. Brigid watched in grim satisfaction as the figure pirouetted and fell to the ground, a tiny spray of blood crossing the air in a flurry of red beads.

But she was too slow—another figure had reached Brigid, perfectly camouflaged in his mirrored outfit, and swiped at her with an outthrust leg. Brigid heard the movement at the same time that she felt the blow strike her behind the knee, and she went tumbling forward, her pistol blasting a useless stream of bullets ahead of her as her finger clenched involuntarily on the trigger.

Brigid struck the snow chin-first, but it was soft, forgiving. She rolled onto her back in an instant, scissoring out with her legs to try to catch her attacker before he got out of range. Liquid fire seemed to burn through her left knee in protest as she moved the leg where her attacker had connected, but she ignored it, sweeping her leg into his feet as he tried to sidestep.

Brigid saw a blur of whiteness, heard the sudden *flump* as her attacker caromed off the ground. She sprung across to him, drawing the TP-9 around to target the face obscured behind the all-encompassing hood. As she looked at it, she saw only her own face, distorted and red-cheeked, reflected in the uneven mirror.

"Who are you?" Brigid spat. "Why are you trying to kill me?"

The man—and she was certain that it was a man now, beneath all that mirrored material—drove his knee up and into Brigid's gut, catching her just below the rib cage. She fell back, gasping for breath.

"I have her," the man announced, saying the words loudly as he pulled himself up to a kneeling position.

Brigid sucked in a breath, the cold air burning her throat and lungs. Beside her, the figure in the camouflaged outfit drew one of the white-painted pistols from a buckled holster at his side, raising it mechanically toward Brigid's prone form.

Brigid grimaced, her eyes narrow as she fought against the pain in her belly and knee. Grant was out there, unconscious and unprotected, and here she was, struggling to draw breath, no use to him.

"Kane, I—" she began, firing up the Commtact without a conscious thought.

The man in the mirrored clothes blasted her then, sending another of those strange dart-like projectiles at Brigid where she lay helpless. It drilled into her chest, just to the left of her breastbone, its tip penetrating the strong weave of the shadow suit beneath her pale jacket.

"—need…" Brigid continued, forcing the words out

as the dart released a powerful drug through her system. The next word didn't want to come and so she lay there, helpless, as the insubstantial shapes of her attackers moved closer, weaving through the trees. "…help," she managed at last before dropping into the frightening and hollow darkness of drug-induced unconsciousness.

Designated Task #013: Child Care.

Child care is performed on Beta Level. And is the responsibility of all citizens of Ioville, although some have the designed task as their main duty. I provide support during three morning shifts a week, before I clock in for my main role at Designated Task #004.

The children are schooled and disciplined through to age eleven, at which point they have gained maturity and join the workforce.

Education is conducted via light screen and private audio, meaning my role is purely as supervisor and to ensure no sickness or other disruption affects the classroom of the six-year-olds assigned to me. Other than the whisper of the private audio leaking through the earphones, the room is silent and, as such, calming. I take these shifts willingly, allowing my thoughts to wander. Sometimes I think back to the man whom I met on the day I was assigned my new apartment, the man with broad shoulders and blue-gray eyes, whose anxiousness seemed to rage like fire. I wonder: Whatever became of him?

—*From the journal of Citizen 619F.*

Chapter 9

The towering vehicle trundled over the icy terrain, its broad chimney spewing cool snow up into the atmosphere. Kane hurried over to the manhole on its rooftop and ran his fingers along the edges. He searched for a moment, feeling at the seam with his gloved hands, cold from the punishing weather and losing a little sensation even despite the best efforts of his shadow suit to keep his core temperature regulated.

It took ten seconds to find a gap in the cover wide enough to slip three fingers in, another five to pull and push it until he had figured which way the hatch moved. It opened inward, Kane discovered, flapping down on a hinge that dropped it inside the body of the vehicle itself before locking against the wall with some kind of magnetic seal, holding it in place to the opposite side from the rooftop handle.

Kane peered down into the open hatchway. The hatch was rectangular and opened into a circular tunnel that dropped straight down into the body of the vehicle, disappearing into darkness after a half-dozen feet or so.

"Belly of the beast," Kane muttered to himself as he grasped the handle and swung himself down into the vertical tunnel. A moment later, he had slipped beneath roof level, snow swirling after him in his wake. He chose to leave the hatchway open—he didn't know what to expect down there, and standard protocol was to leave himself with an escape route.

The tunnel was narrow and cold, with slick sides and a single ladder that Kane estimated ran almost the full height of the towering vehicle until he was almost back at ground level. It made sense—most of the vehicle must have been taken up by that colossal chimney that utterly dominated the roof, and its pumping system would most likely take up almost all of the strange-looking vehicle itself.

It was loud, too, almost deafening, in fact, where the mechanics that ran the pump—or whatever it was that was generating all that snow—churned behind the wall at Kane's back.

Kane moved quickly, his muscles pumping efficiently as he clambered down the lone ladder that was molded into the wall.

As he neared the bottom, Kane slowed his pace and listened, his feet still higher than the bottom of the ladder where they might be seen. Some might observe that it was a vain hope that Kane might somehow detect someone waiting just below him in the chamber that the tunnel opened into. But those observers would not have known about Kane's fabled pointman sense, a seemingly supernatural ability to detect danger before it appeared. It was not supernatural, however. Like everything else in Kane's repertoire, it was the product of many hours of training and drilling, dating all the way back to his days as a Magistrate in distant Cobaltville. Another life, almost another world—but still Kane relied on the things he had learned there, the tricks he had perfected in the name of survival.

For a moment, all Kane could hear was the loud hum of the mechanism powering the chimney, a great bass thrumming that shook through his bones and in his chest cavity. Perfectly still on the ladder, Kane filtered that noise out, listened more intently for something— anything—else. After a moment he picked up a familiar sound, the low hum of fans cooling electronic machinery. There was a pip of electronic chatter, then relative silence once more as the vehicle continued on its journey. Kane could not detect anything else.

Confident that he was not walking into an ambush, Kane clambered down the final few rungs of the ladder, keeping his movements economical and appreciably silent despite the loud whir of fans and pumps just a few feet behind the metal wall at his back. He dropped into a crouch at the bottom, commanding the Sin Eater back into his hand as he landed.

Like the access tunnel, it was unlit here, too.

Kane reached into an inside pocket of his jacket and pulled free what appeared to be a pair of sunglasses, which he slipped over the bridge of his nose. The glasses had specially coated polymer lenses and were designed to draw every available iota of light to create an image of whatever was around the viewer, acting as a kind of proxy night vision. Kane scanned the area through the polymer lenses, allowing them to gather the light.

The change was immediate. The walls came into sudden sharp relief through the miraculous lenses. Kane was in a small chamber, its ceiling just five feet high, low enough that he would need to duck if he tried to walk upright. It was an access area, nothing more, linking the rest of the vehicle to the access tunnel leading to the roof hatch. The walls were plain, flat and straight in a hexagonal pattern, with enough space for two men to work with maybe a little space between them. The chamber featured a cupboard on one wall with an open handle—the kind one puts one's finger in to pull the door open.

The chamber also featured a single doorway, round like a porthole, that a user would have to crouch to step through. Kane peered through the doorway briefly, jabbing his head through the partition for a moment before darting back inside. A corridor ran from the porthole into the depths of the vehicle, unlit but shown in stark relief care of the polymer lenses. The corridor was bland and empty, with blank walls lined with thick pipes.

Kane turned back to the chamber he was in, reaching down for the cupboard. Kane tried it, stepping back just far enough to let the door swing a few inches from the wall. Inside was a fire extinguisher with a small shelf above it. The shelf contained a little case, which Kane pulled out and opened. Inside was a basic repair kit, screwdrivers, a sealed pack of spare screws, a container of multifunction oil, rubber bands and a few other items that could come in handy when making a temporary fix on a machine. There was nothing particularly telling or useful to Kane's current situation, however.

Leaving the contents of the cupboard in place, Kane stepped out through the porthole-like doorway and into the corridor beyond. Pipes ran along both walls, many of them over a foot thick. He touched one of the pipes—it was ice-cold.

Kane made his way along the corridor and stopped when he reached its end. An open doorway waited there, once again round like a porthole. Kane held his blaster ready and listened once more, feeling out with his pointman sense.

Nothing.

He was certain that he was alone. Almost certain, anyway. There was always a chance that this vehicle had a driver—in fact, that would have been Kane's assumption. But even discounting the roar of the processing plant contained within the body of the vehicle itself, he could detect no voices, no sounds of breathing or any of the other unconscious-body noises a person makes even at rest.

He stepped through into the main chamber of the vehicle.

BRIGID AWOKE IN the back of a moving Sandcat—a land vehicle favored by Magistrates with a wide holding area inside and an abbreviated ladder leading up to a rooftop turret. The Sandcat was an armored vehicle with a low-slung, blocky chassis supported by a pair of flat, retractable tracks. Its exterior was a ceramic armaglass compound that could shrug off small-arms fire, and it featured a swiveling gun turret up top armed with twin USMG-73 heavy machine guns.

The dart had contained some kind of sedative, Brigid realized groggily, replaying her last conscious memory in her mind's eye as she lay against the cold metal floor of the Sandcat.

She was slumped against the vehicle's wall, her blaster no longer in its holster pressing against her hip, the side of her face pressed against the cold metal floor. There was a figure sitting beside her, dressed in the strange reflective suit of her attackers—presumably one of them. He had the hood down and the mask off, showing the face of a young man with close-cropped black hair and a scar down the left-hand side of his face, a quarter inch wide of his eye. He held his leg out before him, a bloody smear showing on the torn material there, so Brigid figured he was one of the ones she had shot. The man's teeth were clenched, lips pulled back as he massaged his knee.

Carefully, conscious of the enemy sitting beside her, Brigid tried turning her head and found she couldn't. Whatever was in that dart was still racing around her system, leaving her paralyzed. Her chest felt tight, mouth dry. It would pass, she knew; no one used a tranquilizer dart in that situation unless they wanted their victim alive.

She took some time then just analyzing her situation. Her eyes could still move, although they felt gritty and tired. The top of her head was facing the direction of travel, which made it hard for her to see up front when she couldn't move her neck. She rolled her eyes up and to the side, taking in what she could from the angle. There were two seats up front of the Sandcat, driver and passenger. Both were occupied by men in the reflective camo suits. They traveled in silence, only the growl of the engine accompanying their path across the settled snow.

So, three hostiles in all—one wounded.

She was sure there had been six attackers in the trees, though, which meant three of the enemy were unaccounted for. That suggested another Sandcat, splitting the group in two. Brigid knew that a three-man crew in a Sandcat was SOP for Magistrates. Were these people Mags, then?

Outside, through the windshield, Brigid could see the snow, a great blanket of white with more snow falling in great flurries across the glass.

She shifted her gaze until she spotted the other figure in the back—Grant, a dusting of snow at the edges of his goatee beard, eyes closed in sleep. He had been knocked out good by his altercation with the tree, and it was entirely possible he had been drugged since then when these strangers had grabbed them both.

Brigid tried to hail him on her Commtact but she found she could not work her mouth muscles enough to even subvocalize a message to him. The best she could manage was to click her tongue a few times against the roof of her mouth, and she received no response over the hidden Commtact behind her cochlear.

So she lay there, helpless and cold as the Sandcat bumped over the rugged terrain. Wherever you are, Kane, Brigid thought, I hope you can help.

KANE CLAMBERED INTO the cab of the huge vehicle with the belching chimney stack. The cab was unmanned, though it featured a single seat placed centrally amid a semicircle of information screens and controls.

Warily, Kane paced across the space to the seat, checking behind him—behind the door—in case he was walking into an ambush. There was no one present.

Kane leaned over the console, eyeing the controls. There were five glass-fronted screens, showing computer displays and a radar feed, along with several pressure gauges with wavering needles shaking like wagging fingers behind their glass. There were no windows in the room, no windshield through which a passenger might look out from—just the screens, their twinkling lights casting the only illumination in the room.

Carefully, Kane sat in the seat and looked more closely at the controls. He was not an engineer but he recognized a diagnosis feed on one of the screens. It showed a wire-frame plan of a tower containing a pumping unit at its base, and it took Kane just a moment to conclude what it was—the chimney.

It was a snow machine, he realized now, the great bulk of the vehicle dedicated to the intake and cooling of water vapor, which it then expelled as flecks of ice,

generating artificial snow. In large enough quantities
that ice could affect the weather in the immediate area,
possibly enough to create the snowstorm that Cerberus
had identified as dominating this region for over a year.
But that surely would take more of these chimneys and
perhaps something more substantial, Kane reckoned—
which meant that there was every chance there were
more of these weird "snow wags" trawling the plains.

He activated his Commtact automatically, patching
through to Cerberus in an instant. "Think I've found the
source of our weather pattern," he said. "Acknowledge."

Kane waited a moment for Cerberus to respond.
When they didn't, he tried again, his eyes flicking over
the other screens and taking in what they had to offer.
One showed a rolling wire-frame interpretation of an
undulating plain, no doubt the local terrain as picked
up by onboard sensors in the vehicle. Another was a
radar sweep in familiar green on black, which showed
several fixed-point markers amid its black field, none
of which were labeled. The other screens showed ever-
changing stats that Kane could not begin to fathom in
just a glance like this, but he took them to be related
either to the snow production or whatever was going
on outside.

"Cerberus, acknowledge," Kane said, his voice a little
more urgent now as he spoke into the hidden Commtact pickup.

All that came in response was dead air. The snowstorm was probably affecting the signal somehow, Kane
realized, and he was sitting right in the heart of it.

The mysterious vehicle bumped over a rise, and Kane
clung to the arms of the chair as it shook in place.

STILL UNABLE TO MOVE, all Brigid could do was watch. The man in the seat beside her cleaned his wound with grim efficiency using a medikit housed in the Sandcat. Grant did not stir; he appeared to be dead to the world. Meanwhile, Brigid's senses came back very slowly, and mostly in the form of excruciating pins and needles that she could do nothing about. She still could not move, could not even speak. All she could do was breathe, but that, at least, was becoming easier, the tightness in her chest abating. The air was cold.

She watched from the floor of the Sandcat as the snow batted against the windshield, saw a second Sandcat emerge into view from the right-hand side. This Sandcat was painted white, making it almost perfectly camouflaged in the snow.

Time passed, time spent feeling the incessant irritation of pins and needles in her limbs and all the way down her right flank where it rested against the cold metal floor. Through the floor, Brigid felt the Sandcat begin to slow, the engine humming as the brakes were applied. This sensation was accompanied by a change in pitch of the engine, the barely restrained lion's roar turning to a louder and higher squeal.

Brigid saw something flicker across the windshield where she could see between the two men up front. It looked darker, a shadow in the snow. She strained her head, trying to move her skull so that she could see better, but her muscles would not respond; they were still deadened by the tranquilizer that these strangers had dosed her with.

The darkness flashed again against the brilliance, larger this time, which meant they were getting closer. It took a moment to figure out what she was looking at, with the angle and the snow falling across the windshield like a bead curtain. But she recognized it. It was a ville, eerily familiar with its high walls and guard posts located at each corner and by the main gates. The towers of the ville peered from behind those high walls, set out in the same pattern that every ville followed, from Cobaltville to Beausoliel—a pattern that had been perfected over millennia by the Annunaki and designed to restrict the thoughts and progress of humanity. The snow-capped towers shone with gold.

"On approach," she heard a voice say up front, emanating from a radio speaker. "Stay on your vector."

It all made no sense. Brigid knew the map, could call it to mind in an instant. Nothing should be here, nothing but farmland and small settlements. Not a ville, not one like this.

The Sandcat slowed further, pulling almost to a stop before the gates as its partner passed through. A moment later, Brigid's Sandcat was trailing the other one through the gates.

Come on, Kane, she thought. Where are you?

The Sandcat passed through the ville gates and disappeared into darkness beyond.

Designated Task #001: Air Monitoring.

Air Monitoring is performed in a dedicated room on Cappa Level. Monitoring is overseen by two Magistrates at all times, along with a bank of trained citizens who work the day-to-day chores with the machinery.

I will be assigned here one morning every two weeks, before my shift at Designated Task #004 begins. My first experience here comes under Orientation, and involves a Magistrate showing me the functionality of the equipment and explaining the necessity of the department.

It is my understanding that the intake and monitoring of the air quality in Ioville is considered to be of paramount importance, and that any deviation to its purity is to be reported immediately to the Supreme Magistrate in charge. Protocol dictates that both Magistrates must be informed of any change, and that any sufficient deviation in quality will then be reported to Supreme Magistrate Webb. This protocol must never be deviated from—to do so is punishable by immediate execution.

The ventilation system of Ioville is unusually complex for a ville. It features numerous checks and balances and it feeds all air to the ville and its citizens. No unfiltered air may enter the ville because of the possibility of contamination.

The monitoring equipment is detailed, complete plans of the ventilation system with highlighted areas showing any blockages or traps, potential leaks and any other issues that arise, minute-by-minute, in real time. To be assigned monitoring duty is a daunting task, one which the monitors must train for over many months on a training simulation before they can be allowed to function on the live system. I am informed via comms screen that perhaps I will be assigned this role, once I have proven my worth at Designated Task #004.

—From the journal of Citizen 619F.

Chapter 10

The twin Sandcats passed into the hidden ville via a tunnel, sheltering them from the falling snow.

Sprawled on the floor, Brigid tried to move again, willing her muscles to respond. Her fingers twitched and she felt the agonising pressure as the pins and needles there fired with renewed vigor. But at least she could move.

She worked again, eyes watching the wounded warrior who sat over her and Grant. He was distracted, his head tilted up ahead to watch their progress through the tunnel that sloped down beneath the ville towers. Lights ran along the edges of the tunnel, and Brigid sensed that they were descending on a shallow incline, moving beneath the buildings of the ville. Ville buildings are connected by a series of walkways and wide passages, some of them wide enough to house a Sandcat. Internal roads weave between the buildings, grand tunnels of up to four lanes protected by curving roofs. This ville was no different than any other.

The brake lights of the other Sandcat flashed up ahead and both vehicles slowed, turning in as they reached the end of the tunnel. Wiggling her toes inside her boots, Brigid watched through the windshield as the Sandcat entered a garage area the size of an aircraft hangar.

Brigid watched through the windshield as the other

Sandcat peeled away, parking beside a fleet of identical vehicles. A moment later, her own vehicle pulled to a halt with a hiss of brakes. The driver was the first out of his seat, raising the gull-wing door and stepping out into the garage lot. A moment later, the side door of the Sandcat opened and the passenger—another of the reflective-suited group—appeared to help their colleague hobble out of the rear.

"How is your leg?" one asked—Brigid could not tell which, for both men remained in their hoods, only their masks removed, and she had not gotten a look at their faces up until this moment. They both looked normal, in their mid- to late twenties, brown hair cropped identically short, only the harsh lines of the one to the left's jaw distinguishing him from his colleague—otherwise they could have passed for twins.

"My leg is damaged," the man in the back confirmed emotionlessly. "I'll go to Medical."

The man with the softer jaw nodded. "Acknowledged."

With that, the man that Brigid had shot hopped out of the back of the Sandcat and limped away through the garage area. Brigid watched through the open door, flexing her reviving muscles through the masking cover of her clothes.

The two remaining figures—Brigid had begun to suspect that they were Magistrates—stared into the doorway, taking in Brigid and Grant.

"These two need to go to Processing," said the man on the right.

"Agreed. And Supreme Magistrate Webb needs to be advised of their arrival," said the other with the same lack of emotion.

Supreme Magistrate? Brigid thought. Well, that was interesting.

She had never heard of a Supreme Magistrate before. Supervisors, yes—the Magistrate system, like any other military structure, had a hierarchy. But the use of the term "Supreme Magistrate" was new to her and it wasn't something either Kane or Grant had ever mentioned. *Dammit*, if only Grant were awake to confirm this.

Brigid may not know the full inner workings and hierarchy of the Magistrate system but she did know one thing—being shot at by Mags without warning was bad, even if they were using tranqs. It meant they weren't interested in negotiating. They probably intended to toss her and Grant into a cell somewhere and forget about them. She could not allow that to happen.

One of the men stepped into the back of the Sandcat, eyeing Grant and Brigid. Then he reached for Grant, getting his hands under the bigger man's armpits, and dragged him through the open door.

Brigid would be next, she knew. She tensed her muscles and prepared herself as the other figure reached in for her. He knelt down on the deck and placed one arm under Brigid's knees, the other under her shoulders. As he did so, she moved, kicking out with her left leg, striking the man in the chest. The blow was not ideal, but it caught the man by surprise and he toppled back against the frame of the Sandcat, momentarily losing his balance. His breath expelled through his mouth in a whuff of rushing air.

Brigid moved swiftly, rolling over, muscles complaining, dragging her knees up under her. She triggered her Commtact—now was not the time for subtlety—and called for Kane. She knew that with the biolink transponder she had embedded subcutaneously, the Cerberus control room would be tracking her and would be able to pass that information to Kane so that he could come find her and Grant. She just hoped he wasn't too far away because she didn't much fancy her chances with fighting off a whole army of these guys.

But when she tried to speak, Brigid discovered her tongue was still struggling under the tranquilizer—it lolled in her mouth like a beached fish, and all that came out from her voice box was a kind of "Allallall" sound.

As Brigid tried to hail Kane or Cerberus, the man in the vehicle recovered himself, bracing for impact with his forearms held up protectively before him—a typical Mag move. At the same time, his partner outside the vehicle dropped Grant, leaving the slumbering Cerberus warrior on the floor of the garage, and was pulling his blaster from its holster at his hip.

Lying on her back, Brigid kicked out again. She directed the heels of her boots against the first Magistrate's upheld arms—once, twice, thrice—until he cried out in pain and drew his arms down just a little. In that fraction of a second, Brigid changed aim, one long leg kicking out at the gap between the man's upheld arms and booting him in the chin. Blood erupted across the man's mouth and he slumped back into the wall of the Sandcat a second time.

In continuous motion, Brigid shifted her trained body once again, taut muscles coming back to life as the second figure poked his head through the open side door, the white-shelled gun thrust out before him. Brigid shoved herself backward into the back of the passenger's seat and kicked out, using the firmness of the seat to anchor herself and send more force into her kick. Her outstretched foot met with the blaster's muzzle as it poked through the door, kicking it up as the Magistrate—if he was a Magistrate—fired. There was a *pfft* of expelled air as the gun fired, sending another of those tranquilizer darts wildly through the Sandcat interior until it embedded two feet to Brigid's right.

Brigid triggered her Commtact again, struggling desperately to send a message—however garbled—to Kane.

Hopefully Kane would hear the message and realize that there was trouble brewing, big, unexpected trouble just over the snow-capped horizon.

The other Mag was in the rear of the Sandcat now, standing with his head ducked so as not to knock into the ceiling, leveling his dart gun at Brigid's retreating form.

Brigid's emerald eyes fixed on the long nose of the gun and a dozen thoughts rushed through her mind. Why had the Mags attacked her? How had they known the Cerberus exiles were even in the area? And this ville existed where no ville was listed, a rogue tenth in a strict structure of nine.

All of this went through Brigid's mind in a scant few seconds as her attacker sighted down his weapon and pulled the trigger, sending another dart into Brigid's chest, high on the left breast.

Brigid fought it for a moment, clenching her eyes closed, balling her fists. But whatever was in the dart squelched her determination, and a moment later she had fallen into unconsciousness, sagging back against the steering column of the Sandcat.

Her final thought was a hope that Kane had received and understood her warning. Because it was all over for her.

KANE CHECKED OVER the screens in the cab of the colossal vehicle again, examining them more carefully this time. He had no way to contact Cerberus for the moment, though whether that was a by-product of the vehicle's casing or of the weather system outside, he couldn't say.

Kane looked at the display that showed the rolling terrain and compared it to the sweeping radar. The radar showed several fixed points, including one to the west that seemed larger than the others. That could be another vehicle or a building, Kane guessed, but it was hard to tell the exact size from the simplistic radar image.

He watched for a while, figured that the vehicle was making a slow circuit around a predetermined course. Everything was automated, of course—that much had been obvious from the moment he entered the cab. But it was programmed and followed a very definite pattern, passing around the area that, he guessed, Cerberus had identified with the artificial snowstorm.

So, say there were two of these vehicles. Would that be enough to create the snowstorm? Not likely, Kane figured. Then maybe three or four or six or a dozen. The continuous need to intake water vapor, the fuel expended in the operation, and the costs involved—it was astronomical. No wonder it had taken at least three barons to fund this op.

As Kane watched the displays, regularly hailing Cerberus to no avail, he thought that he had begun to detect the pattern of his journey. The vehicle was performing a very wide circuit, several miles wide perhaps, with a specific point remaining in the center. That fixed point was the blot he had noticed earlier on the radar—then to the far west and now roughly the same distance but to the north. They were circling that point, keeping it to their left at all times.

"So," Kane muttered, touching his index finger to that point on the radar display, "what's there?"

When Brigid awoke next she was lying faceup, strapped to a table in a starkly lit room that smelled of ammonia and chlorine. The table was warm beneath her, which made her suspect she had been there for some time.

Her blaster was gone still, of course, the holster feeling light against her hip.

She turned her head, but the muscles felt slow, lethargic, and they complained at every fraction of an inch she gained. As before, her eyes responded, but her tongue felt thick and swollen, like it was inflamed.

A figure moved about the room, passing through a doorway that had either been propped open or did not have a door at all. Brigid watched as the figure—a woman clad in white with blond hair slicked back from her forehead and tied in a neat ponytail—paced out of the room and disappeared, only to return a minute later carrying a datapack on which she was using a stylus to make notations. She stopped before Brigid and offered a slight smile. The smile was barely there, a social construct, and Brigid noticed that it did not extend to her eyes.

"You're awake," said the woman. Her voice was surprisingly deep.

"Mmm," Brigid responded. She tried to ask "Where's Grant?" but it came out more as "—errs Gand?"

The woman leaned a little closer, tilting her head so that her ear was above Brigid's mouth. "I'm sorry?" she asked.

"—errs Gand?" Brigid repeated more slowly. "Nigh par-ner?"

"Your friend?" the woman prompted and Brigid nodded slightly, still unable to really move. "He's here. He's fine. Doing well, in fact. He's in another section of Processing right now but you may see him again soon enough."

Brigid blinked slowly, holding her eyelids closed for a moment to acknowledge the woman's statement. "Hangh ooo."

The woman returned to her datapad and tapped something on the screen. "The sedative can take a while to wear off," she explained without looking up, "but it will do no permanent harm. You probably feel a bit silly just now."

Brigid eyed the woman and the room around her, silently testing the straps that held her, trying not to draw attention to herself. The room was a lot like the medical examination rooms in the Cerberus redoubt. She wondered then what they might be doing to her, or planning to do.

Brigid took a slow breath and tried to speak again. Her mouth seemed less swollen now, and words came more easily. "Where'm I?" she drawled.

The woman glanced up at Brigid as she replied, "In Processing."

"Brocessin...what?"

"New arrivals are processed before they can be entered into the ville. It's SOP," the woman explained, ticking off something on the datapad with her stylus. "Standard operating procedure."

"Whar...ville?" Brigid asked.

"Ioville," the woman answered without looking up. "Don't worry—you're quite safe here. We'll do all your thinking for you."

Brigid leaned back against the examination table and gathered her thoughts. She had never heard of Ioville, knew of no baron of that name. It made no sense, which meant she wasn't seeing the whole picture yet.

As she lay there, waiting, Brigid triggered her Commtact again and subvocalized a message, her teeth clamped shut. "Kane? Help me." It was all she could manage before another figure entered the room—this one a man in his forties wearing white pants and a white blazer with a white shirt beneath, buttoned up to the neck, but collarless.

The man took the datapad from the blonde and Brigid saw his eyes scan the notes she had put there. He cast a disinterested look at Brigid, then handed the datapad back to the woman.

"The subject is awake," the woman told the newcomer.

He simply nodded before leaning over Brigid and unbuttoning her top. Strapped down and still recovering from sedation, Brigid could not fight back as the man and woman stripped her then checked her body, measuring various aspects and checking for signs of disease or damage. They were drawn by the scar that ran down the nape of her neck where Ullikummis had removed her old transponder, but otherwise they concluded that she was healthy and in an acceptable condition for ville induction.

"How was the other one?" the woman asked as the two of them pawed at Brigid like a hunk of meat.

"He performed admirably," the man replied. "He's already being taken through Orientation prior to being assigned a role."

Grant, Brigid realized. They were talking about Grant. She closed her eyes in frustration as the man measured the length of her legs and took holos of her naked body lying on the slab.

THE SNOW VEHICLE seemed to lurch and the terrain showing on the rolling display before Kane shuddered as the display adjusted.

Kane watched, his eyes flicking to each of the screens arrayed before him. They had been circling a long time, but now they were heading inward, running a slow spiral that would take them—*where*?

Kane looked at the radar, compared it to the other displays and to what he had seen before. They were heading toward that bright spot that had been fixed in the center of the circuit the whole time—that one spot which the snow-making vehicle had been circling at an even distance for the past three hours.

Kane watched as the displays flickered and refreshed, making the slow change that indicated they were on their way...*home*?

Designated Task #014: Education.

Parents do not raise their children; instead, that task is left to dedicated citizens assigned to child rearing in grand residences on Beta Level. All children must be educated. Ioville has an admirably high birthrate, thanks to the use of a dedicated eugenics program, and birth survival rate is held at a steady 99.8 percent.

All children are assigned an identifier at birth that utilizes an *N*—for *New*—next to the identifying letter. Hence, the most recent birth, a boy, was registered as Citizen 304MN. The *N* is important—Supreme Magistrate Webb wishes to differentiate the population by those born here and those, like me, who were inducted. My understanding is that this relates to a medical program which studies the effects of viral control.

From birth, the children are schooled for seven hours of every day. They are taught language and math along with practical skills that will serve them well in their service to the ville.

Weren't these...? Weren't there once workstations there? On Beta Level? I can picture them in my mind's eye. Yet...

The thought passes and I perform my tasks with due diligence. I am asked to teach the Year Three children reading and writing skills so that they can understand written commands. They are keen learners.

Beta Level feels familiar in its unfamiliarity. I raise this question to my superior, Citizen 455F, who dismisses it with a shake of her head. "This area has always been dedicated to child rearing and child education. No other tasks have been performed here in the entire history of Ioville."

The word *history* makes me baulk, and I dwell on this while my class of six-year-olds perform their exercises. Once the lesson is over, I return to the supervisor and raise the question that I have framed during the hour I have had to think.

"Should history not be taught to the children, too?" I ask.

"It is," Supervisor Citizen 455F assures me. "Once they are older, they learn of the Program of Unification, the history of the baronies and the villes, and the role the benevolent barons have played in the establishment of Ioville."

I accept this with a curt nod, but I feel that it has not answered the real question—the question at the heart of my question, the one I cannot frame into words.

—*From the journal of Citizen 619F.*

Chapter 11

Kane watched the vehicle displays slowly alter over the next three-quarters of an hour, confirming his suspicion that he was moving toward the central spot that the behemoth had circled for the past three hours. The ride was bumpy; no consideration had been given to a passenger's comfort. Presumably the vehicle was designed to run unmanned and this cabin-type area was only provided for diagnostics checks and repairs. But even that told Kane something—that there was someone behind this, someone who sent out and maintained this vehicle as it trekked its slow circuit of the snow-shrouded terrain.

As they drew closer to the central spot, Kane saw another illuminated spot moving across the radar. He watched it for several minutes before confirming that it was moving, headed toward the central spot. That suggested perhaps another vehicle like this one, also dedicated to the creation and distribution of the artificial snow.

Kane watched the display screens as his ride took him toward that mysterious central spot. The terrain tracker showed something in the distance, displayed as a computer-generated wire-frame model. Kane felt a sense of eerie familiarity as the model became more detailed—it was a ville, like the one he had grown up in and served as Magistrate for so many years prior to Cerberus.

Kane continued tracking his progress on the displays as the great wagon rumbled toward the ville, lining up with a set of tall gates on the eastern side. Something flickered on one of the control panels, and Kane watched as the gates—still shown as wire models—drew back into the ville walls to allow access into the ville itself. Something else happened then, which Kane noticed out of the corner of his eye—the pressure gauges dropped suddenly, the needles sinking back to their start points. All around him, the great rumbling that he had associated with the chimney ceased, leaving the cab suddenly feeling very quiet and still.

Kane took that moment to try his Commtact again, hailing Cerberus, hailing Grant, hailing Brigid. To his frustration, no answer came back.

Without an exterior view, it was hard to be certain, but Kane sensed that the vehicle had given no indication of slowing. A vehicle like this took so much power to accelerate that it was likely that it was designed not to slow unless absolutely necessary, and even then it would most probably coast to a stop rather than braking. The vehicle rumbled on toward and through the gates before finally shuddering to a halt. Panels shook and Kane's seat jounced as if he were caught in an earthquake. But it wasn't the stop that caused this—rather, Kane suspected that they were dropping down on some kind of elevator platform. All around him, the displays held fixed images, no further input required. Which meant, Kane realized, that wherever it was they were going they were almost there.

He moved swiftly then, moving with a sense of urgency as he climbed out of the seat and hurried back along the access tunnel within the colossal vehicle. Arrival meant one thing—people. And if someone caught him inside here before he had had a chance to figure out just what was going on, then he could find himself in serious trouble or worse—on the wrong end of a blaster with an ask-no-questions attitude working the trigger.

Kane trotted swiftly along the shaft and scrambled back up the ladder. A small mound of snow had settled at the bottom where he had left the roof hatch open and the rungs were wet with a dusting of ice. There were no lights in here, no illumination. Instead Kane had to rely on the polymer lenses to keep everything straight—otherwise he would have been in absolute darkness right now.

The chimney pumps had ceased, and the tunnel containing the access ladder now acted like any other tube, echoing the sounds coming from outside. Kane heard the low, duo-tonal whine of a motor—probably the elevator platform as it sunk beneath the ville.

Kane was about six feet from the uppermost rung when the elevator stopped with a great echoing thump. He stopped, too, holding himself in place and stilling his breathing. The loud rumble of a door sliding back carried down the access shaft, accompanied by a faint trace of light. Then the vehicle began to move again, shuddering ahead and into a lit area that cast bright shadows through the hatchway above.

Waiting there, Kane watched, taking in what little he could from his restricted view. There was a plastered ceiling up there with long strip lights descending from rigs. As the vehicle rumbled on, Kane saw more of the lights pass overhead.

Then came a lurch—not too powerful, but enough that Kane had to secure his balance on the ladder—and the wagon finally came to a halt amid a growl of shuddering engine. Kane waited a few moments, listening to the sounds of the vast room he was now in. There were echoes of movement, the screech of compressed air and pumped water, pressure hoses and the whirring spin of nuts, screws or perhaps whole panels being removed.

Kane decided to risk a peek up top. He clambered up the last few rungs of the ladder. As he reached the topmost rung, the vehicle shuddered once more and he was forced to cling tightly for a moment as the column he was poised in shook. Above him, he saw the ceiling with its strip lights slowly rotating, accompanied by the high-pitched sound of a straining motor. After ten seconds, the sound of the motor came to an abrupt halt and the rotation stopped. Kane waited again, situated just beneath the roof hatch, watching the space above. Nothing more happened, and all he could hear were the general sounds he had detected as soon as the vehicle entered this room.

Kane warily popped his head up over the manhole rim and peered outside. All he could see was the flat, snow-covered rooftop of the vehicle, beside which the white-painted chimney towered like a lighthouse. From what he could see of the room, it was a high, enclosed space with strip lighting, plastered walls and ceiling. Definitely man-made.

Kane waited a moment, the top of his head just poking out of the hatch, ready to command his Sin Eater back into his hand at a moment's notice. But nothing came to threaten him—it seemed he had not been spotted, if there were even anyone to spot him in light of the automated system driving the snow wagon.

Kane drew himself up above the manhole edge until he could pull himself up, sitting on the rim and leaving his knees dangling inside. From this position he could see more of the room. It was some kind of garage; that much was obvious. The space was as large as a football field and encompassed several bays where repairs and construction were ongoing. There were two more of the towering wagons besides the one he was sitting atop, one of them showing a similar coating of snow on its rooftop while the other was clean. The latter had been placed up on jacks and a side panel had been removed where two men in gray overalls were working inside, a wheeled bed of tools sitting beside them.

Kane looked around the room, counting the number of people within. He could see thirteen in all, dressed in matching gray overalls and all of them working intently, with no chatter, no distractions. Unlike many garage areas, there was no music playing here, just the steady sounds of work as men and women repaired the towering vehicles, the hiss of acetylene torches being used to weld panels into place.

Repair shop, Kane told himself as he turned his head, taking everything in.

Reassured that no one seemed to have noticed him— there were no walkways or guard positions high up at least—Kane pulled himself out of the hatchway and walked at a crouch across the rooftop, searching for a way down.

There were people down there—just mechanics, he guessed, but it wouldn't do to alert them to his presence.

From up here it appeared that Kane's vehicle was resting on a gigantic turntable and he saw similar turntables located around the room, included beneath the other parked wagons. Down below, a team of three mechanics was marching across the floor toward this new arrival, carrying work tools and bags, heads down. Kane noticed something else, too—the floor itself was clean, so clean that it gleamed. That was unusual for a servicing area like this; usually one would expect oil stains and the trace of old tire tracks, metal pieces and discarded screws. But no, this room was evidently kept meticulously clean.

Kane looked around. There were three obvious exits visible from this position, and possibly others that were currently obscured by the towering smokestack of the vehicle.

One exit was a wide set of very tall doors that closed top on bottom, like a set of jaws. Kane deduced that this was the elevator through which he had entered the chamber.

The other two exits were normal doorways found past the other snow-speckled wagon, located against the walls. Where they led, Kane could not guess, so he watched them a moment to see if anyone appeared. After about ten seconds, a woman in gray overalls came through the right-most door carrying a large leather tool bag, her frizzy blond hair cinched back in a tight ponytail, bangs tucked under a gray cap. Could be a tool storage area, could be an exit. Kane could not be certain—the only thing he could reasonably assume was that it was not a restroom, as no mechanic should need to carry their tools within—well, not unless the toilets had backed up. So, that told him something anyhow.

One of the team below him moved toward the ladder while the other two pulled back a panel on the side of the unit and brought over a hose-like attachment, which they placed inside. Refuelling, Kane guessed.

He watched for a moment as the figure stood at the base of the ladder and began his ascent, then Kane ducked back out of sight, sweeping his foot through the snow behind him to cover his tracks from casual examination.

The man had to be coming up here to check on the hatch, look at the insides maybe. Which meant Kane couldn't be found here.

Swiftly, Kane moved back to the hatch and pulled it closed. It wouldn't do to alert the engineer too quickly to his presence.

That done, he moved around to the edge of the chimneylike pipe, covering his tracks, and waited, watching the space where the external ladder emerged. The head of the mechanic appeared about fifteen seconds after, climbing the final rungs before pulling himself up over the side. Kane tensed, watching the man from his hiding place around the curve of the chimney. The man was oblivious to him, stone-faced, eyes dull almost as if drugged, a head lamp attached to his cap.

Kane waited, watching as the mechanic disappeared, walking across the far side of the chimney. Kane kept pace, keeping his movements fluid and silent. He halted when he reached the far side of the chimney. The gray-garbed engineer was already there, crouching down to lift the hatch that led inside the hulking vehicle. Kane hurried forward, creeping up behind the man before grabbing him from behind, his hand over the mechanic's mouth.

The mechanic struggled for just a moment as Kane put pressure on his windpipe. His legs kicked out and he released a muffled yelp that sounded more like a whisper through the sleeve of Kane's jacket. It took thirty seconds, holding the man like that, moving in sympathy as he bucked this way and that. The fight went out of him first, followed by the breath. In under a minute, the man was unconscious.

Kane laid him out on the snowy roof, then stalked away. A moment later he stood at the back end of the vehicle, studying the room beyond. There was no easy way down—if he used the ladder he would be spotted and challenged, but he needed to get across to one of those doors or he would simply be trapped here, waiting for the unconscious mechanic to wake up and raise the alarm.

Kane looked around the room until his eyes settled on one of the other colossal vehicles that were here for refuelling and maintenance. The one on the jacks was a little higher than his rooftop, but it was close enough that—with a run up—he could jump across to it. Without any further thought, Kane backed up to give himself a running start, then leaped from the edge of his wagon and onto the next. His arms reached out, grabbing the side, and he used his forward momentum to swing himself up. A moment later he was secure atop the second wag.

No one had noticed.

Kane trotted along the length of the vehicle, making his way to the rear. Once there, he peered down, eyeing the twin doorways positioned along the wall. From here he could reach the nearer of the two with ease and, crucially, without being seen. All he had to do was get down to ground level, which meant using the rear-mounted ladder, which was backed up against a wall.

After giving the area a once-over to make sure that the mechanics working on it were still at the open panel, Kane slipped over the side of the vehicle and clambered down the ladder, moving swiftly, hand and foot.

Ten seconds later he was at the base of the ladder, stepping out onto the floor of the vast maintenance room for the first time. Without a backward glance, Kane trotted hastily over to the door he had spied the frizzy-haired mechanic exit and slipped through it, pulling the door closed behind him so that it did not slam.

Kane found himself in a corridor, amid cool still air with no sense of warmth. Blank, pale walls and dull overhead lighting cast it in a grayness of eternal shadow. The walls were a kind of dirty white in color, like snow turning to sludge. The corridor had other doors leading from it and the smell of cafeteria food wafted from somewhere close by, a kind of greasy, stewed pungency that made Kane want to sneer. There were noises, too, rotary fans and air coolers, the clatter of footsteps coming from somewhere within.

Kane hurried along the corridor, glancing into each of the open doorways as he passed, careful not to slow his pace. He passed a communal room featuring plain furniture; a sink beside which stood a handful of mugs that had been placed upside down to drain; two toilet stalls, separate, doors open; a darkened cloakroom with lockers at one end and pegs lining both walls on which hung a half-dozen coats.

At the end of the corridor was a closed door that opened onto a lobby. The lobby featured a single elevator, beside which was a stairwell running upward. Kane recognized the elevator design—it was the same type that they had used in Cobaltville.

He took the stairs, preferring to see where he was going and to keep his options open.

The first level was a long way up and it opened onto a maintenance area of low ceilings and twisting pipes: the inner workings of the ville.

Above that, a further maintenance level, this one featuring a wide service road that ran in a tunnel beneath the ville proper. A Sandcat moved steadily along the tunnel, painted white and with headlights on to illuminate the darkened tunnel.

Kane ducked back into the stairwell before he was spotted, and hurried up the next flight of stairs.

Two more flights—meeting no one along the way—and he ducked out at last on a familiar-looking level. He was on Epsilon Level of the central tower, called the Administrative Monolith. Villes adhered to a strict hierarchical system, with each level of the monolith named after a Greek letter of the alphabet. Administration was conducted in the highest—or Alpha—level, above where the baron dwelled alone and unapproachable. Beneath this was Beta Level, where the Historical Division was located, then Cappa Level, which housed the Magistrate Division, including their training and medical facilities. Beneath that was Delta, which was dedicated to the preservation, preparation and distribution of food, then Epsilon, where the construction and manufacturing facilities were located.

In the standard design, the lowest level below this was known as the Tartarus Pits, a level of semi-lawlessness where cheap labor could be procured and the possibilities of the wilder side of life—prostitution, illegal literature, recreational drugs—remained available for those brave enough to look.

That did not appear to be the case here, however. Kane should have passed from the maintenance levels through Tartarus—and any movement between the Enclaves of the ville and the Pits should be tightly controlled and restricted by the ville Magistrates. But this ville had no Tartarus Level, which in itself was not objectionable—just odd. Barons were creatures of careful design, and each had controlled the human populations under them by enforcing the same strict system of levels. To deviate from that suggested that something was different about this ville.

Kane stepped out and strode down the warren-like corridor, keeping his head down and eyes wary, moving quickly and with purpose. The walls were blank, painted in a bland, oatmeal gray-white.

Beyond this, a wider walkway emerged with windows running along one side. Kane slowed, gazing out the windows. Snow was falling out there and it covered the towers of the ville. The towers still gleamed beneath their frosty white covering, metallic silvers and golds, windows gleaming as they reflected the falling snowflakes. It was marvelous. What was more, it felt a lot like coming home.

Despite his exile from Cobaltville following dismissal from his role as Magistrate, Kane had revisited his home ville on several occasions, most recently to deal with a virus outbreak that had threatened to cull the entire population. Even so, he never grew bored with the feeling of being back—it always felt exciting and familiar and comfortable all at once.

As he looked out the vast bank of windows, Kane engaged his Commtact and hailed his partners hopefully. "Grant, Baptiste—I've entered a ville hidden in the snow. Do you copy?"

The response was nothing but dead air.

He tried again. "Cerberus? Do you copy? Please acknowledge."

Nothing. It seemed that wherever he had wound up, he had no comms and no backup. He could only hope that Grant and Brigid were all right.

There was a certain eeriness to the ville that he had noticed subliminally from the moment he had entered Epsilon Level. He couldn't put his finger on it at first, but within a few minutes it dawned on him just how quiet the place was. There were mechanical noises, of course, emanating from the various construction areas that littered this level. But there were no voices, no clip-clop of running feet or strains of music or carrying laughter. It was strangely bereft of those normal sounds of human life.

For now at least, it seemed that Kane had entered into the ville undetected. He was on a major thoroughfare, however, and a group of people were coming along the walkway toward him. There were thirty people in all, walking in step, eyes forward, shoulders sagging. Kane eyed them swiftly, assessing the level of threat they might pose. They were dressed in utilitarian clothes, gray on white, overalls and buttoned-down shirts with high, stiff collars. They looked bored.

Kane watched as the group filed into one of the grand doorways to his right, along the opposite wall to the windows. He peered inside as he strode past, saw them queuing for entry into what looked like a decontamination chamber. That made sense—if this was the manufacturing level then sometimes it was necessary to decontaminate before handling sensitive components or machinery.

Kane wondered what it was they were constructing out here in the British Columbia wilderness. More snow machines maybe?

He carried on, consulting with a map affixed to the wall for a sense of direction. The map gave the name of the ville—

Ioville.

He had never heard of it. He wished Brigid was with him right now—with her freak-show memory she would no doubt produce a whole raft of facts and figures about

Io, Ioville and *E-I-E-I-O*-ville. Damn, that woman was smart.

According to the map, he could either carry on along Epsilon, maybe get a sense of what kind of stuff was being constructed here, or he could reach a nearby bank of elevators and ascend farther. But without communications he was on his own, and he knew it was only a matter of time before someone challenged him and the authorities got involved. What he needed right now was a bolt hole, somewhere to hide out and figure out his next step—then he could maybe locate a comms unit that could broadcast to Cerberus through this abysmal weather.

Kane turned, memorizing the location of the nearest residential block, and hurried along the walkway that led to it.

It took four minutes for Kane to reach the residential units. White-walled, they stood on a broad passageway that was wide enough to accommodate a Sandcat, but that seemed cramped because of the seemingly endless walls of apartments and the lack of natural light. Kane guessed this level alone could house three hundred people.

He stood beside a lamppost, watching the doors to the residential blocks for a few minutes while he calculated his next move. The doors, like the walls, were a washed-out white, like day-old snow.

The introduction of the Program of Unification years before had ensured that no property had a locked door, and Kane suspected he could just walk into any one of the apartments. But he wanted one that he knew had an occupant—that way he could place them somewhere secure and be reasonably certain no one else would surprise him.

He waited, watching the street as a likely group of people arrived in an electric trolleybus. The bus's movement was accompanied by the sound of the electric motor, a kind of cheery "yeaaah" noise. Its side had an open doorway and as it pulled to a halt at a designated stop, Kane saw a group of people shuffling to disembark. They were uniformly dressed in gray and white, and Kane watched as they filed from the trolleybus before it took off on its route again.

Twenty feet away, Kane watched, trying to decide who would be the easiest to pin down and deal with. There were three women in the group of eight, two young and one older with graying hair cut in a short bob that framed her face. Kane figured the older woman would be easy to control, but the younger women boded more chance of living alone and hence not being interrupted. The younger women wore hats over their heads, pulled low to keep their hair back. The hats, like their clothes, were gray. He would watch to see how they split up, to see where each person went.

None of them spoke. That was unusual. Maybe they had had a long shift at the manufacturing plants, or maybe they just didn't know one another, but still, it struck Kane as odd.

But as he watched, something even more odd caught his eye. One group had paired off from the others and initially Kane had ignored them, not wanting to take on two people at once for the risk that one might escape and raise an alarm. Then he looked at them again and realized that one of the men was directing the other to an apartment. The man doing the directing was five foot eight with close-cropped blond hair and the familiar gray shirt and slacks.

The other man was Grant.

Designated Task #002: Intake.

Ioville is self-sufficient. However, not all materials can be created on-site. Some require input from items found farther afield, in the barony that the ville inhabits.

Mineral deposits including metals have been brought in by the thousands of tons, and await smelting and molding into the many machines that we construct and rely upon. This raw material is stored deep below the ville itself, in a sublevel called Iota. Iota is carved out of bedrock, its walls like a cavern, and is piled high with deposits awaiting transportation to manufacture. There is also a great well here, which supplies much of the water for the ville. The remainder comes from rainwater gathered on the roofs of the towers, and distilled until it may be drunk.

I am asked to attend this deep basement level, known as Intake, only once, better to appreciate the hard work that is performed here by the diligent team of citizens. My attendance is overseen by Magistrates, and I am asked to wear a helmet over my head at all times. The helmet protects my face and covers my ears, and it produces a baffle sound loud enough to combat the roar of the water and other noises down here. It is the first place where I have seen color since I came to Ioville and it makes me feel anxious. The walls here are not gray or white.

My visit is brief. I report my sense of anxiousness to the proper authority. I am assured that this reaction is normal.

—*From the journal of Citizen 619F.*

Chapter 12

Kane watched as the blond-haired man guided Grant into one of the residential blocks. Grant was dressed in the same gray overalls as the blond man, and Kane guessed he was undercover, having reached the ville before him. That was the trouble with having their Commtacts offline—he could not discuss tactics and neither of them could inform the other of their movements.

He would get the full story as soon as Grant was alone—he just needed to wait for the other man to leave his partner's side. Kane watched as the two men entered an apartment block together and disappeared from sight.

Kane waited ten minutes, twenty, hanging around the artificially lit street, pacing its length and stopping now and then in an effort to draw less attention to himself. Another trolleybus came after about twenty minutes, dropping off a half-dozen passengers before trundling away on its automated circuit. The people seemed bored and listless as they filed away to their respective dwelling units, moving in silence.

Finally, Blondie left the apartment building and Kane watched him go. He walked a few doors down before entering another building. Kane waited a little longer, making sure that the man was not coming back, then he trotted across the street toward the building where Grant had disappeared.

In a moment, Kane was through the lobby door and

inside the residential block itself. The gray-walled lobby was illuminated by dim lighting, set high on the walls. There were eight doors feeding off from this communal entryway. Kane paced forward, selecting which door to try.

Be bold, he reminded himself. He may not be a Magistrate anymore but he could still carry himself like one if he needed to.

He tried the first door, pushing it gently until he could see inside the main area of the residential unit. The door opened straight onto a living area which featured a dining table with a single chair molded into it, a kitchenette positioned before it with a low counter backing directly onto the table. An open door to the right showed a compact, neatly kept bedroom area with a single bed and a low table containing a lone glass of water. The unit appeared empty, and Kane took just a moment to listen for sounds of a shower or bath running, a toilet being flushed. Nothing caught his ear.

Satisfied that there was no one here, Kane pulled the door closed and made his way to the next unit, peering inside. With the advent of the Program of Unification, no door here was locked, which made searching for Grant a little easier.

The next apartment featured a gray-looking man with bags under his eyes and a dull expression. The man was sitting in a low seat, staring at a glowing panel on the wall.

"'Scuse me, wrong door," Kane bluffed, stepping out and pulling the door closed.

The man didn't even look up.

Kane tried three more doors before finally locating Grant in the sixth apartment. Two of them had residents within, one a pretty young woman eating a bowl of what looked like gruel from the countertop, the other a young man with spiky hair that seemed at odds with his blank expression. Neither resident challenged Kane.

When he opened the sixth door and saw Grant, Kane stepped inside and closed the door behind him. Grant was in the bedroom, standing before the open wardrobe where empty hangers were fixed to the rail.

"Grant," Kane began. "Hey, buddy."

It took a few seconds for Grant to turn, and when he did there was a look of confusion on his furrowed brow.

"So you got here before me," Kane barreled on, marching across to his friend. "How did you get here? I hitched a ride on that juggernaut that almost ran us down, ended up in a garage area way, way downstairs. How about you?"

Grant looked at Kane with that same bemused expression.

"Grant…?" Kane asked, waving a hand before his partner's eyes. "You okay? Cat got your crotch?"

Grant looked Kane over slowly. "You don't belong here," he pronounced in his low rumble.

"Say what?"

"You must be returned to Processing, I think," Grant explained. "You shouldn't be walking around like that."

"Processing?" Kane spit. "What the hell are you talking—?"

Grant stepped behind Kane in an instant, the old Magistrate training as strong as ever. He grabbed Kane from behind, pinning one of his arms tightly behind his back. "Come with me," Grant said emotionlessly. "I'll get you some help."

Kane struggled against the grip, recalling his own training and breaking Grant's lock with a roll of his shoulders.

"Help?" Kane barked, glaring at his buddy. "I don't need help. What the hell has got into you? Look, partner—"

Grant swung for him then, right fist whipping out like a ball from a cannon, cutting the air to strike solidly against Kane's jaw.

Kane saw the blow coming and he responded without conscious thought, dropping back and rolling with the punch. He was up in a second, but Grant stalked toward him across the bedroom, a look of intolerance and determination on his face.

Kane leaped out of the way of Grant's next attack, slipping to the side of his partner before stepping in closer and grabbing him around the shoulder. Now the two men were face-to-face.

"Look, Grant," Kane whispered, keeping his voice low. "If this is some act, just give me the sign."

Grant didn't give Kane any signal. Instead he shoved Kane away so that the younger man slammed against the nearby wall with a crash.

Okay, Kane realized. Something's going on here and I don't have one clue what.

He figured that Grant had some answers, but getting to them may take time—and he didn't relish fighting his brother-in-arms to get to those answers right now, not until he had a better idea of what he had walked into. Instead, Kane weaved past Grant, leaping over the single bed and springing from it to the open door to the room.

Grant stalked after him, lumbering and slow as if his energy level was low.

Kane grabbed the front door handle and pulled the door open, stepping outside. Grant was a few paces behind him and losing ground quickly. Kane ran through the lobby area of the residential block and out through the main door, his mind racing as he wondered where to go now.

On the one hand, he wanted to stick with Grant—if his partner was in trouble, then abandoning him felt like a traitorous thing to do. On the other hand, while Grant was like this there was little benefit in Kane fighting with the man and potentially drawing attention to them both with the commotion. It seemed that this apartment had been—assigned maybe?—to Grant, perhaps by the blond man. The way Grant was fiddling with the empty wardrobe certainly suggested so. Which meant that Grant should still be here when Kane came to look for him again—only the next time, Kane would be prepared to restrain his buddy before things escalated out of hand.

Kane thought all of this as he dashed through the door and out into the covered street beyond. But as he ran, another trolleybus pulled up and something else caught his eye. No, not something—some*one*. There, sitting on the bus with her head against the window, was Brigid Baptiste.

Designated Task #001: Air Monitoring.

Why is Air Monitoring so critical to the running of Ioville? This is a question which has haunted me since my experience in training and observing the monitoring area on Cappa Level. I know of no ville that has a history of problems with air circulation, and yet the precautions here seem unduly stringent and meticulous.

The obvious way to learn more is blocked to me, because asking questions is discouraged. Furthermore, I suspect that few in my circle of experience would know the answers. Thus, I shall need to employ the resources I have at hand in a more imaginative way, albeit with discretion.

—From the journal of Citizen 619F.

Chapter 13

Kane stopped in his tracks, watching as the electric trolleybus glided past on the far side of the covered street.

Brigid wore a peaked gray cap over her head, pushing her hair back behind her ears, but she was immediately recognizable, despite the uncharacteristic way she slumped against the window glass of the trolleybus. Kane could not see much more of her, only her head and neck, but he detected a hint of gray collar there and presumed she was wearing the same gray overalls that many of the women he had seen here were wearing. Gray or white seemed to be the only colors here.

Behind Kane, the door to the residential block swung open and Grant appeared, lumbering after his teammate with a look of vexation on his dull-eyed face.

Kane turned, pondering Grant and their altercation, a dozen thoughts rushing through his mind. He couldn't get into something out here with Grant—that was just asking for trouble. Plus, who knew where Brigid was headed—without Cerberus to back him up with the satellite telemetry, he needed to keep track of her, tell her what had happened to Grant.

There was a sinking feeling in the pit of his stomach when Kane thought that. He knew there was a chance that Brigid would be in the same irrational state as Grant now—especially if they had entered Ioville together.

Decision made, Kane sprinted after the trolley, hurrying down the middle of the thoroughfare and outpacing Grant in a few seconds. Grant watched him go, his expression unreadable.

The trolley took a turn down another narrow thoroughfare of white-walled residential blocks before pulling to a halt with a whine of its electric motor.

Kane waited at the corner of one of the residential blocks. Like the one where he had found Grant, these, too, were painted a kind of washed-out, lifeless white, as were their doors and the lampposts that lined the street. The streetlamps were on, casting a low, yellowish glow that made the whole area look drab.

Brigid Baptiste filed off the bus along with two other women, and all three made their way toward one of the residential blocks. Kane followed, glancing behind him to see if Grant was still on his trail. He could not see him, but there was a gathering crowd of gray-garbed people back there and Kane worried that maybe Grant was recruiting reinforcements, that word of Kane's unlawful appearance in the ville was spreading. He needed to get off the street, out of the open.

A little way along the street, the trolleybus was just pulling away as Brigid and her two companions disappeared into one of the residential blocks. Kane jogged along the walkway in pursuit, ducking into the block's lobby a few seconds later.

The lobby was almost identical to the one in Grant's building—poorly illuminated gray walls, this time with six doors rather than eight. A door to Kane's left was just closing, and he guessed that this was where Brigid and her companions had gone. Kane followed, glancing back just once to check no one was following him, before he pushed the door to the apartment open.

This apartment was smaller than Grant's, and it was

crowded by the three women within. There was a single, understuffed couch propped against one wall and a walk-in wardrobe that was empty apart from a few hangers and a bag of toiletries on the floor. A closed door beside the wardrobe led to the bathroom, Kane guessed.

As Kane stepped inside, pushing the door closed behind him, Brigid and the other women looked up at him with dull comprehension. Kane hurried forward, ignoring the women and addressing Brigid.

"Baptiste, you gotta come with me," he urged. "I think Grant's in trouble and—"

"Step away from her." One of the women broke into Kane's speech. She was dark-skinned and in her early thirties, Kane guessed, with a halo of black hair framing her face beneath the gray cap she wore. Her overalls were the standard gray, unzipped just enough to reveal a white undershirt beneath. "Who are you? What's your citizen number?"

"I'm an old friend of Brigid's," Kane told the woman before dismissing her and turning his attention back to his Cerberus colleague.

Brigid looked at Kane with something akin to confusion on her pale face, before recognition finally seemed to dawn. "Kane…?" she asked, drawling the word slowly and with what appeared to be some effort.

"Yeah—it's Kane," Kane replied, grabbing her by the arms and shaking her. "You know me. What's the game, Baptiste?"

"Game?" Brigid repeated, sounding just as confused as when she had uttered Kane's name.

One of the other women in the room—a brunette in her early twenties with a wide jaw that made it seem she was about to break into a smile—tapped Kane on the upper arm. "This is a women-only block," she said with grave earnestness. "You must not be in here."

Kane shot her a withering look. "Butt out. I'm talking with my friend here."

"Is this correct?" the brunette asked Brigid. "Do you know this man?"

Brigid looked confused, her emerald eyes searching Kane's face with barely a flicker of their usual luster. "It's Kane," she said at last. "Yes, I think I know him. I must."

"Okay, Baptiste," Kane growled, "this just ceased to be funny."

But before he could continue, the apartment door swung open and four Magistrates came striding in. Kane turned and saw the familiar uniforms—the very uniform he used to wear back in Cobaltville—only instead of jet-black leathers they wore slush-gray, and the bright red insignia that Kane had worn over his left breast had been replaced by a white letter *I* over a circle—*Io*.

"Step away from the woman and explain your purpose," the lead Magistrate requested.

Kane let go of Brigid, not following the directive but rather to keep his hands free. He didn't much relish taking on four Mags, wasn't sure if he could take them alone like this. Maybe with Grant, maybe with Brigid—but not alone.

As he thought those words, Kane spotted other figures waiting behind the Mags—more of the gray-clad residents of this block, presumably, blocking the only exit. And among them stood Grant, dull eyed and standing limply as Kane was challenged by the local Magistrates. Kane could only guess that Grant had had a hand in bringing them—but if he was right it confirmed that something was seriously wrong here.

Slowly—reluctantly—Kane raised his hands above his head and nodded in surrender. "I guess you boys don't take kindly to seeing a rooster in the ol' hen house, huh?" he said.

A MAN HAD to know when to fight and when to watch, Kane reasoned, and just then it had been the time to watch and conserve his energies for later. Something wacky was going on here, and Kane figured that in surrendering himself to the authorities he stood the best chance of discovering just what that something was.

Two things worried him as he was disarmed by the Magistrates outside the residential block: first, that Brigid gave no reaction to his capture, and second, the evidence that Grant had possibly been at the root of it. Neither was in keeping with his allies' methods, and had they intended him to be captured—perhaps as some bluff to get inside the system—the three of them knew one another well enough to have passed Kane some kind of signal no matter who was observing.

Once he had been disarmed, Kane was escorted to an access tunnel hidden by an unobtrusive door between residential blocks, accompanied by the four-man foot patrol.

"So," Kane began as they walked through the unmarked door, "where are we headed?"

None of the Mags replied—which was protocol for dealing with a prisoner.

UNDER ARMED GUARD, Kane was taken to a service elevator and from there he ascended to Cappa Level, where the Magistrates were based. When the elevator doors parted, Kane had that strange sense of déjà vu once again. It was a Magistrate area just like the one he had worked from, but there was something subtly differ-ent about it—the walls were painted in that same dirty white that covered the residential buildings and the access walkway he had first emerged on when he had exited the garage.

The Mags, too, were subtly different, working at desks or drinking water from a cooler, dressed in a dull gray interpretation of the Magistrate uniform. It felt to Kane as if all the color had been drained from this ville.

He held his hands loosely at his sides as he took everything in, eyes darting left and right and making a note of possible exits, number of personnel on shift, location of unguarded weapons and the armory. He did not want to start a fight here, as there were too many Mags on shift and Kane abhorred hurting Magistrates, despite the action sometimes proving necessary. But in case it came to it, he mapped out an efficient route to get him armed and out of here with as little interference as possible. It would be risky.

Kane was taken to a medical room where a sample of his blood and skin was taken by a white-haired woman while the Magistrates waited, the whole performance conducted in absolute silence with Kane standing the whole time. A small adhesive bandage was placed over the wound after she had taken the samples, and Kane was made to wait while his tissue and blood was run through a spectroanalysis.

"You want me to pee in a cup, too?" Kane asked cheerfully.

The woman ignored him, never saying a word.

After a little wait, the analysis data appeared on the woman's computer terminal and she read through it and printed out a copy, which she filed efficiently in a cabinet behind her. Once that was done, she nodded to the

Magistrates who had remained to guard Kane and said a single word: "Proceed."

Kane was made to turn and was then escorted from the room. He was marched along a white-walled corridor to the supervisor's office, a room he associated with his old boss Salvo, even after all these years. The room had a lone occupant who was standing with his back to Kane, gazing out the window at the impressive view of the snow-capped towers of the ville. The man was tall and clad in a tight gray uniform like the other Magistrates, though its tightness suggested a little paunch around his middle. His hair was long and gray, tied back in a thin ponytail that stretched halfway down his spine.

As Kane entered the man let out a loud breath. "Sit," he instructed.

The accompanying Magistrates—just two now, but both of them armed—guided Kane into one of three empty chairs that waited on the near side of the desk. Kane tried to make himself comfortable as he waited for the man to acknowledge him.

"Magistrates, you may leave," the supervisor said, his back still facing the room.

The Magistrates stood up straighter and clicked their heels before marching out of the supervisor's office in silence.

Alone now with the super, Kane waited, eyeing the items on the man's desk, weighing their merits as makeshift weapons in his mind. There were paperweights and a letter opener that might conceivably double as a knife, as well as the usual selection of computer, filing cabinets, in- and out-trays, and piled reports that appeared not to have been opened.

"Kane," the man at the window said, finally breaking the silence as he turned to face him. The man had a craggy old face with blue eyes the color of the ocean off the West Coast, and a thin scar running just above his left temple that showed white on his already pale skin. "Cobaltville Magistrate, retired in disgrace, expelled from the ville in 220—"

"Yeah, I know this story already," Kane interrupted sourly. "Care to tell me who you are?"

The gray-haired man nodded as if to accept Kane's point. "DNA analysis provides a good insight into a man's history," he explained, removing a small electrical device that had been hooked over his left ear, unseen by Kane until now. "And you have a lot of history, ex-Mag Kane."

"It's just Kane," Kane told him. "I dropped the Mag thing pretty much the same time Cobalt dropped me."

The gray-haired man sat down behind the desk opposite Kane and steepled his fingers, smiling indulgently. "Yes, your file says you were a troublemaker with no time for authority. I can quite believe it."

Kane glared at him. "Is this going somewhere, ponytail, or are we just shooting the breeze? 'Cause I've got other places to be and other breezes to shoot."

"I'm sure you have," the man agreed, inclining his head in a slight nod. "I am Supreme Magistrate Webb. I run this ville."

Kane stared at the man, hiding his disbelief. "Supreme Mag? I don't recall hearing that rank before."

The man called Webb nodded demurely. "There have been very few of us," he explained. "It is a rank conferred only where there is no baron present."

"So this place," Kane asked, "Ioville—doesn't have a baron?"

"At this moment in time, no," Webb confirmed.

Kane knew of other villes that operated without a

baron, but they had only done so once their baron had departed in the great changing that had heralded the reemergence of the Annunaki. Never had a ville been established without a baron to rule it, not to his knowledge anyway.

"You seem surprised, Kane," Webb said after a few moments of silence.

"Me? No," Kane replied. "Just trying to work out how a place this big gets set up without a baron pulling the strings."

Webb locked eyes with Kane as if trying to warn the ex-Mag not to press his luck. "'Pulling the strings' is a very weighted phrase, though not entirely unexpected seeing that it comes from a man who has a history with rebelling against authority."

Kane held the man's gaze, the challenge clear in his own. This discussion was getting him nowhere—it was time to tip his hand and see how Supreme Magistrate Webb reacted. "So, this is all a part of Terminal White, is that right?"

Webb said nothing, but Kane saw the recognition flash behind his eyes.

"Three barons collaborating to build a ville, hidden out of the way in an artificial snowstorm," Kane continued. "Who was it? Cobalt, Ragnar and Snakefish?" He counted the names off on his fingers. "Did I leave anyone out?"

"You've done your research before coming here," Webb responded. "I'm impressed. Who are you working for these days, Kane?"

"No one in particular," Kane lied easily. "A freelance agent can still get a lot of data if he pays the right information brokers."

"I wouldn't know," Webb gloated. "It's been a long

time since I last had cause to step outside the security of these walls."

"So what is this? A prison or a ville?" Kane asked.

"This?" Webb responded. "Why, this here is the future, Kane. The future of the whole human race."

Designated Task #014: Education.

All children in Ioville must be educated. My role in this education process is admittedly minor but it gives me access to the body of historical facts that are deemed appropriate for children. These facts are quite dense, and include full histories of the nine walled villes that are located to the south of Ioville.

While my charges work quietly at their set exercises, I scan the facts with vigor, searching for information about the ventilation systems used by each ville. There is scant information, but what exists gives no indication that there has ever been a problem with ville ventilation, and certainly not one that would warrant the filtration and constant monitoring of air intake.

The question is "why?" but questions are discouraged and frequently go unanswered in Ioville. To control air is to control breathing—could this be the reason that it is monitored so keenly?

—*From the journal of Citizen 619F.*

Chapter 14

"It began as a collaboration between three barons," Supreme Magistrate Webb explained from behind his desk. "Barons Ragnar, Cobalt and Snakefish. They were concerned with the potential for humankind to turn on itself, just as it had after the nukecaust when the whole world had seemingly gone feral in the era we now know as the Deathlands Age.

"Mankind's civilization, they reasoned, was fragile—it fell apart easily. Recent history had shown how one small change had been like removing the kingpin, causing the whole of civilized society to implode."

Kane nodded. The Historical Division in Cobaltville and elsewhere had been tasked with making the past more palatable and had hidden many of the excesses that had occurred in those dark days after the nuclear war. But, prior to her position at Cerberus, Brigid Baptiste had been an archivist in the Historical Division, and she had told Kane many horror stories of what had really happened then. Cannibalism had been rife, inhuman mutations running wild and the whole dog-eat-dog world had taken on a terrible new level as the survivors of the nukecaust had strived to go on living.

"The barons set about searching for a way to iron out mankind's propensity to kill itself," Webb continued, "at first separately, later combining their research into one grand study once they learned of the others' programs.

"I cannot tell you how many years they researched this, only what the culmination of that research produced. And that was Terminal White, as you've already surmised. Terminal White was an experimental way to control mankind's emotional extremes, such as fear, jealousy and anger, to make humans more...stable. It functioned through well-known psychological principles, utilising environmental factors to keep people in an acceptable emotional state."

"Drugging people?" Kane asked.

"Not at all," Webb told him. "Terminal White is far more convenient than that. It uses spatial structures to affect a subject's emotional state, through the principles of curved air."

"You've lost me," Kane admitted.

Webb smiled, indulgently. Kane suspected it had been a long time since he'd had the opportunity to have a discussion like this, and could see that he rather reveled in being able to talk with someone new.

"Have you ever heard of a phenomenon called Sick Building Syndrome, where one's environment is said to affect one's physical and mental state?" the Supreme Magistrate asked. "Curved air applies that principle to affect the human mind by a subtle change in air currents. This structure you find yourself in—and really, we must establish just how you came to be here, but there's time enough for that—is built to incorporate the very ventilation methods outlined in the research, affecting an individual's inner ear and thus upsetting the production of negative thoughts. There's more to it, of course, but that is the foundation of the system."

Kane looked mystified. "Am I being affected now? Because I sure don't feel like I am."

"It takes a little adjustment for a newcomer to fit in,"

Webb told him, "but once that's done you'll find you let go of all that anger I can see bottled up within you."

"What if I like my anger just the way it is?" Kane asked.

Webb shook his head and smiled. "Before long, you won't care," he assured Kane. "You'll just let it all go like it never was. You've looked around Ioville a little, I take it?"

Kane nodded grudgingly.

"It's efficient," Webb trilled. "No problems here, no issues, no fighting."

"You have a Magistrate Division," Kane pointed out.

"Yes, but it's one primarily dedicated to service work and operations outside of the ville walls," Webb told him. "We have very little trouble with the population itself."

"No Tartarus Pits," Kane recalled.

"Not necessary," Webb explained. "Here in Ioville we have all the docile and amenable labor we need. No job goes undone, no task is rejected. If I were to command the people to kill themselves right now, in my name, they would do so. And they would do it so swiftly that you and I would be sitting inch-deep in their blood before I could even retract the command. Think about that, Kane. A docile and utterly obedient population in a ville where crime will never exist. It's quite the achievement, isn't it?"

"Quite," Kane said sourly.

"You sound unconvinced," Webb said, picking up on Kane's tone. "Would you like me to show you around so you can get a real feel for things here in Ioville?"

I would like to know what you've done to my friends, Kane thought, but he didn't say that. That would wait.

Instead he just said: "Sure, show me around. Let's see what perfection looks like when it's running smoothly."

ACCOMPANIED BY A discreet armed escort comprised of two Magistrates, Supreme Magistrate Webb showed Kane around Ioville, from Epsilon Level all the way up to Alpha. Kane saw a model of efficiency in action, but it was a dull kind of efficiency, people turned almost into mindless robots as they worked at their tasks, building huge military transports or boiling food down to its core components, maintaining the substructure of the ville and polishing the plain gray-white walls that could be seen everywhere.

A whole swathe of white-clad citizens were being drilled in a vast chamber on Cappa Level, traditionally the level dedicated solely to Magistrates. Kane wondered what this augured. Supreme Magistrate Webb's words were not reassuring—he said that everyone in the ville was expected to remain in the peak of physical fitness and was trained for certain eventualities. Kane did not ask what those "eventualities" might be, but he suspected it was nothing positive—the man was building an army, whether he meant to use it offensively or not.

Kane asked a few questions, hiding them in the nature of genial conversation, and concluded that Grant and Brigid had only just been inducted a few hours before he had found them here, that they were being familiarized with their new lodgings from which they would conduct their new, regimented lives in Ioville. Kane wanted to ask if they had fought back, and, more crucially, why they were not still fighting now, but he could think of no way in which to phrase this without giving himself away. Thus, he settled instead for a discussion about the snowstorm that seemed to have racked the area for as long as Cerberus could divine.

"Ah, yes, the northern climate," Webb chuckled. "A little cold, the risk of frost and snow—it's all perfectly normal. Of course we have had to take precautions, because the weather can be punishing to the buildings of the ville long-term. But the barons understood that before they began construction."

"And when was that, exactly?" Kane asked as the two men looked out through the windows of a high walkway on Beta Level. Above them, the plastiglass of the walkway showed the sky where the snow fell in flurries, and the snow had settled on the crest of its rounded roof in a straight white line.

Webb took a moment in thought before answering. "This experiment was begun twelve years ago," he stated. "It took three years to build Ioville and to perfect the ventilation system that would deliver air along the curved air principles."

"So you've been here nine years, then?" Kane checked.

Webb shook his head and the long strand of ponytail swept to and fro behind his back. "There were other structures that needed to be put in place before the whole system could function. Even now we're still not at full capacity for a ville, but it's all a learning process as I'm sure you can appreciate."

"Where are you…recruiting your citizens from?" Kane asked.

"The villes initially," Webb said. "Each baron allocated one hundred and fifty people to populate Ioville, along with a cadre of trained Magistrates whom I chose personally to serve under my command."

"And you came from…Ragnarville?" Kane prompted.

"Ragnar, yes," Webb confirmed. "How did you know?"

"I have a good ear for accents," Kane told him. "So, by my calculations you have four hundred and fifty people, plus Mags, here. That's not enough to keep a ville this size running."

"We have also recruited locally," Webb said with a selective vagueness. Kane suspected what he meant was that people were press-ganged into the ville and brainwashed.

"In the longer term, we're now looking at a natural turnover and replenishment of the ville population," Webb continued. "We have an admirable birthrate. The early bloomers of Ioville's second generation are almost ready to join the workforce, just a couple more years."

Kane nodded, still watching the incessant snow falling on the towers. "Kids? And they're obedient to this Terminal White system you have going? They're usually unruly, especially as they reach the teenage years."

Webb laughed. "Not our children." Then he looked at Kane and smiled. "You ask a lot of questions, Kane, but they're good questions. Insightful," he said. "Your profiling did not overestimate your intelligence. You'll be a real asset here."

Kane turned to take in his surroundings. The gray-clad Magistrates and the gray-clad citizens, all of them quietly going about their duties without any chatter. It certainly wasn't a life, not from what he could see. "I'm not sure I'd fit in."

"You will," Webb assured him. "Processing only takes a little over an hour and then, I can assure you, you will never look back."

Kane didn't like the sound of that. "Where are your

orders coming from, Supreme Magistrate?" he asked as they walked back along the skyway toward the elevator.

"I follow the instructions as laid by the barons," Webb replied primly.

"Baron Cobalt, Ragnar…?" Kane queried.

"That's correct."

"So they are the ultimate authority over this…experiment?" Kane checked as he and Webb entered a waiting elevator accompanied by their Magistrate guards.

"Yes, that's correct," Webb assured him.

"But the barons are dead, Supreme Magistrate," Kane said. "They upped and left a long time before, and they all died over a year ago."

Kane did not delve into the way that the nine barons had transformed into the Annunaki ruling family. If Webb pressed him on it, Kane would explain, but from what he suspected Webb had been out here so long just following orders that he was entirely unaware that the world outside of his artificial snowstorm had long since moved on.

"Dead?" Supreme Magistrate Webb asked, not quite masking his incredulity. "Then what of the villes? What of the baronies? What is happening out there? Surely the world must have descended into chaos!"

Kane shook his head and smiled. "No more so than it did under the barons themselves."

Webb looked ashen as he considered the implications of Kane's revelation.

"Been a long time since you got any new orders, I guess," Kane teased.

Webb fixed him with a serious stare. "Someone must correct this," he said gravely.

It was only then that Kane began to wonder if perhaps he had overplayed his hand.

Designated Task #011: Cleaning.

The question remains: Why is Air Monitoring so critical to the running of Ioville?

I had wondered if it had something to do with breathing but I can find no evidence of any breathing difficulties in Ioville. In fact, there is little sickness that I can find any evidence to speak of.

I tentatively ask Citizen 058F, my colleague on Designated Task #011, if she is aware of any breathing-related problems in Ioville. My shift with her is one of the few occasions when I am alone with just one other individual. I have deduced from her low identification number that she has most likely been here since construction of Ioville, and as such she would likely have more knowledge than most. She looks at me strangely as we clean the gray doors to an elevator on Epsilon Level, surprised that I have spoken.

"It is a reasonable concern," I assure her. "Each citizen should be concerned for the welfare of their fellow citizens and of the ville."

She accepts this with a slow blink, then replies in a timid whisper. "No incidence I know of." Her voice sounds as if it is an alien thing to her, an instrument rarely used.

—*From the journal of Citizen 619F.*

Chapter 15

Kane was taken to Processing.

Processing was located on Delta Level, which struck Kane as perverse. In the standard ville structure, Delta Level was dedicated to the preparation, storage and distribution of food—to process humans here suggested that, perhaps unconsciously, the designers of this ville considered humans to be just more meat going through the system.

Webb accompanied Kane, now escorted by four Magistrates like an honour guard in their stiff gray uniforms.

"You deal with all your prisoners so personally?" Kane asked as they emerged from the elevator on Delta and paced into a dimly lit, white-walled corridor.

Webb shook his head and laughed. "You have exceptional genes, Kane," he said. "We'll be glad to have that here. Longer-term, yours will be the seeds of a strong strand of humanity that will help guide us into the twenty-fourth century and beyond."

Kane looked at the man askance. "And what makes you think I'll give up my...*seeds* willingly?" he asked.

"Free will is an outdated concept, I find," Webb replied without pause. "*That* great experiment failed a long time ago and the concept of free will should have been put out to pasture at the same time that the barons introduced the Program of Unification."

Webb watched Kane a moment as the posse walked

toward a set of double doors at the end of the dimly lit corridor. The doors were tall, twelve feet or more, twice the height of Kane or the other men. They were designed to impress, to intimidate. Kane recalled the theatrics that Baron Cobalt had used when people were brought in his presence, of how they had been frightened and disoriented by a whole series of psychological tricks, the better to give the baron the upper hand. And here it all was again, those same tricks, carefully chosen to make a man feel small.

"I see from your expression that you know what I am talking about," Webb observed after a moment. "The Program of Unification was a masterstroke, but one that did not go far enough. You, even as an ex-Magistrate, can surely see that now."

Kane slowed his pace and locked eyes with Webb. "People have problems," he said, "and sometimes people can create problems. But they—*we*—are also capable of brilliance, Supreme Magistrate. I didn't learn to appreciate that until I'd left the service. Maybe you should try doing the same."

Webb shook his head and chuckled as the double doors opened, revealing a medical complex with numerous security protocols in place. These included two Mags at the doors, and an auto-gun affixed to a ceiling mount on a swivel point. "You do have spirit, Kane," Webb said. "The file was right about that—"

Before the man could say another word, Kane moved, taking a long step backward and swinging out his left arm so that it connected with the nearest Magistrate's chin in a solid blow. On seeing the medical wing that passed for Processing, Kane had realized that it was now or never—if he didn't make his move in these moments then he would be trapped in Ioville forever more, caught under the hypnotic yoke of Terminal White.

The Mag stumbled back as if he were drunk. Kane dropped low, even as the other Magistrates pulled their blasters and took aim at him. They were not standard-issue Sin Eaters, Kane noted as he ran at the closest of them, keeping the Mag between him and the other Mags to block their line of fire.

Kane leaped as he ran, barreling into a gray-clad Magistrate in a powerful shoulder barge that sent the other man hurtling backward. Kane landed in a running turn, spinning on his heel as his opponent crashed to the floor. He was unarmed of course—time to change that.

The two remaining Magistrates, who had accompanied Kane as Webb had given him the tour of the ville, discharged their curious weapons at Kane, loosing twin dart-like projectiles at their suddenly energetic captive.

Kane spun, twisting out of the path of those projectiles as they zipped toward him. Then, without any loss of momentum, he kicked the Mag to the right, bringing his foot high so that it connected with the man's chest in a blurt of expelled breath. The Magistrate staggered backward, dropping his weapon as his colleague reeled off a second shot.

Kane leaped over the incoming missile, moving in great strides toward the dropped firearm as it skittered across the tiled floor. He dropped low as he ran, reaching down so that his knuckles almost scraped the floor, snatching up the dart gun without slowing his pace.

Another dart came racing toward Kane from behind, smacking into his left shoulder, impacting harmlessly against his shadow suit.

Webb was giving orders now, calm but urgent: "Carefully, this one's a keeper. We don't want to damage him."

The two Mags who guarded the white-walled Processing area were hurrying out from their posts, surprised at the scene that had been playing out before their eyes in the past five seconds. Kane turned to them, taking swift aim with the stolen dart gun, and fired off two shots.

The first missed its intended target entirely, spinning off to the far right of the man's armored flank.

The second, however, struck the other Magistrate full in the chest, imbedding itself just beneath the flash of white that decorated his left breast. The Mag did a kind of uncoordinated two-step dance backward before slumping against a wall and wrenching the dart from his chest.

More darts peppered the wall by Kane, drilling into the white space there like debris from a meteor shower.

Kane turned again, conscious that his first two victims were even now pulling themselves up off the floor, ready to reenter the fight. He could run for the elevator, but that would take precious seconds to call, and then he needed to get the doors closed without getting shot. Or he could head inward, into the area known as Processing, but that was fraught with its own dangers— the primary of which was he had no idea whether it contained another exit. No, his best option then was to overpower these Magistrates and maybe hold Webb hostage to give himself the bartering chip to get out of here with his partners.

Sounds easy, Kane thought grimly.

He ducked and rolled across the floor, eyes locking on the other Mag who had emerged from the medical center, squeezing the trigger on the dart gun even as another burst of fire snapped at his heels.

The Mag cried out as Kane's dart hit him in the neck,

at the vulnerable fraction of an inch between helmet and leather. But his blaster fired, too, delivering a dart of sedative to Kane's right bicep, the impact sending a spike of pain through Kane's arm and chest.

"Yeargh!" Kane howled as the dart struck. He kept rolling, reaching for the dart with his free hand and ripping it out of his arm. Once again, the shadow suit had saved him from more serious harm, deflecting the dart's needle and preventing the liquid within from discharging. Kane tossed the dart aside, its nib bent where it had struck against the shadow suit.

"He's just one man, dammit," Webb was saying over the sounds of the scuffle.

Then Kane was up, like a sprinter leaping from the starting blocks, powering toward the Mag who had just taken the dart to the neck, landing a vicious left hook to the side of his helmet so that he caromed to the deck.

As the Mag crashed to the ground, Kane spun to face the others, the dart gun raised ready in his right fist. Another dart whipped through the air toward Kane, and he sidestepped out of its path so that it caught him only a glancing blow on the right leg. Then Kane was moving forward, sprinting for Supreme Magistrate Webb in his bland gray uniform, a determined grimace on his face.

Supreme Mag Webb saw Kane's attack coming, processed it in an instant, and subtly shifted his weight so that it rested on his back foot. Kane reached for him, and Webb leaned back and grabbed Kane's grasping left hand by the wrist, pulling him forward and down in the same movement. Wrong-footed, Kane skipped forward, tumbling toward the Supreme Mag as he sank to the floor.

Webb drew his hand in, pulling Kane over and down.

Kane crashed to the floor with bone-jarring finality, Webb standing over him and still holding his wrist.

"Surprised?" Webb taunted. "Don't be. You don't get to be Supreme Magistrate without knowing how to rough-and-tumble."

Kane squirmed there, struggling to get leverage as he lay front-first on the floor, drawing the older man down toward him. A moment later, Webb's face was close to Kane's as the Supreme Magistrate strained to free himself from the grip that he had instigated.

"Tell me something," Kane snarled as the other Magistrates swarmed around the two men. "Why aren't you affected by Terminal White?"

Webb's lips pulled back in a superior smile despite the sudden pressure that Kane was putting on him. "Because somebody has to be there," he began as two Magistrates point-blanked tranquilizing darts into Kane from both sides at once, "to make the decisions."

Those final words were lost on Kane as the combined sedatives buzzed through his veins, sending him into a dark and chaotic sleep.

In Processing, they took Kane's slumbering body and subjected it to several tests to determine the subject's level of health and detect any signs of disease. He had, of course, been scanned when he had been brought into the Magistrate department on Cappa Level, but this battery of tests was more rigorous, for the fear of disease and the threat of it spreading in the closed community of Ioville could not be underestimated.

Once the white-clad medical staff conducting the tests were satisfied that Kane was in acceptable health, now stripped naked and restrained on an examination table the same way that Brigid and Grant had been when they had entered the ville, they filed him through to a room that was referred to as the Surgical Theater. This room was entirely automated. The same process had been performed on every resident of Ioville, all except for Supreme Magistrate, to help amplify and thus ensure the success of Terminal White. As Webb had intimated, this system was still in the experimental stage, a proof-of-concept test being performed for the long-dead barons. What Webb had not explained was that the experiment was scheduled to run twenty years, one full generation of the human lifespan.

The theater itself was dark, the only light emanating from the laser guidance system that operated the sensitive robot arms to perform the so-called surgery needed to induct a new member into the ville. The procedure itself was very minor. One robot arm reached across Kane's unconscious form, guided until it was perfectly placed above his eyes. Then the eyes were opened mechanically and a small amount of liquid was dropped into each eye to ensure that the pupils expanded as wide as they could go. The patient remained sleeping the whole time.

Once Kane's eyes were open, a new light source appeared on the ceiling above him, directly in line with his face. This was the only light in the room. The light was a bright white in color and perfectly square in shape, with soft, rounded edges. In the center of the square a shape began to form, projected onto the previously blank canvas. The shape was a spiral, jet black so that it fiercely stood out against the pale background.

An automated voice gave a command over speakers set in the unit where the gurney rested. "Concentrate on the pattern," it said in a gentle, soothing tone.

On-screen, the spiral began to rotate slowly, becoming larger until it almost touched the edges of the square.

"Concentrate on the pattern," the soothing voice said again.

The rotation became a little faster and the spiral seemed to shudder where it spun, as if it was not quite balanced. The whole time, Kane remained sedated, tripping along at the very fringes of unconsciousness, obeying the command without any question.

For a moment, the spiral seemed to escape the square.

Other than the voice, the procedure was conducted in silence, with only the faint whirring of the motors powering the robot arms and the regular hiss of the machine that regulated the patient's breathing via a breath mask that had been attached to Kane's mouth.

Kane remained asleep the whole time.

Once the "surgery" was completed, and it took less than twenty minutes from start to finish, the wheeled gurney on which Kane's sleeping form resided was moved by powerful electromagnets until it passed through the double doors that had ostensibly been designed, air-lock style, to keep the theater sterile. In actuality, it was there to prevent any resident of Ioville learning of the procedure.

Kane looked the same to the naked eye. However, deep in the channels of his ear, his vestibular system, which controlled balance in humans and other mammals, seemed to sway as if he was at sea. This change in the subject, whose only name was now a sequence of numbers like a bar code, adapted to and reinforced a subject's responses to the curved air system of ventilation that was at the heart of the Terminal White project. In very simple terms, it worked a little like a hypnotist's spinning pocket watch or coin, transfixing the subject with a vertiginous sense of unbalance, which created a high level of susceptibility. It also ensured that the wearer was no longer concerned with their own thoughts, that they became more like vessels who would accept and obey instructions.

And so Kane was inducted into the Terminal White program as a compliant citizen of Ioville, where he would join Brigid and Grant, serving the Supreme Magistrate, who in turn served the almost decade-old orders of the inhuman barons. Had Kane still had anything like his individual thoughts, he might have observed knowingly that wherever he and his crew went, they could always find someone trying to subjugate mankind for their own ends. Fear and subjugation—the old saws that had been at the heart of man's history since the Annunaki had first set foot on the planet millennia ago.

But of course Kane had no thoughts left. Everything was Terminal White.

Communiqué to Ioville Magistrate 620M:

Check corridor 4-76, Delta Level. Food spillage may result in loss and personal harm. Please respond to protect citizens until cleanup crew arrives.
Message ends.

Chapter 16

The operations room at the Cerberus redoubt had taken on a solemn quality. It had been five hours since anyone from CAT Alpha had made contact. In itself, this was not unusual—a field mission might see an agent out of touch for an extended period. However, what made it a source of worry for all concerned was the fact that the biolink transponders had ceased to register, which meant that not only did the Cerberus ops team not know where Kane and his crew were precisely, but also they could not confirm if they were even alive.

"Time since initial loss of signal?" Lakesh asked, one eye on the clock as he paced the large operations center.

"Five hours and oh-seven minutes since LOS," an ops member called Farrell replied emotionlessly from his desk. Farrell had a shaven head, goatee beard and a gold hoop earring in one ear, and had served with Cerberus for a long time. He was skilled in surveillance and the operational procedures of the mat-trans among many other disciplines. Like most of the Cerberus staff, he was used to multitasking.

"Donald? Any progress with the transponders?" Lakesh asked, turning to his red-haired colleague.

"Nothing yet, Doctor," Donald Bry replied from his terminal desk, shaking his mop of unruly red curls.

"Brewster? Any success with the satellite imaging?"

Lakesh asked as he moved to stand behind Brewster Philboyd's unruly desk.

Philboyd shook his head, receding blond hair slick with sweat. "I can't penetrate the cloud cover of that blasted storm," he admitted. "Heat imagery and triangulation are negative. It's a bust, dammit."

"Reba? Extrapolation from last received readings from the transponders?" Lakesh requested, turning to Reba DeFore where she sat at her own terminal to the side of the room, close to the doors. "Are our people still alive?"

"Nothing to indicate otherwise," she confirmed. "They should be fine, despite the cold. Their shadow suits will protect them."

"From the weather, yes," Lakesh mused grimly, "but what I really want to know is what else is out there. Did they run into something that has blocked our signal just as effectively as that snowstorm is blocking our view of the site?"

A youthful woman spoke up then from the back of the room, where she lounged catlike atop Lakesh's own operations desk, bare legs raised as she cleaned her toenails with a six-inch combat knife with a serrated edge. The woman, whose name was Domi, was a strange sight in any environment, and perhaps more so here where technology and uniform dominated. Domi was an albino, with chalk-white skin and bone-white hair cropped in a pixie style, along with bewitching, bloodred eyes. She was a petite woman, barely five feet in height and built like a ballerina. Unlike the rest of the personnel in the room, Domi did not wear the white jumpsuit associated with the Cerberus staff. Rather, she chose to wear as few clothes as possible, just a crop top that clung to her small, pert breasts and a pair of cutoff shorts, leaving her legs, arms and feet bare. Many in the Cerberus staff were wary of Domi, believing her to be half-feral thanks to her Outlander upbringing, but she was a fierce combatant and loyal to her friends, who included not just Kane, Grant and Brigid, but also the other personnel of the Cerberus operation, most especially Lakesh with whom she was in love. "Get me a mat-trans window, an interphase window, and I'll buzz out there and check out the situation," she urged.

Lakesh looked up and smiled benignly as he fixed his gaze on his albino lover. "Domi, no," he said. "As I've told you before, until we have some indication of what is going on out there it's too dangerous to send another field team."

"But that was an hour ago—" Domi whined.

"Forty-seven minutes," Lakesh corrected.

"And besides, you don't need to send a field team," Domi insisted, ignoring him, "just me. I'll scope things out and report back ASAP."

Lakesh shook his head. "No, Domi."

Domi propelled herself from the desk in a graceful, catlike leap that sent her almost halfway across the room, landing between the aisle of desks before pacing over to where Lakesh was standing. "I'm perfectly camouflaged for snow day," she maintained, "plus I can handle myself out there. You know I can." This last was said with a fierce jut of her jaw as she fixed Lakesh with her bloodred glare, her face close to his.

Lakesh took a deep breath and gathered his thoughts. "We are all concerned about the current circumstances of our colleagues, dearest one," he told Domi gently, "but rushing in half-cocked has the potential to be catastrophic, putting both you and Kane's team in jeopardy. Be patient, dearest one. Your time will come."

Domi screwed up her face in irritation, her eyes still locked with her lover's. "Fine," she said finally. "I'll ask again in an hour's time, and then every hour after that."

Lakesh smiled. "I look forward to that."

Domi turned with a shrug of her shoulders and strode back across the room.

Lakesh turned back to Farrell at the comms desk. "Try hailing them again," Lakesh said in a quiet tone. "Keep trying—not just vocal but use Morse code, use coded message. Let me know as soon as you hear anything. And Farrell?"

"Yes?"

"Don't blurt anything out to the room," Lakesh told him. "Just me for now."

"Yes, sir."

BRIGID BAPTISTE WAS BAFFLED.

She sat alone now on the sofa that doubled for a bed in the apartment that she had been allocated and stared at the blank walls, thinking about the man who had burst through the door barely a minute after she had first been introduced to her safe new home. Was he the previous tenant maybe, disgruntled at having been ousted? He had seemed hot about something, that was for sure.

And yet—

And yet he had called her by a name, had seemed to know her. There was something in his gray-blue eyes when he had grabbed her—recognition.

Brigid wondered who the man was. Did she know him? She didn't remember meeting him before. Not now.

And yet—

And yet when she said "before" she really meant before Ioville, before today, before her life had been affixed in this spot, with these tasks, with these clothes.

Had there been something before this? she wondered. Had she lived somewhere else, perhaps not even a ville? The orientation she had passed through after Processing had told her that there were other villes, nine in all, ruled by the baron elite who had only her best interests at heart. Of course they did—why would she ever doubt that if that is what she had been told?

And yet—

And yet the man with the broad shoulders and the dark, tussled hair and the steely gray-blue eyes had sparked *something* in the back of her mind. A memory, maybe, but one hard for her to reach. A handsome man walking into her life, albeit just for a moment. It had to mean something.

Brigid thought back to the incident with the intruder. He had been sure of himself when he had entered the apartment. He had certainly known where he was going and for whom he was looking.

The authorities had responded quickly, praise the baron. The strange intruder had barely called her that name when they had arrived at her door and escorted him from the property. One of the other women, the ones who had shown her to her apartment, had told Brigid that the stranger had to be disarmed, that he had been carrying some kind of blaster, which, as she knew, was only allowed for Magistrates.

Brigid puzzled over the whole sequence of events, trying to recollect all the details.

He had addressed her by a name, she knew, but already that name was fading from her memory. What had it been?

Bap—?

Cap—?

Happiest—? Was it Happiest? A nickname of some

kind, perhaps? That would imply that she knew the man, and there was a nagging feeling in her mind that maybe she did. She could not be sure now, but had she maybe addressed him by a name, too?

Game—?

Was that it? No, they had talked about a game and he had a name that sounded a little like that, she felt, but she couldn't pin it down in her mind.

How long had she been here in Ioville? That was a question that she could not answer, for already Processing and Orientation felt like they had happened months—maybe even years—ago.

It was all a great big mystery.

Brigid adjusted the gray cap that resided on her head, straightening its peak so that she looked just like all the other workers who contributed to the manufacture on Epsilon Level. Whoever the man was, she felt reassured that if it mattered then the barons would tell her so and would instruct her what to do. They knew best, after all.

Brigid Baptiste stood up and paced over to the front door, ready to catch the trolleybus that would take her to her shift in the manufacturing rooms of Epsilon Level. She was not Brigid Baptiste in her mind, however—now she had another name, a designation, really. Her name now was Citizen 619F.

Communiqué to Ioville Magistrate 620M:

Restrict access to Epsilon Level, Tower 3. Sandcat armaments malfunction. Please respond to protect citizens. Engineering has been dispatched to address mechanical failure.

Message ends.

Chapter 17

Kane would never have given himself willingly to any regime. Not after everything he had suffered to gain his freedom—true freedom—from his days as a Magistrate under the iron heel of Baron Cobalt.

No, Kane would never have given himself willingly. But the newly designated Citizen 620M emerged from Orientation keen to serve the regime and uphold the principles of Ioville. He did not remember his talk with Supreme Magistrate Webb, did not recall anything that had been said in that long discussion about Terminal White and the conspiracy of barons, of how they had refined a perfect system with which to control humans, to iron out the wrinkles that were known as *free will.*

In essence, Kane was no more. Sure, the man who stood now as Citizen 620M looked like Kane and sounded like Kane. He had the same cropped hair and steely gray-blue eyes, the same muscles and the same scars. To the keenest eye, Citizen 620M held himself a little differently to Kane, more erect and a little stiffer perhaps, closer in fact to the day of graduation in the Hall of Justice back in Cobaltville, when Kane had turned eighteen and been inducted full-time into the Magistrate Division. Now Kane—which is to say Citizen 620M—would carry himself that stiffly on all occasions, would march wherever he was required, would hold that same fixed, emotionless expression, eyes taking in everything around him, face giving nothing away.

He was Kane but he wasn't. He was something that Salvo and Kane's other trainers, going all the way up to Baron Cobalt himself, could only have dreamed of—a perfectly obedient, perfectly reliable soldier.

When the newly christened Citizen 620M emerged from Orientation he was ushered to Preparation, where he was suited up in a gray Magistrate's uniform like the ones worn by the Mags who had captured him. At the breast, the uniform featured a white circle through which an upright line had been scored: *Io*.

Io was the name assigned to the ville but its significance was more than that. Unlike other villes, Ioville had not taken its name from its ruling baron. Indeed, on paper the ville was ruled equally by three barons—Ragnar, Cobalt and Snakefish, all of whom had evolved a few years previously into the would-be rulers of the earth, the Annunaki. No, Ioville drew its name from simple binary code used in computer programming. IO, one and zero, on and off. It was a chilling indication of just how the barons viewed humans—as nothing more than functions with flesh form.

Kane was kitted out as a Magistrate, assigned a beat in the west tower of the ville. He nodded once in understanding as he was issued these instructions by a similarly emotionless man in a long white coat like a doctor's.

"There is no trouble in Ioville," the man assured Kane, "but the patrol is needed for security. There is a lot of a sensitive material being held and built here, and enemies of the barons are keen to acquire it. As such you must always be on your guard on behalf of the barons."

"On behalf of the barons," Kane repeated, staring into the middle distance of the quiet, gray-walled room.

"You may be called upon, on occasion, to patrol the exterior of the ville," the man continued, "but that assignment will be explained to you at a separate time. You will also receive other designated tasks, which you will perform to the best of your abilities. These will be assigned to you once you have been shown your residence."

Kane said nothing, taking on board the man's points without a word.

"You are expected to perform all duties at all times as though a baron was there with you, watching you," the whitecoat explained. "Remember that always. Do not slide in your perseverance or dedication. Otherwise you will be retrained and assigned to another primary task. The role of Magistrate is an honour. You act as the baron now, your authority only superseded by the Supreme Magistrate's. Do you understand?"

Kane nodded once solemnly. Kane no longer. Magistrate 620M exited the room and was met by a male with graying hair and a stooped walk. Kane eyed the man aggressively, wondering at his walk—was this acceptable in Ioville, this walking like a hunchback? He would need to consider this once the man had performed his duty.

The man introduced himself as Citizen 091M and explained that it was his duty to show Kane to his residence. Together, they ascended in an elevator that took them up to Cappa Level, where the Magistrates had their operational hub and training facilities. The two of them disembarked the elevator car and walked down one of the gray-white corridors in silence, Kane easily keeping pace with the stooped man who seemed to drag his heels.

They came to a bank of compartment doors, which opened onto single-room sleeping quarters featuring a bed, a computer terminal and a shelf containing a surgically clean glass and a book detailing the Program of Unification. Citizen 091M led Kane to one of the rooms and showed him inside.

"This is where you shall sleep," Citizen 091M explained, standing to the side of the doorway.

Kane nodded. "Acceptable."

"Sleep is designated to last 6.2 hours," Citizen 091M informed Kane. "After that, you will be assigned your next task, which you will be expected to begin immediately."

Kane nodded again. "Acknowledged."

"Further information is contained in your task pack," the gray-haired man told the Magistrate, indicating a gray-covered book that had been placed on the flat pillow of the bed. "You may call on me if you have any questions, I reside at Room 147, Residence Block 9, Level Delta."

Kane stood in his new room, his eyes still fixed on his advisor.

"Is there anything else, Magistrate?"

"Do you need to be examined, Citizen 091M?" Kane asked. "Your walk seems uncomfortable."

Citizen 091M thought for a moment. "One of the barons will instruct me if I require examination or surgery," he replied.

"And if they are not available?" Kane pursued.

"Supreme Magistrate Webb holds the authority to make a decision in their stead," the man told him before turning on his heel and departing back down the corridor toward the bank of blank-walled elevators.

Now alone, Kane stood stiffly in place as he examined the room. It featured walls of a dirty, washed-out white, a white shelf, a white computer terminal and dull gray covers on the bed. It felt entirely adequate. This was home now for Magistrate Citizen 620M. This was home now for Kane. He was content.

CITIZEN 618M HAD given little thought to the man who had invaded his apartment and grabbed him. He could have overpowered the man with the cropped dark hair and the blue-gray eyes, but the stranger had evaded his grasp and run, and so Citizen 618M had called for the Magistrates, as was protocol.

Now Citizen 618M was in a repair shop on Zeta Level, far below Epsilon, the traditional bottom of a ville. Citizen 618M was working on the panel repair of the chassis of one of the snow machines. The machines ran in vast circuits around Ioville, absorbing the moisture in the air, chilling it and producing snow in continuous streams. The ville also sent a pulse spike into the atmosphere every hour, which helped chill the area and seed the clouds with enough moisture that they would snow almost without cessation. The result was an ongoing snowstorm that had lasted almost six years.

Citizen 618M was satisfied in his work. He needed his brawn—his muscle—to batter out the dents in the side of the panels, and he was able to lift more than most of the other citizens who worked here. They did not speak—there was no need. Their tasks required no negotiation, no discussion; they were set out and performed in strict order, with each man working at his own set function.

Citizen 618M had another name once, not so long ago. That name was Grant and his functions as Grant had been very different. If he remembered that life it was at a stage once removed from himself now, like remembering a film one had seen or a painting once admired. It was the memory of a story.

Grant/Citizen 618M struck his hammer along the metal panel of the snow wagon, flattening out the dents that the vehicle had received in the rough terrain outside Ioville walls. He was content.

CITIZEN 619F HAD been inducted into the ville at the same time as Citizen 618M. When she had entered the ville she had been called Brigid Baptiste and he had been called Grant, but now he was Citizen 618M and she was Citizen 619F and any thought of her past life was forgotten.

Citizen 619F pushed at her long red hair self-consciously as the day's tasks were outlined by the supervisor. There were twenty of them in the work crew, divided into four even groups, with each group tasked to work together to construct Sandcat vehicles.

"You are to check all work twice before confirming that it is complete," the supervisor—a gray-overalled woman with short blond hair in a pixie cut—intoned. "Errors cost lives, so make none."

Citizen 619F got to work, marching with her crew to the wide conveyor belt where the premolded Sandcat chassis would be delivered from the workshop behind this area. The thought of the stranger in her apartment was barely a whisper now, already almost forgotten by her occupied, even-keel mind. Citizen 619F was content.

Communiqué to Ioville Magistrate 620M:

Any weapons used by a Magistrate are his responsibility for the duration of his shift. Weapons are to be field stripped and reconstructed in the Magistrate's own time.

Message ends.

Chapter 18

Seventy-two hours had passed since anyone from the CAT Alpha field team had made contact with Cerberus. There had been no further word from Kane, Grant or Brigid, no reignition of their biolink transponders, no clue where they had gone. It was as though they had quite simply dropped off the map.

Now, in a desolate, snow-dappled field, fifty miles from a place still called Whitecourt in spite of all the devastation and changes wrought upon the North American landmass in the past two hundred years, two figures stepped unobserved from a rent in space, appearing as if out of nowhere.

The figures emerged from the momentary haze of the quantum window seen between the falling snowflakes. They were the chalk-skinned albino, Domi, and a man called Edwards, an ex-Magistrate who had been a field operative for Cerberus for several years. Edwards was a tall, broad-shouldered man in his early thirties, with rippling muscles and hair shaved down to a brief fuzz of shadow. His short hair drew attention to his bullet-bitten right ear, a memento from an adventure several years before.

Both Cerberus personnel wore shadow suits augmented with civilian clothes suitable for the cold weather of the north, fur-lined hoods pulled high and cinched close to their faces. The snow began to settle on their hoods and shoulders and in the creases of their clothes in seconds, creating narrow white streaks all over them as they stepped onto the snow. To a casual observer, they would look like any other travelers, with their tired clothes and carrying their possessions on their backs. However, Edwards's backpack contained tracking equipment that could be instantaneously linked back to the Cerberus headquarters through a dedicated satellite uplink, while the other pack, which Domi had strapped to her back, featured a specially molded interior within which the interphaser unit rested when not in use.

The rent in space from which they emerged looked like a blossoming lotus flower, budding into existence from nowhere with one hundred different colors swirling in its impossible depths where lightning flashed like witch fire. The budding lotus appeared to mirror itself, creating a second swirling triangle beneath it—existing impossibly beneath the ground and yet still visible to the human eye—if any such eye had been there to observe its rapid materialisation. This was the quantum window generated by the interphaser, a method of instantaneous transportation available almost exclusively to the Cerberus personnel. This window had formed over a scrap of ground where once tribal elders from the North Plains Indians had communed and, long before that, where primitive man had felt fear without knowing why. Such were the places where the interphaser, that incredible bit of technology made available to the Cerberus operation through the diligent efforts of Lakesh and his scientists, could access, transporting an individual to a new location instantaneously.

The interphaser was in fact based on an alien artifact that could tap the quantum pathways and move people through space to specific locations. While more amenable than the stationary mat-trans, the alien technology of the interphaser was limited by certain esoteric factors. The full gamut of those limitations had yet to be cataloged, but what was known was that the interphaser was reliant on an ancient web of powerful, naturally occurring energy lines that stretched across the globe and beyond. These invisible pathways could be accessed at key locations that were called parallax points. This network followed old ley lines and formed a powerful technology so far beyond ancient human comprehension as to appear magical. In some ways, the interphaser operated along the same principles as the mat-trans, but its logic was more obtuse to modern eyes. As one might expect, the interphaser's destination points were often located in temples, graveyards or similar sites of religious value. These sites had grown up around the interphaser's use, ancient man sensing the incredible power that was being tapped for such instantaneous travel.

Cerberus personnel's access to an operational interphaser was the combined work of Brigid Baptiste and Cerberus scientist Brewster Philboyd, and had taken many months of trial and error to achieve.

Edwards took a deep breath of the chill air, noting his surroundings with the alertness of a trained military man entering a known hostile environment. The snow was hard-packed underfoot. "Looks like we got here just in time to miss piss all," he said grimly, commenting on the lack of any signs of human habitation.

Behind him, the interphase window closed, dematerialising as though it had never been there. Domi shrugged out of her backpack and leaned down, reaching for the interphaser. "Desolate is good," she reminded Edwards as she watched the unit power down. "Less chance of being seen."

The interphaser was a foot-high pyramidal structure with a mirrored silver finish. Its surface seemed to be almost liquid to the naked eye. Domi took the unit and set it in the molded case she had brought with her before replacing it on her back.

"Yeah, that's all to the good," Edwards grumbled as he pulled his Beretta 93R pistol from his hip holster. Less than ten inches in length but accommodating a rate of automatic fire of 1,100 rounds per minute in 3-round bursts, this compact pistol could do a vast amount of damage for its size. Edwards never traveled anywhere unarmed. "But let's not start walking around with our eyes closed just yet."

Domi nodded solemnly in agreement. She, too, was armed—in her case with a Detonics Combat Master with a silver finish as well as a fighting knife, which she had carried with her since her days as a sex slave in Cobaltville, long before joining the Cerberus setup. Her knife featured a serrated six-inch blade that had tasted blood more times than Domi had kept track of. She reached out with her heightened senses, searching for any threats hidden by the falling snow.

Edwards logged in with Cerberus operations, confirming their arrival as he consulted a handheld tracking device to find the last known location of Kane's team. Domi trotted after him, catching up in a few moments but keeping a good six feet between them to make it that little bit harder should someone try to pick them off from a distance.

Putting a man on the ground had been a difficult decision. Lakesh had certainly wanted to get someone out here once CAT Alpha had lost contact and disappeared from the Cerberus surveillance system, but at the same time he was wary of moving too soon and jeopardizing the op before it had even begun. Thus, for three days the comms experts in the Cerberus redoubt had run through protocol, attempting contact with their missing team once every four hours, using several communication systems in case their colleagues were unable to respond with words. At the same time, Donald Bry and Brewster Philboyd had repositioned the satellites to focus on the area in question, the hidden snowy plains of British Columbia, but to no avail—the ongoing storm proved impenetrable to even the fiercest satellite sweep and no additional information could be garnered by remote.

Thus, on the third morning, the conclusion had been reached that an observation squad be sent out on a recce of the area. Domi and Edwards were under strict orders to observe and to locate their colleagues, but not to engage with anyone else unless they absolutely had to. Edwards had something of a reputation for creating static in these situations, while Domi was a law unto herself. At the same time, they were probably the most capable field agents that Cerberus had with Kane, Grant and Brigid lost.

Snow fell in aimless, wayward spirals, fluttering down to earth on the chill breeze as Edwards and Domi trekked across the barren landscape toward the last known location of their colleagues.

"Brewster said that they left the Mantas somewhere around here," Edwards stated, reading from the hand-held tracking unit, "before checking out the zone on foot."

He began setting up the more advanced tracking system, which he had packed in component form in his backpack. The tracker featured the ability to run tests on the whole gamut of the electromagnetic spectrum, as well as containing a signal booster for radio communications.

While Edwards set up the analysis unit, Domi looked bleakly around. Stretching in every direction all that could be seen was the white blanket of snow. It covered trees and bushes and the gradually undulating ground, obscuring every detail with its chill whiteness. "How close are we to where they set down?" Domi wondered.

"Mile, mile and a half maybe," Edwards said, powering up the little unit he had unpacked. The unit stood six inches high and a little wider than it was tall; and it looked reminiscent of an old-fashioned radio set with a small, circular screen molded off-center on its front panel. "Brewster couldn't get more specific—satellite tracking had lost them in the storm by the time they set down. Maybe we'll have more success."

A man on the ground could see much more than a satellite, especially with the ever-present storm restricting the view from above to anywhere between three and zero percent of optimum.

Edwards set the tracking unit to Scan, wedging it in place in the snow. Then he stood, letting out a slow breath that hung in the air like fog. Domi had already padded off, checking the immediate area in her own way, searching for evidence of her allies' disappearance and for clues as to their whereabouts now. Edwards was momentarily surprised that he could not see her through the falling curtain of snow, and he calmly fired up his Commtact to call to her.

"Domi? You wandered off or you been kidnapped?"

"Just wandered off," Domi responded in a playful tone. Her voice came back to Edwards marred by static, the effect of all that snow coupled with the satellite bounce required even for a signal to transfer a few dozen feet, even using the signal booster on the tracking device.

"See anything?" he asked, turning on the spot to try to locate the albino girl.

"Not yet," she said.

Edwards went back to the sensor scan, eyeing the circular screen. The screen featured just two tones, gray and black, and interpreted a scan of the immediate area surrounding the tracking unit, running a basic sweep pattern and widening the field of scan with each rotation. Edwards saw a black blip showing very close by, and realized it was Domi checking out the immediate area. The screen showed nothing else—no Mantas; no life signs; nothing.

Close by, Domi continued to check the area. She was a tracker by nature, more at home in the open wilderness than she would ever be in the fussy and restricting corridors of the Cerberus redoubt. She applied her keen senses the way a chef flavours a dish—instinct and combination, reacting to one element and countering another. But there was no sign of the Mantas, and certainly no sign of Kane, Grant or Brigid.

"Nothing," Domi muttered, picking up a handful of snow and letting it sift through her pale fingers.

WHILE DOMI WAS out there searching, Edwards paced around the tracking unit, peering through the snow cover. It was hard to see out here. Kane or Grant or the redhead could be twenty yards away and he might not even see them. Heck, they could be twenty feet away!

Edwards engaged his subdermal Commtact again, speaking aloud. "Kane? Grant? You out here? You read me? Brigid? Brigid Baptise? This is Edwards, please respond."

He waited. The booster aerial on the tracking unit would power his signal through the difficult conditions, and maybe—hopefully—reach the members of CAT Alpha if they were anywhere nearby.

Snow fell, creating that muffled silence that snow always brought. And with that silence came the silence of Edwards's Commtact, receiving no response from Kane and his crew no matter how many times he tried hailing them.

BEING ON THE ground was proving very disappointing. It should have come as no surprise—the area was just snow, lots and lots of snow, stretching in every direction, falling from the sky, hiding and masking and *smothering* everything that existed here. Things lived, no doubt—things always did—but any sign of habitation, animal or human, was utterly masked by the falling snow. Domi could not even find animal tracks in the white blanket; she suspected that she would have to dig if she wanted to locate any of the indigenous creatures.

Domi turned around, heading back to where she had left Edwards fifty minutes earlier, her ghostly form almost lost amid the falling snow.

Edwards was standing beside the advanced tracking unit from his backpack, clapping his arms together to keep warm, his breath hanging about him in a clump of foggy moisture. "We're the only heat source in a two-mile radius, Domi," he stated glumly. "Wherever Kane and company are, it sure ain't here.

"Seventy-two hours is a bastard long time in this game," he added through gritted teeth. "Kane's team could be on the other side of the globe by now, even without a mat-trans or interphaser at their disposal. I'm calling it."

With that, Edwards crouched and shut down the scanning unit, watching the screen as it committed one last sweep of the terrain before it shut off.

Domi shook her head in disappointment. It felt as though they were failing their colleagues and, to Domi, that felt like a very personal shortcoming. CAT Alpha had found her not very long ago when she had been taken off world in a hijacked spaceship. There was no tally of who owed whom, not with Cerberus, but still there was that sense that Domi should try harder, should not quit until she had found her friends.

But it was needle-in-a-haystack territory; they both knew that. That was the only possible conclusion they could reach once they experienced the true enormity of searching this barren landscape with no clues and no promise that their colleagues were still here.

"We'll try another site," Edwards explained, "but I don't hold out much hope. If the scan was going to pick up anything it would have done so by now."

Domi nodded absently, watching the falling flakes of snow. "Brewster said that the snow never ends," she said.

Together, the two Cerberus rebels trekked a half mile in the treacherous terrain, tried another scan and then a third from yet another locale, but every result was the same—nothing showed on the scanner, and there was no evidence of Kane's team anywhere on the ground.

Eventually, as darkness arrived, casting the snow in an otherworldly blue, Edwards and Domi agreed to head home.

They could not know, could not guess, that the Mantas were less than a mile away, but that they had been so perfectly buried by the snow that they could not be seen. The only way to find them under all that snow was by pure fluke.

Eventually, Domi and Edwards traipsed back to the parallax point, the air turning even colder. There they fired up the interphaser and dematerialized in that lotus blossom of rainbow colors, returning home. Had they been just twenty feet to the west, and twenty minutes later in their departure, they might—perhaps—have spotted a snow-generating wagon of the type that Kane had clambered aboard and which had taken him into the heart of Ioville, passing by on its automated circuit around the vast terrain of this hidden barony.

Communiqué to Ioville Magistrate 620M:

Enact Protocol 1-9-9, gates sentry duty during receipt of snow wags. Please respond to protect citizens. *Message ends.*

Chapter 19

"Brigid? Brigid Baptiste? This is Edwards, please respond."

Citizen 619F heard the words in her head and wondered where they came from. She was busy on the production line in the Sandcat factory on Epsilon Level at that moment, using an electric screwdriver to attach the screws that held the vehicle's back plate in place. Each screw had to be tightly put in place from behind, so that it could only be reached from inside the vehicle. The screwdriver whirred in her hand with a high-pitched whine as she fastened the fourth screw on this plate, her fifty-sixth today.

Citizen 619F stopped, letting the screwdriver power down, curtailing the high whine it made. Around her, other citizens were working at their own designated tasks, stretching the caterpillar tracks over the wheels and affixing them there, pushing in reinforced arma-glass windshields and side windows, oiling the swivel mounts that would hold the twin USMG-73 heavy machine guns in the bubble at the roof. Citizen 619F ignored the noises, listening more closely to the voice in her head.

It came again, distinct, almost as if someone was standing a foot behind her and speaking right into her ear. She turned in place, looking behind her, her brows furrowed in confusion.

There were people in the Sandcat. She was half lying on the deck beside the back plate, her butt pressed against the side in a cavity where a fire extinguisher would be placed before the vehicle was deemed combat ready. There were four other people working on the 'cat that she could see—one in the turret, its bubble not yet in place, one close to the front smoothing down the runners where the seats would fit, and two more attaching one of the gull-wing doors—on the passenger side—to its hinges. None of them looked up from their respective tasks, and none of them spoke—as was the norm. Working diligently and in silence was the only way to get the jobs done efficiently; anything else was tantamount to a challenge of the baron's authority.

Citizen 619F turned back to her own task, reaching for another screw before pressing her hand against the metal plate that would protect the rear of the Sandcat from entry.

"Brigid? Brigid Baptiste? This is Edwards, please respond."

It was a man's voice, gravelly and subtly accented, and it was there inside her head. She let go of the back plate and reached for her cap, pushing her flame-red hair back from her ear to listen more closely.

"I hear you." She mouthed the words, too afraid to say them.

The voice in her head said nothing for a very long time, a full three minutes of silence where she was certain she had heard a man speak. When he spoke again, the voice was harsh with static, like a poorly tuned radio: "CAT Alpha, we are at your last known location. If you can hear this message, please respond."

CAT Alpha? Who was that? A woman's name? A citizen? But all citizens here were known by their designated numbers, which they had been assigned at induction. Names were considered frivolous for the citizens of Ioville; only barons and the Supreme Magistrate had a name.

But if that was the case, why did she recognize the name? CAT Alpha? Could that be her? CAT—Catherine, maybe?

"Catherine Alpha," Citizen 619F said, the words barely a whisper. As she said it, she glanced surreptitiously over her shoulder, eyeing the other members of the shift crew. None of them heard her speak; none of them were even looking in her direction.

Could CAT Alpha be her name? Maybe. But there had been another name that the voice in her head had used, which the man who had burst into her apartment on that other day had also used when he had grabbed her by the arms. Baptiste. She had almost forgotten it, forgotten that he had said it to her. It was a strange name, not functional like Citizen 619F was functional. *That* name told her fellow citizens everything they needed to know about her—that she was a citizen of Ioville, that she was the six hundred and nineteenth to be inducted here and that she was female. Baptiste, however, told a person nothing.

Who was Brigid Baptiste?

AFTER HER SHIFT in the factory, Citizen 619F was dispatched to Designated Task #008. Food Distribution. Food Distribution was performed on every level of Ioville, several times a day. Each citizen attended at the start or end of their shift at any assigned task, where they would be served a nutritiously balanced but otherwise bland meal. Some meals were designed to be taken from the grand cafeteria area and consumed at home. They called these "baggies."

Citizen 619F worked the slop, her red-gold hair tied back now in a hairnet so that it would not touch the food, a ladle gripped in each hand where she would operate two separate meal groups—proteins and bulkers. Each person was assigned one spoonful of each group, which they could choose as either warmed or cold, and which was then eaten with the designated cutlery. Magistrates and other key players of the ville were assigned additional food and drug supplements as required, and this additional supplement was granted to Citizen 619F on those days when she attended Designated Task #015, Fitness.

Designated Task #008 was monotonous but it gave Citizen 619F time to think. She watched the blank eyes of the other citizens as she served them, watched the way they sat and ate in silence, choosing to sit alone or together; it didn't matter which.

The dining hall was silent, the only sound coming from the scraping of cutlery as a bowl of slop was scraped dry, the hiss of the water coolers as diners filled glasses with water to drink.

"Catherine Alpha," Citizen 619F whispered to herself during a lull in the queue for food. That could be her name. That could be who she was before.

She tried to imagine a life outside of Ioville, a life devoid of meaning and designated tasks. A life of aimlessness and caution and fear, where one did not know where one would be expected to appear next. It seemed chaotic in her mind's eye, and doubtless fraught with danger. But she could not be certain if what she thought was memory or just imagination, a conjuring of the worst possible scenarios or a life she had truly escaped.

She tried the other word instead, letting it tickle across her lips as she formed it: "Baptiste."

That could be a name. It could be her name. It felt strange that she had heard the word said by two different male voices, that two strangers had seemed to say it to her, one of them in her mind.

Was the one in her mind just madness? The emergence of some mental issue she was unaware of, maybe? And would such a thing prevent her from being productive for the barons? That did not bear thinking about, surely.

She continued slopping the gruel on the trays of the arriving diners, pushing all thoughts of Catherine Alpha and Brigid Baptiste to the back of her mind.

WHEN SHE RETURNED to her apartment, limbs aching, exhaustion pronounced, Citizen 619F ate a little from the baggie and sat down before the terminal that was built into the wall at the end of her couch-bed. She had begun keeping a journal there, as had been proscribed on her first day at Orientation.

In the earliest days of the Terminal White experiment, the barons had discovered a strange quirk of human behavior that they could not seem to eradicate. That was the need to retain and process thoughts, to hold information, to make one's mark, as it were. This need dated all the way back to cave paintings, and could be found in other mammals in their desire to mark their territory. Humans, it seemed, functioned more productively if they were assigned a place to mark. The terminals provided that place, as well as an opportunity to communicate new tasks and requirements to the citizenry.

Citizen 619F used her terminal to keep a journal of her experiences in Ioville. The journal was perfunctory and lacked imagination, instead detailing the routine she was expected to adhere to along with her occasional insights into a particular aspect of that routine.

She sat before it now, perched uncomfortably on the poorly cushioned sofa, unable to get quite the right height for typing. Still, she made her entry, this one about Designated Task #008: Food Distribution, the task she had been performing in the preceding three hours after her shift at the factory had ended.

As she sat there, her red hair finally freed of the clips that held it tightly beneath her gray cap during the work day, Citizen 619F stared into the screen. She had stopped typing, almost without realizing it, and was now studying the tinted pixels that made up the glowing white screen, the infinitesimal flicker as they waited for her to add more to her journal entry.

"Brigid Baptiste," she typed, before stopping and staring at the words. They meant nothing to her. She sensed disappointment as she stared at them; perhaps she had been hoping that seeing them written down might jog something deep down inside her, might miraculously answer the questions that she could not quite seem to frame.

She backspaced, deleting the strange words.

Citizen 619F looked at the blank space on the screen where the words had been, and slowly typed another: "Catherine."

She stared at that word, the gray-black letters clinging to the white background at the foot of her incomplete journal entry, and tried to make sense of it. Was it her name? It was a name, she knew that much. But hers?

She typed a second word beside the first, until it read, "Catherine Brigid." Was that her name before? Was that who she really was?

The red-haired woman shook her head in despair, backspaced through the names until they were no longer there. Then she typed the rest of her entry about Food Distribution, not noticing the elementary typing error she had included therein.

The journal was wiped forty seconds after Citizen 619F completed it. No recollection from a citizen could be saved in Ioville, as the terminals were strictly to ameliorate the sense of being adrift that a complete lack of such facilities would give. It was very efficient.

Citizen 619F went to the meager basin facilities and washed and cleaned her teeth, in preparation for sleep. Cleanliness in self, as well as ville, was important to the efficient running of Ioville.

AT NIGHT SHE lay on her soft couch-turned-bed with its gray blanket and low, too-soft pillow, waiting for the commencement of her designated 6.2 hours of sleep.

The names were still with her, rattling in her head like a dice player *rollin' dem bones*.

They had been with her throughout her shift at the Sandcat manufactory, with her through her three hours at the cafeteria serving food to her fellow citizens, there on the trolleybus ride home.

CAT Alpha.

Baptiste.

They meant something; she was sure of it. Something that did not exist in Citizen 619F's life, but that existed outside the walls of her apartment and her designated tasks. But what?

Citizen 619F, the woman once known as Brigid Baptiste, drifted into an anxious sleep, one marred by dark, oppressive dreams and the disconcerting sense that everyone around her knew more than she did.

Designated Task #008: Food Distribution.

I am expected at the serving area of the west tower, Epsilon Level one day per week, where I perform a three-hour shift after my work at the factory is over. Here I am taught how to distribute food to my fellow citizens with efficiency and fairness. The food is of nutritional value but of little taste.

The components for the food are grown in the hydroponics labs on Delta Level, where all preparation occurs. It is then transported to the serving areas, vast rooms with seats and long tables that can sit forty at a time. Despite the size of the room, the smell of the food is ever-present, and stays with me long after my shift is completed.

The food itself is unappetizing, two paste-like slops of *brigid* gruel. The food functions to fuel the citizens, and in that it is successful.

—From the journal of Citizen 619F.

Chapter 20

Alpha Level was spotless, all white walls and sterile corridors running in perfectly straight lines. It had that new-car smell, of dust in the sun, of things sealed in airtight packaging. It was hardly used.

Alone, Supreme Magistrate Webb paced the walkways of Alpha Level toward the baron's suite, a spark of uncertainty nagging at his mind. Kane had said something when he had arrived three days before, as the two men had toured the towers of Ioville with its admirable cleanliness and order. He had said that the barons were all dead.

Webb had dismissed the statement when Kane had attacked him and his cadre of Magistrate guards, naturally assumed the comment to be a last, desperate bid by a man still wanted by Baron Cobalt for his crimes. But the thought still nagged at him.

The walls were blank white canvases, with gray piping to delineate the edges and where the doors resided. The elevator doors were a faint gray, as if a single spot of ink had been dropped into the whiteness, changing it, but subtly.

Everything was big here, too, the proportions of the corridors wide, their ceilings subtly higher than the ville standard so as to dwarf a visitor, making them subliminally feel shorter. The barons used a lot of tricks like that, employing subtle ways to make men feel inferior.

Some were not so subtle—rituals that involved clanging gongs, swirling incense and the use of gauzy curtains to create a kind of ethereal world within which they seemed to dwell. Supreme Magistrate Webb had visited that odd, unreal world three times, when he had been selected by Barons Ragnar, Cobalt and Snakefish for this task, to head up Project: Terminal White. Three times he had been interviewed by a baron, three times experiencing the same ritual of dark glasses and dazzling lights, mystical voices and curtains that shimmered like moonlight on water. And he had passed, been considered an acceptable choice to head up this barony until the barons themselves were ready to assume control or raze it to the ground, depending on the results of the protracted test.

Supreme Magistrate Webb had wondered how many others had been considered for the role, how many had been tested, going through the obtuse rituals of meeting the unearthly barons and showing no fear, or perhaps just the right amount of fear. How many had been made to forget what they had seen after they had failed those tests? He remembered. He was the one man in all of Ioville who remembered anything before the orders began.

So now he was on Alpha Level.

The center of Alpha Level had been set aside for the barons when they chose to visit; perhaps one day when one decided to live here instead of in his or her old barony, a summer vacation, a home away from home. It had stood empty since its construction almost nine years ago, waiting silently for the barons' arrival.

Alpha Level—still unoccupied years after it had been constructed and sealed, its elevators restricted by nothing more than a written rule, a spoken instruction. Such was the power of Terminal White.

Webb visited the level infrequently, coming up here

now and then just to check that things were as they should be, that nothing had disintegrated or rotted or spoiled in some other way. He had had to have a window replaced once, when the constant battling snow had revealed a very tiny break in the seal that, over time, had rotted away to create a full-scale leak, mold running up the wall in dark streaks. That had been seven years ago. The cleaning squad who had come to deal with the intrusion had been executed after the work was complete—their obedience was not in question, it was simply that no citizen should be here in the barons' suites, not even people whose ability to retain memories had been controlled.

Webb paced past the unmanned guard post and up toward the open glass doors of the suite. They had never been closed—the decision had been made that they should be left open to welcome the first baron when he or she finally arrived.

Webb could not help but glance back over his shoulder before entering, checking that no one was following him. He was allowed here, as that was a part of his remit as Supreme Magistrate, but still it felt uncomfortable to him, as if he was using a bathroom designated for members of the opposite sex only.

Inside, the suite was fragranced with a trace of incense, a heavy scent long since departed, only its whisper still lingering. Barons liked scents around them because it helped enhance the otherworldly allure that they exuded.

Webb was in a lobby, a long room with patterned walls and two long, white couches lining either side. The patterning on the walls was carved into the plaster, white on white, the only way to see it by the shadows that it cast. It showed part of the design of the elaborate ventilation system that formed the foundation of Ioville, the air circulation process by which Terminal White was administered. Webb admired it a moment, his brow furrowed in thought.

The barons cannot be dead, he thought as his eyes traced one of the lines that represented the flow of air in Beta Level.

There was only one way to be certain, however, and his knowledge of that had nagged at him for three days. Ioville was located in a communications black spot, one artificially created by the snowstorm. It was a necessary sacrifice—the storm helped hide the ville, preserving its secrecy from all but the most determined traveler.

However, here in the central tower was the means to communicate with the outside world. This tower, higher than the others, featured a powerful antenna that poked high above the ville itself, adding an extra fifty feet to the already colossal structure. The antenna was enough to penetrate the snowstorm, so that Webb could send and receive messages from the barons. Other booster units were located in a few spots around the ville, including Webb's Supreme Magistrate office on Cappa Level and the Mag radio comms, but he preferred to send this message in private, away even from the dull-minded Magistrates who served him.

He strode through the meeting room, nine chairs arranged around a long, rectangular table, all of it finished in white. The communications suite was located to the side of this, through a pale door that had been almost perfectly hidden within the wall it was located in. Webb stopped before it and drew a deep breath before entering.

The automated lighting of the baron's comms room flickered to life, bulbs *plink-plink-plink*ing before they finally came on with a sound like a fingernail tapping a champagne glass. Webb paced across to the radio receiver and checked the display. No message had been received since he'd last been here seven months ago; no communication. In over four years, he had heard nothing from the barons. But until just three days ago he had not thought to question this. Why would he, a man loyal to the cause, question the ways of the barons? Such a thing was beyond contemplation!

He picked up the microphone headset, adjusting the mic until it rested comfortably before his mouth.

"Test," Webb said, enunciating the word, watching as the radio readout display altered to show it was picking up the sound waves.

Satisfied, Webb sat down and fired off his first message. "Calling Baron Ragnar. This is Supreme Magistrate Webb at Ioville. Important query has arisen. Please respond."

Then he waited, sitting before the radio set, watching the display as it told him the Hz rating of the current input and received nothing but dead air.

Webb sent two further messages, one to Baron Snakefish in the west and one to Baron Cobalt to the east of that in Cobaltville. Both messages were identical, as was the disappointing response—dead air.

Webb sat in frustration, staring at the mindless radio display as it confirmed his signal was strong and his messages had been sent. He sat, and he waited, and he considered the implications if what Kane had said was true. If it was, it meant that there was a power vacuum that could only lead to chaos and a resurgence of the barbarism that had predated the Program of Unification. That was something which Supreme Magistrate Webb could not allow.

Subliminal Instruction to Ioville Citizen 618M:

Attend Zeta Level from 0100.
Service Snowcats by rotation. Check armaments. Assist fellow citizens on duty.
Shift: 12 hours.
Designated break: 0400, 0900; 900 seconds each.

Chapter 21

Three weeks had passed. The Cerberus ops room had moved on to other tasks, while still monitoring the signals hopefully for a sign of Kane and his team. Just now the vast majority of the staff on duty were observing and recording the effects of an earthquake in Southeast Asia, and wondering if this was a natural disaster or a hint of some weapons test where a new world power might be coming to the fore.

Mohandas Lakesh Singh's thoughts were far away when Donald Bry placed the report on his desk. Lakesh responded with a jump of sudden surprise.

"I'm sorry," Bry apologized. "I didn't realize you were—"

"Think nothing of it, Donald," Lakesh assured with a dismissive wave of his hand. "I was just…away with the fairies."

Bry pierced him with a fixed stare. "Real fairies or imaginary ones?"

A smile broke across Lakesh's solemn features. "Ah, yes, we have seen a few things that could make us question the existence of such, haven't we, my friend?" he said. "But, in answer to your question, no—I was just thinking."

Bry looked at his mentor and detected the man's need to talk. "Penny for your thoughts?" he prompted.

"Save your money," Lakesh told him. "They're nothing but the circular thoughts of an old man who's wondering where things went wrong. Unproductive. I should know better."

"CAT Alpha?" Bry asked after a moment's consideration.

Lakesh nodded grimly. "Yes. It's been twenty-one days since we heard anything from our dear friends."

"Longest they've been out of contact," Bry agreed solemnly.

"And that snowstorm is still raging," Lakesh stated, bringing up the overhead satellite image on his computer screen.

"The nukecaust disrupted our environment beyond comprehension," Bry reminded his superior. "Inexplicable weather patterns have been logged before now."

"Inexplicable," Lakesh repeated with a shake of his head. "We are scientists, Mr. Bry. Nothing is inexplicable. There is a reason for this storm and that reason is related to the disappearance of Kane and his team. I am certain of it."

"We can keep monitoring," Bry replied, "but we don't have the personnel or resources to follow a dead lead indefinitely. The automated message is still broadcasting over their Commtact frequencies, but their transponders are no longer broadcasting and have not been for three weeks. Without that tracking signal, we are left with no way to know where they are."

"Yes, yes," Lakesh agreed with an air of defeat. "Still, three weeks is a long time to be lost in the field. A very long time indeed."

"We've done all we can, Lakesh," Bry reassured his colleague.

"No, we haven't," Lakesh responded, "because we have not found them, Donald, and that is the acid test."

Bry looked at the man at the desk and sighed. "I don't know what else we can do," he admitted.

"Nor do I, Donald," Lakesh replied wearily. "Nor do I."

MAGISTRATE CITIZEN 620M paced the lower realms of Ioville, following his standard patrol route. He had once been Kane, a warrior in the Cerberus organization, but that was long ago and in another life. Now, all he knew was his life as an Ioville Magistrate, and all that his life was was the orders he was given.

He was in Epsilon Level, close to the heart of the ville beneath the Administration Monolith, which towered above all else. Every Mag patrolled here at least once a day, because it was here that the heart of Ioville and the most important piece of engineering was held.

The room was unlocked, like everywhere else in Ioville. Despite its importance, there was no need to secure it—no citizen would ever countermand the orders of the Supreme Magistrate who spoke on behalf of the barons.

Kane entered, one hand on the gray hip holster he wore that contained the tranq gun. It was a vast room, fifty feet across and circular, its ceiling stretching all the way up through the building to the top, where the great white cyclopean eye resided. Midway down that vast tube lay the fan, a whirring blade that cycled the air through the ville. The blades were as large as the rotors on a Deathbird helicopter, and much thicker. Most debris that came through from the external intake vents was diced into powder when it met those rotor blades.

The sound of the fan was like standing next to a massive waterfall, the great rush of air and the whir of the powerful blades enhanced by the tube effect of the tower in which they stood to make the noise almost unbearable.

Kane stood on a catwalk-style balcony that jutted out beneath the giant fan itself. The catwalk had a single safety bar that a visitor could hold if needed, to counteract the effects of the rushing air.

Kane stood beneath the fan, watched the whirring blades as they rotated over and over, cycling the air through the system.

It was here that the air began to circulate through Ioville, this giant fan distributing every iota of air through a complex network of vents and tubes, following the principles of curved air where it would react to the counterbalance that had been hypnotically instilled into every citizen, assuring their obedience.

Kane's task, like all the Magistrates who patrolled here, was to ensure that the blades were free of debris and that they were turning. There was continuous computerized monitoring of this unit occurring on Cappa Level, but it was too important to leave merely to an automated system. One visit with human eyeballs could detect a problem that might not have been obvious to a computer.

Kane stood there, eyeing the rotating blades, eyeing the tower above—where even now another Mag would be checking—and the vents and ducts, reassuring himself that everything was working precisely as he had been shown. It was.

He stood a few moments longer, watching the whirring blades, feeling the rush of air against his face.

"Breathe," Kane said, taking in a deep lungful of the air.

For a moment, he felt different, almost like he was another person, no longer Citizen 620M, Magistrate of

Ioville. For a moment, here where the air was still raw, before it had been shunted through the complex network of pipes that filtered and distributed it through Ioville, he felt the twinge of a memory, deep and long-buried, rushing back to the surface.

"Cerberus," Kane said, plucking the word from his mind where it seemed to lie like driftwood washed ashore. Saying the name brought the next memory, solidifying the first in place.

He saw a home carved out of rock, a man with dusky skin given him instructions, and not just to him; there were two others with him, a broad-shouldered beast of a man with skin like midnight and a woman whose hair was as bright as fire. Who were those people? Kane wondered.

He tried to remember. He was Citizen 620M; he knew that much. But those other people, people outside of Cappa Level, places he had never seen—it was frustrating trying to process such images and thoughts.

Kane remembered something but he could not fix it in his mind. He said the strange word again: "Cerberus." That meant something to him, or it had meant something, before Ioville.

Kane determined to think this through further, but his time here was over. He was expected in decontamination—no visitor to the central intake tube could be allowed back into the ville without this, for fear that a rogue substance might enter Ioville—before continuing his patrol of the ville.

Kane exited the room via the air lock, stood and waited for the door behind him to seal. Then, the whir of cleaning air and a blast of chemically treated water descended on him as he stood and thought of the word *Cerberus* and the people he had seen in his mind's eye.

As the jet of cleansing air played across his face, however, he found the thoughts slipping away, and by the time the decontamination cycle was completed he had all but forgotten what he had been pondering. Something about a flame, he thought as he exited the ventilation structure. Even that thought was gone by the time he was on the main walkway that ran through Epsilon Level.

CITIZEN 619F SAW the Magistrate as she finished her shift at the Sandcat factory. She had an irregular free evening because she had been teaching children for two hours before her shift began this morning.

She watched him stride along the walkway which led to the trolleybus stop, and she halted, pulling herself up short as he came closer.

Things had been worrying Citizen 619F over the past weeks, things that did not seem to add up. Why was so much attention paid to the air flow of Ioville? She had investigated this as much as she could without drawing attention, had found no mention in the educational resources of a concern with air flow in other villes.

There was the other thing, too, the word that she had heard in her head and from this very Magistrate: *Baptiste*. What did that mean? Where had it come from? Was it her name? Why had it appeared in her ear as if someone was speaking to her in the same room when no one was there? That and the other phrase: "CAT Alpha."

Citizen 619F had begun to wonder about her own history. The villes had history, one she taught in her classes, and the barons had a history, and even the world had a history—from idyllic to nukecaust to the Program of Unification. And yet she and the other citizens here seemed to have no history. She had asked about this a few times when she had been alone with another citizen and when she could be reasonably certain that she was not being overheard, but none of them had had an answer. To be truthful, none of them seemed much to care; it was a concern that was apparently solely her own.

She had memories—she was sure of it. She could sense them now and then, pluck at them in her dreams like the strings of a harp. Memories she could not seem to draw forth and yet she knew were there, like a coin glinting from the back of the sofa.

The broad-shouldered Magistrate strode closer, his stride formal, dressed in regulation gray with his helmet visor hiding his steely blue-gray eyes. She watched him, making a swift and crazy decision to step into his path.

The Magistrate almost collided with her, and Citizen 619F reeled at his glare.

"Aside, citizen," the Mag growled in a fierce tone.

Citizen 619F stared at him, challenge in her emerald eyes. "You," she said quietly, so that only he could hear as the other citizens continued filing past on their way to the trolley stop. "Say it to me again."

The Mag looked at her, his teeth gritted with barely contained rage. "Say what?"

"The word," Citizen 619F said. "The word you said before."

The Magistrate looked confused, then pushed her out of his path with one strong arm. "Return to Orientation, report in by 0500. Report that you may be delusional, and give my number as reference—Magistrate 620M."

Citizen 619F nodded once, solemnly, looking down at the floor. "Acknowledged."

Citizen 619F watched the Magistrate walk away. But in her head, she heard the word again—the one he had said to her weeks ago, when he had stormed into her apartment. *Baptiste.*

CITIZEN 619F RETURNED to her apartment, taking the later trolleybus with the other citizens, almost falling asleep right there in her seat. The man was something to her—she was sure of it. He had been connected to her once, in some way she could not recall.

Her stop came all too soon, as her mind wandered and her body threatened sleep. She disembarked by instinct, a maneuver practiced a dozen times a week, and made her way back to her apartment. It was getting harder to think out here in the enclosed walkways. She struggled to hang on to what had happened, to cling to the memory of the Magistrate with the familiar face and the strange word.

She entered her residence block, through the lobby and into her apartment, not saying a word to her neighbors who were doing the same. They did not speak; there was no need and, besides, no time—every hour was accounted for in Ioville, every hour and every minute and every second.

Citizen 619F closed the door to her apartment, leaning with her back against it and letting out a weary sigh. "Baptiste," she said, remembering the word that the Magistrate had said. She wasn't certain that he had been a Magistrate then, since the memory was too fuzzy.

She moved through the apartment, sat, ate, washed. All the while she was trying to cling on to the word and remember what had happened. She could hardly recall what had happened after her shift now, every memory was transient, like a fading Polaroid.

Eventually, Citizen 619F lay down on her couch, which doubled for a bed, plumped up its meager cushion and switched off the single lightbulb of the room. She had not written a journal entry today, because there was so much to remember and so much that kept slip-

ping from her mind that she knew that the process would
only be frustrating.

She lay there in darkness, listened as the apartment's
ventilation system whirred into action, bringing clean,
new air into the meager living space. Gradually, her
mind relented and she went to sleep.

MAGISTRATE 620M ENDED his shift and returned to his
own residence. He was thinking about the citizen who
had bumped into him, the woman with the red hair. The
hair had been clipped down and tucked neatly beneath
her cap, but it was impossible to hide its vivid color, the
color of burning flames.

620M stood before the basin in the communal bathroom, cleaning his teeth. He looked at himself in the
mirror as he thought about the woman with the flame-
red hair, wondering where he had seen her before,
wondering how the meeting had seemed familiar. A
Magistrate is trained to notice details, to piece information together, but he was having trouble doing that
for some reason.

He spit toothpaste into the stream of rushing water
running from the faucet. "Description of suspect," he
said aloud. "Late twenties, Caucasian, five-seven, slen-
der." He took a mouthful of water and rinsed. "Green
eyes. Red hair."

The face in the mirror stared back at him as he rinsed
again, but 620M—Kane as was—was looking past it,
searching his mind for the image of the woman, the familiar face in the crowd.

CITIZEN 619F DREAMED of a dark space lit only by volcanic rock. In the dream, she was with the man—the
Magistrate—and they were working together to stop a

disjointed monster made of hunks of shale. It seemed impossible. It seemed familiar.

Subliminal Instruction to Ioville Citizen 618M:

Attend Cappa Level at 1320.
Fitness training. Obey Magistrate instructions.
Task: 2 hours.
Designated break: None.

Chapter 22

Citizen 619F awoke feeling unrested. The lightbulb had automatically switched back on, bathing the room with light. 6.2 hours had passed since she had closed her eyes, the 6.2 hours of sleep prescribed to every citizen of the ville.

She lay there in the tangle of her bedclothes and tried to remember what it was that had so bothered her the day before. Her electronic journal would give no clues— she had long since learned that, the way it wiped its memory—her memories—with every shutdown and boot-up cycle.

There had been something, though, she was sure of it. A face maybe? Or a name? A name.

She lay there a moment longer, taking another breath in the glare of the single light source, reaching into her mind for some hint of what it was. The air con hummed and whirred, blowing cool air into the apartment.

There was no time. She had to keep moving. Designated Task #004 was waiting for her. Tardiness would not be tolerated.

She climbed out of the unsatisfying bed, threw the covers aside and strode across the tiny room of the miniscule apartment and into the refresher cubicle.

The refresher was small, not much bigger than a large wardrobe, and featured a shower, toilet and basin, above which was a mirror. Citizen 619F switched on the shower, stripping out of her clothes and letting it run hot.

She could not think in the communal areas. Could not think in the apartment. Something kept making her mind jump back, return to the concept of instructions and designated tasks and orders, orders, orders. Even here, as she conducted her ablutions before getting into the shower, she felt violated, like there was something always in her head, buzzing, distracting her from her own thought process.

The ventilation.

The history.

The man and the word he had said.

All these things were bobbing around in her mind, like survivors from a sea wreck, bobbing about in the ocean.

"Put them all together," Citizen 619F told herself gently. "Keep focus and put them all in the right boxes in your head."

She stepped into the shower, luxuriating in its heat, the way that heat ran across her skin with each sluice of water. Water washed over her body, her neck, her hair and face and, in that moment, the whistling in her ears from the ventilation finally stopped and Citizen 619F remembered something.

Dripping wet, she stepped from the shower and stood before the mirror, wiping at the misted glass with her forearm until she could see her face.

Baptiste.

It was *her* name.

Not Cat Alpha, Catherine, whatever that was. That name didn't fit, although it was tantalizing in its familiarity. She just could not place it yet.

The mirror in the tiny bathroom was misting over

again already. Citizen 619F wiped at its surface with the side of her hand, then picked up the towel and wiped it down properly. In the reflective surface she saw herself, naked, red hair and emerald eyes. She moved close to the mirror and stared into her own eyes as the shower continued to spray.

"Baptiste," she said in a voice barely more than a whisper. "Who am I? Baptiste?"

Her mind seemed to ache with the memory, the yearning to remember.

"Come on," she told herself fiercely. "You had a name. What was it? Baptiste. Baptiste something, something Baptiste. Something. B— B—"

The eyes in the mirror watched her eyes, moving when she moved, but always rolling to keep pace with her eyes. She stared harder into them, harder into her own eyes, once believed to be the windows of the soul.

"B—" she began, feeling the familiarity of the movement of her vocal cords, feeling the way that the name yearned to be spoken, to be freed from its prison. "Brigid," she said finally. "Brigid Baptiste. I am Brigid Baptiste."

The mirror had begun to fog over again as the shower continued to generate condensation. Citizen 619F— Brigid Baptiste—let it run, trusting the sound to mask anything she said while she was here, masking her words from any bugs that the regime might have. She leaned forward and pressed her index finger against the fogging glass of the mirror, carving two letters in the mist: *BB*, for Brigid Baptiste.

Then, still naked, she pulled the towel around her shoulders and sat down on the edge of the shower cubicle, where the warm, flowing water continued to drizzle against her back.

"Brigid Baptiste," she said, the words coming more confidently now. "Kane and Grant and…and Cerberus. Oh, son of a baron, I remember it all. It's all inside here, inside me." She pushed her hair back, clenched her hand tighter against her forehead. "Come on, what else do you have? Don't let it stop now, Brigid Baptiste. Don't let all this stuff get forgotten again."

The shower continued to flow as Brigid remembered as much as she could of her previous life, the condensation obscuring the two letters she had written in the mirror's surface. With each recollection, another ten were triggered. Somewhere along the way, she recalled making her way here to Ioville in the billowing snow, meeting the mirror-clad Magistrates and getting captured by them and the things that had happened after she had been drugged, when she had awoken in the area known as Processing. She remembered how the people there had spoken to her, instructing her, performing the hypnotic process in darkness. They had put something in her brain, she realized, a subliminal trigger that affected her ability to reason, to think.

"But you didn't count on this, did you?" she muttered, tapping the side of her head. "You didn't count on a woman with an eidetic memory, who could never really forget anything no matter how much you did."

At Brigid's back, the water in the shower had gone cold, spraying against her and the cubicle walls in a chilly drizzle like autumn rain.

BRIGID TURNED OFF the shower, dried herself and dressed in the gray overalls and peaked cap of Citizen 619F. It was just a costume now, like playing dress-up, a persona she would put on so that no one else suspected who she really was.

She moved through the tiny apartment, eyes sharp as she studied everything. There was nothing here that she might use as a weapon, nothing sharp, nothing solid or easily concealed. In fact, there was barely anything in the apartment at all, just an unforgiving couch that doubled as a bed, a food bowl and a spoon that was more like the handleless end of a shovel, roughly the size and shape of a credit card. None of that could be used, which meant she would just have to rely on her other weapons—her mind, her body, the most dependable weapons in her arsenal.

She moved toward the door, still tucking rogue locks of red-gold hair beneath her cap. "You are Brigid Baptiste," she muttered to herself as she stood at the closed door. "Do not let them make you forget this. Remember it no matter what they say or make you do."

Outside of her apartment, the lobby was oatmeal gray with a coolness that made her shiver involuntarily after the warmth of the shower. She marched through the lobby, out into the thoroughfare beyond.

A trolleybus was just pulling up across the street where a half-dozen people waited—each of them dressed in identical gray overalls and peaked caps that matched hers.

"Brigid Baptiste," she whispered under her breath. "You are Brigid Baptiste."

She watched the other people get on the trolleybus, watched it pull away with a purr of its electric motor. She should have been on that bus, she knew—that was her ride into Epsilon Level and her work at the manufactory, performing Designated Task #004 for the good of the ville and the barons. The people who had got on the bus had all stood the same way, Brigid realized—kind of stooped, heads down, watching the ground. She tilted her head down, adopting the same pose, but she kept her eyes looking up, looking forward, watching everything from under the peak of the cap.

"Brigid Baptiste," she whispered, just mouthing the name now, not even saying it aloud.

She could not be late for her shift. That would draw attention to herself, and she was already running late after the time spent in the shower. No need to find an excuse, if she could just move quickly.

She began to run in the direction of the trolleybus, down the main thoroughfare that led into the central core of the ville where the factories were based. She ran easily, long legs eating up the distance in great, easy strides, arms pumping in easy rhythm, picking up speed and navigating obstacles in her way without conscious thought. It felt good to run—all that combat training with the Mags had kept her trim and in shape, as had the steady diet of nothing but tasteless proteins, but she had not really cut loose like this in three weeks. Now she ran like a gray blur through the walkways, ducking down tight alleyways where the trolley did not go, one time running through and out the lobby of another residential block that was intended for men only—there was no unauthorized fraternizing in Ioville, she realized. Every step of her life for the past twentysomething days had been dictated to her, running her like a robot.

You're not a robot, she told herself. You're…Bap… Brigid. Brigid Baptiste.

The name almost wouldn't come. It scared her how difficult it had become already, how much harder it was going to become. Already she was beginning to lose the sense of identity that she had discovered in the shower, the puzzle pieces slipping from their slots, the great deception lowering back into place to cover her eyes, her mind.

"No," she hissed to herself. "You're Baptiste. Brigid Baptiste."

She cut through the gray-walled communal lobby of another residential block, slipping out the rear door and rushing onto the street once more, finally outrunning the trolleybus that was making its scheduled stops as it made its way to the manufactories of Epsilon Level.

THE WALKWAYS WERE SILENT, the gray-white walls bland and characterless. Brigid eyed them differently now, saw the way they seemed to drain the color from the world. It was as if this whole ville was dedicated to the mundane, to making things listless and dreary. There were vents on every wall, she noticed, set behind shaped grids, circulating the air into the walkways, the buildings.

She trotted into the entrance doors to the Sandcat factory, stripping out of her clothes to prepare for decontamination.

SHE HAD BEEN on the production line for three hours. Her break was almost due, but its imminence promised no letup in her duties, only its arrival. She had been thinking about Brigid Baptiste—thinking hard. And yet, each time she thought she had it she had lost it again, almost feeling the thoughts slipping from her grasp.

There was something here, Brigid realized. Something out here, in the factory, in the walkways, maybe—probably—everywhere, that was doing its utmost to hinder her thoughts. Every time she stopped thinking about it she would start to lose that grip on her name, like it was being washed out to sea and she could only barely keep hold of it.

Brigid Baptiste.

The voice in her head, weeks ago now, the one that had plucked at her conscience long after its echoes had faded, had called her Baptiste. That voice had been inside her head, and she knew now what it was—a communications signal, a broadcast aimed directly at her.

Working on the back panels of a Sandcat, Brigid screwed up her eyes and tried to remember the communications device, the thing that she and…and Kane and…Grant… What they had used to speak to the people in…in… Dammit, what was the name of that place?

Brigid…Baptiste, she reminded herself grimly, forcing the name into her head.

"Citizen 619F, is something wrong?" The voice came from behind Brigid. It was her shift supervisor, Citizen 240M, a tall, gaunt man with dark skin and traces of iron gray in his black hair.

Brigid turned to look at him, opened her eyes when she realized that they were still screwed tight.

"You stopped performing," Citizen 240M stated emotionlessly. "Is something wrong? Are you sick?"

"My…" Brigid began, fumbling for an excuse. "Something in my eye. Dust from the panels."

The gaunt man looked down at Brigid from his position behind the partially constructed Sandcat at the side of the assembly line. "Wash your eye out under cold water until it is clear," he ordered. "Then return to work."

"Acknowledged," Brigid said. She wondered if this was the first conversation that had occurred in this factory this week—perhaps even this month.

Relieved from her workstation for a moment, Brigid made her way to the tiny-but-functional restroom to wash out the imaginary speck of dust that had fallen in her eye. As she walked she realized, frighteningly, that she was forgetting her name again. *Citizen 619F.* That's what the man had called her, that felt like it was her name. No, she told herself. Baptiste. Baptiste was her name.

She remained in the bathroom a long time, running the faucet and just staring at her face in the mirror. Without the cap she looked more like herself, more like that stranger called Brigid Baptiste.

All around her, the air vents pumped filtered air into the room. Her gaze was drawn to one as she looked in the mirror, and she turned to look at it directly. A wired grid with an aperture to direct air down, so that it blew through the room. There were ten of these in the room, more than seemed necessary, and Brigid remembered what she had been looking into before, about the air monitoring in Ioville and the emphasis on artificial ventilation and how this seemed unprecedented compared to the historical records of the other villes.

With a sudden inspiration, Brigid strode purposefully across the room and reached up for the vent. It was above her, so high she was barely able to reach it. But holding her hand up she could feel the breeze it generated, the way it played lightly across her fingers and the palm of her hand.

She drew her hand away very slowly, feeling the path that the breeze took, tracing it through the air. It was blowing against her, she realized. Blowing against her face in a soft, subtle whisper.

Brigid strode across the room, put her hand against one of the vents on the opposite wall and traced its breeze as she had the first. This one, too, blew against her, licking against the sides of her head.

"Brigid Baptiste," she reminded herself as she felt

the air play against her ear. She knew she could lose the memory again, if she wasn't careful.

Now, why would an air-con engineer design a system that blew air in people's faces? she wondered. And if they did, why so subtly?

There was something here she was not seeing, not quite able to comprehend. The elaborate air flow plans in Cappa Level, the exhaustive ventilation system that ensured no outside air entered the ville without being filtered—it all meant something, but what?

She knew she had been gone too long. She trotted back to the door and hurried outside, pacing across the factory floor to her work crew on the production line. The supervisor said nothing, as if he had not noticed her protracted absence. Even stranger, he reminded her to take her break just ten minutes later, which she did.

Brigid sat in the penned-off area of the factory that had been designated for breaks, listening to the roar of the massive conveyor belts and the hum of machinery, the hiss of the acetylene torches and the whir of screws being fastened in place. But her attention was elsewhere. She gazed around the room, sipping from a beaker of water as she traced the vents on the walls. They were evenly paced and ran the whole length of the vast room, each one designed just like the ones in the bathroom with their strange, open central aperture like a spout.

They were blowing air at people, Brigid realized. Not circulating it in the room—well, not just that anyway— but blowing it at people's heads.

"Brigid Baptiste," she mouthed to herself, subvocalizing the words.

The act of subvocalizing triggered something else in her mind, another piece of the puzzle. The Commtact, she remembered. She had a Commtact, a remarkable piece of hardware wired up inside her skull that could send and receive radio communications in real time. And one trick to using the Commtact in awkward situations was to subvocalize, because the way its microphone was built into her skull meant that it would pick up and augment the words when it broadcast them to a colleague. *A colleague like Kane.*

Brigid thought hard about the Commtact, remembering how to make it function. "Kane, this is Baptiste," she subvocalized. "Where are you?"

Subliminal Instruction to Ioville Citizen 618M:

Attend Delta Level from 1532.
Location: Tower 3, room D11.
Nutrition intake. All food must be consumed.
Any food not eaten in situ may be packaged up and removed to be imbibed in your sleeping quarters. Only use designated packaging and log the removal with one of the wall-mounted analyzers, including the weight of the package.
Duration: .75 hours.

Chapter 23

The elevator doors parted and Supreme Magistrate Webb emerged on Cappa Level, in the headquarters and training facility of the Magistrates. It was here that everyone in his ville was schooled in physical fitness. Even now as he passed the training gymnasium, Webb could see a small group of citizens being put through their paces as he peered through the reinforced glass panel set in the gray double doors.

Webb's face was set in a grim expression. He had been thinking about what that ex-Magistrate Kane had told him when he had arrived at Ioville, before he had been sent through Processing and Orientation and had lost his mind to Terminal White.

He marched on, striding familiar corridors, passing through another set of doors and into one of four incident rooms where the Magistrates toiled to retain the fixed order of Ioville. Gray-clad Mags worked at their desks, following through on a grand project to create laws that could govern all of the continent. To govern one needed rules. Webb had thought this an idle dream of noble intent but a dream all the same; now, however, he was beginning to realize the necessity of such an endeavor.

Webb had been waiting three weeks for a message to come through from the barons, setting his request message on a loop so that it would play over and over, twice a day at random intervals. No response had been received.

Webb stepped into the Magistrate communications suite, a large room, twenty feet square, its walls hidden behind equipment—all processors and flashing diodes and the whir of cooling fans. Two Mags manned the control desk, which looked like the instrument panel of an aircraft, sending instructions to the Magistrates on duty out in the ville.

"Mag 390M, please report to sector 3-G for cleanup," one of the controllers was saying into his microphone headset.

The two Mags turned as Webb entered, offering a clenched-fist salute. Webb nodded soberly, then instructed them to wait outside. For what he had to do next, he wished to be alone. The two men filed out of the room, marching in step.

Still standing, Webb went over to the comms array and tapped in his private code. The unit switched to monitoring the dedicated frequencies for baronial communication. Webb glared at the transmitter display, holding little hope now that the barons would contact him. The display was blank, confirming what Webb had suspected—that no response had been received.

He grimaced as he took a place at the comms desk, seating himself in the swivel chair. Could what Kane said be true then? Could the barons be dead? It seemed incredible, preposterous even, that such beautiful creatures could have died.

But without them, as he had told Kane, the world would surely descend into chaos, as man turned on man, exposing his violent nature. This could not happen—not when the Program of Unification had drawn everything together and imposed order on the world.

Webb made a decision then. He took it upon himself, in that quiet moment alone in the Mag comms center in a perfectly ordered ville named in binary code, to take charge of the reins, to correct the dangerous path that the world outside the snowstorm must surely be on, to bring Terminal White to the masses.

He had his army, trained and ready, every citizen schooled in the techniques they would need to conquer the madness snapping at the world's heels.

When Webb was done, the whole of North America would be in his control, eradicating all the petty rivalries and wars and dissatisfactions that had driven mankind to the brink of extinction once before.

The discipline, the fitness, the manufacturing—everything was in place for this moment. Everything was ready. It had to be—the world was depending on him. It was time for humanity to experience the day after it lost free will.

He turned away from the radio receiver, stood up and strode out of the room with renewed purpose. It was time to begin again.

"Call my personal guard," he told the waiting comms officers outside.

What he had to do next, he would conduct from Alpha Level—a new baron for a new age.

"KANE?" BRIGID TRIED AGAIN, subvocalizing the request through the pickup mic of her Commtact. "I'm in Ioville with you. Do you hear me?

"Grant? Are you there?"

Just as the first time, there was no response to her request.

Brigid stood self-consciously, eyeing the citizens working at their designated tasks in the factory. She had to get out of here, find Kane, figure out a way to stop this madness that was slowing her mind. Her eidetic memory had shaken it off, but even now she could feel her thoughts misting over again.

Brigid tried the Commtact again. "Grant? It's Brigid. Do you read me?"

Nothing.

Her crew supervisor was pacing across the room toward where Brigid was standing in the break area, a stern look on his wrinkled features. Her break was over, she realized, and Ioville always ran to schedule. There was no leeway to deviate.

"Hello, Cerberus? This is Brigid Baptiste. Please respond," Brigid subvocalized again as she watched the supervisor get nearer.

The supervisor stopped before Brigid, standing on the other side of the low barricade that delineated the "room."

"You are dangerously late, Citizen 619F," he said.

Dangerously? It was five seconds since she should have been back at her post. Just five seconds.

Brigid nodded as if chastised and hurried back across the room to her position on the production line. But she was thinking things through now, putting together all the tiny slivers of evidence that told her something was very much amiss.

One, she had trouble recalling her memories. She knew they were there, but pulling them to mind took effort. Which meant that something was blocking her normal thought processes.

That something was likely coming through the vents, which she realized were in every walkway, every room, every apartment. A narcotic, a beat, a subliminal suggestion of some kind—it was hard to tell, but it was almost certainly there.

How that suggestion worked she did not know yet, but it was making people obey. Brigid herself had been made compliant by whatever it was, working in this grim factory for the betterment of a ville she owed no loyalty to.

Two, she had a means to contact her allies and the outside world. That means was the Commtact, but for some reason no one was picking up her signal.

From what she could recall, the Commtact was surgically inserted beneath her skin, which meant it was next to impossible for a stranger to happen upon it. So she felt safe to assume it was still there. Furthermore, its hiding place meant it should have sustained no damage, so maybe there was another factor in play here.

She settled into her groove at the rear of the semiconstructed Sandcat, considering all these points as she set about affixing another rear panel to another vehicle. And as she did so, Brigid wondered: Just how many Sandcats does one ville need?

IN ZETA LEVEL, Citizen 618M was working on the final armament checks for a Sandcat, his sixteenth today. Each Sandcat and Deathbird was checked after being produced by the factories on Epsilon Level, and each was checked regularly after that to ensure it was in optimum working order.

Citizen 618M went through the checklist of tests required for each vehicle, never hurrying and never slowing. Each was granted precisely the same amount of energy and time, each a regimented test of its capabilities and efficiency.

He climbed into the turret of the snow-white Sandcat he was working on, ran a series of tests on the control board before activating the twin USMG-73 turret guns located there. The guns cycled to life, the control panel switching to a faint red color to indicate that the weapons were live. Citizen 618M commanded the turret to swing around, watching on the targeting controls while the crosshairs tracked across the vast garage and repair shop, past his fellow workers.

Citizen 618M brought the twin heavy machine guns around counterclockwise until their target fell on a bull's-eye located on a distant wall. The bull's-eye was two hundred and fifteen feet away from the Sandcat and was marked in rings of gray, white and black with an outer ring in silver. Citizen 618M depressed the twin triggers, sending a short burst of fire—just two bullets—from the turret guns. The twin bullets streaked away and struck the target an instant later.

Citizen 618M checked a portable display he carried with him, linked to a camera that had been positioned facing the target but out of the line of fire. The image on the display unit confirmed that the bullets had struck, dead center. The guns were perfectly balanced and in working order.

Citizen 618M commanded the turret chair to swivel back to the starting position, following the counterclockwise circuit. Once this was done, he climbed out of the turret blister and back into the main body of the Sandcat before exiting via the side door. Around him, the other mechanics continued their own checks.

If Citizen 618M had any inkling that he had ever operated one of these turret guns before, either in his previous life as the Cerberus warrior called Grant or even in the preceding three weeks in his current role as an Ioville mechanic, he gave no hint. In fact, he seemed to be exactly what he was—a blank slate, ready to be shaped to the will of his superiors.

CITIZEN 619F'S SHIFT was over. Citizen 619F—Brigid Baptiste as she knew herself to be now—was expected next in the food distribution room in the adjacent tower at Epsilon Level. As she left the factory, she took a moment to let her thoughts settle. Her thoughts had raced while she was working, so many questions and problems that needed to be addressed before she could get herself—and her allies—out of this mess.

She was standing before a large bank of windows that looked out over the snow-covered ville. It looked beautiful, like a frosted cake in an art deco style. Snow continued to fall, generated by the artificial engines and the seeded clouds.

Brigid stopped in surprise, eyeing the falling snow through the windows of the walkway as if for the first time.

Extreme weather could affect the Commtact's signal strength, she realized, and it was snowing up a blizzard outside the ville, had been ever since she could remember.

That man's broadcast had reached her, the man she had heard in her head—no, through the Commtact, she corrected herself—weeks ago. He must have had some system to penetrate through the blizzard, some way to boost his signal.

Brigid's mind raced, drawing on all the radio broadcast knowledge that she could recall. Antennae and signal boosters and receiver stations—that was the basic triangle of radio broadcast.

Could she find something to boost her signal here in

the ville? She racked her brains, thinking about everything she had seen but nothing came to mind.

But that was looking at the situation of herself alone. Kane was here, performing duties as a Magistrate, and a Magistrate would know more about the inner workings of the ville than any normal citizen. Which brought her to her next question— How do I find Kane?

Chapter 24

Brigid stood to the side of the broad walkway, watching the milling crowds switching shift at the Sandcat factory. Like them, she was due somewhere now, too, at one of the designated tasks, this one involving serving food.

Brigid felt the pull to her next task, felt the compunction to follow that edict, to go to the vast food banks elsewhere on Epsilon Level, where she should be serving her fellow citizens in ten minutes' time.

"You are Brigid Baptiste," she whispered to herself, holding her head, rubbing at her face. "Don't let them make you forget that."

She had more important things to do now. She needed to find Kane and locate Grant. Grant would be harder—she had not seen him since she had been indoctrinated into ville life, could not even be certain that he was really here. But Kane—Kane should be easier to locate. She just had to apply logic, because in a world as ordered as Ioville, logic was the most effective weapon of all. Use the logic, flip the process—simple.

She strode toward the nearest elevator bank, tapped the call button and waited for the elevator car to arrive. A few seconds later the elevator let out a dull chime and a set of elevator doors opened. Two Magistrates came marching out, and Brigid stepped back automatically, pushing herself against the wall, trying not to draw at-

tention to herself. The Mags strode past, ignoring her—
they clearly had business elsewhere on this level.

Once they had passed, Brigid stepped into the elevator—gray-walled, of course—and pressed the button
for Cappa Level.

"You are Brigid Baptiste," Brigid muttered to herself as the elevator ascended. "Do not let them make
you forget that."

The elevator ground to a halt, issuing just the faint-
est of wheezes as the hydraulic brakes functioned. Then
the doors opened, revealing a corridor on Cappa Level.
The corridor was gray with horizontal white lines running along it at waist and ankle level.

Brigid stepped warily from the elevator, searching
right and left for anyone who might be observing her.
Two Magistrates in full uniform—gray with the white
Io insignia over the breast—were marching toward her
from the far left, but as she watched they peeled away,
turning into a doorway located farther along the corridor.

Self-consciously, Brigid pushed her hair back, pulled
down the peak of her cap and began to stride purposefully along the featureless corridor.

She made her way past several open doorways, glancing inside to see various workings of the Magistrate
Division. There was an armory, heavily secured and
guarded, a computer room and a lab where samples
might be taken for analysis. Another room looked like
a morgue, lines of open drawers waiting between its
cool walls, each drawer empty. I guess no one has died
lately in Ioville, Brigid thought with a sense of curiosity.
She wondered if maybe no one ever did, if that would
be against the Designated Task system that was applied
so cruelly to every resident of the ville.

She hurried on, uncertain of where she was going. There were no signs here, and no wall maps as there were in other areas of the ville.

She walked straight into an evidence room without realizing it, found herself facing a wall of identical lockers, each one identified only by bar code. A network of robot arms descended from the ceiling like an upturned octopus, motionless now but ready to spring into action if anything was required from this room.

Another doorway opened into a long corridor that served as a communal shower, stretching forty feet, open like a carwash. Brigid stepped out, almost walking into a Magistrate who was about to get washed. The man was stripped down and held a gray towel in his hands.

Brigid said nothing and neither did the Mag, and she wondered if by saying nothing the man presumed that she was following orders and thus had no need to challenge her. If that was the case then it made things easier—so long as she did nothing to specifically draw attention to herself she should theoretically be able to move about this area freely.

Brigid hurried on, trotting away from the showers until she reached a junction where four corridors met. She halted there, eyeing each direction. Ahead, a doorway, wide enough for a Sandcat to pass through, opened into an operations room. A dozen Magistrates worked at their desks there, and Brigid searched their faces—or what she could see of them from under their helmets— looking for the familiar strong lines of Kane's jaw. He wasn't there.

The other two directions showed more featureless corridors. Brigid wondered how to choose a direction, stood for thirty seconds seemingly unable to make a decision.

You are now late for Designated Task #008, her mind pleaded. Please report to Epsilon Level immediately, Citizen 619F.

Brigid turned and began to stride back to the elevators, something like a sense of dread clawing at the pit of her stomach. She was late for her duty, and in not performing that duty to the utmost of her ability she was letting down the ville.

"No," Brigid muttered, halting midstride, the elevator bank still twenty feet ahead of her. She screwed her eyes shut tight and shook her head. You are Brigid Baptiste, she told herself. Do not let them make you forget this. "Brigid Baptiste," she whispered.

Regathering her thoughts, Brigid turned herself around and strode back down the corridor, repeating the mantra of her own name in her head. If she kept focused, it seemed that she could retain her own thoughts and personality—but any momentary lapse and she risked losing sight of herself and reverting back to her prescribed role as Citizen 619F.

BRIGID REACHED THE junction of corridors a couple of minutes later, back where she had become confused. She halted for just a moment, spun clockwise on her heel scanning all routes, telling herself that she was Brigid Baptiste the whole time in her mind, occasionally muttering the words under her breath. Then, making a decision, she turned around and retraced her steps, then continued on into the Residential Enclaves, where she knew the Magistrates would also have their apartments. They would spend their time there when they were not on shift.

Kane could be on shift, that was true, but he might be here. Statistically, she had more chance of finding Kane here than anywhere else anyway—after all, it would be the one location where he would remain in a static place for any significant amount of time, the rest of his hours taken up with patrolling the myriad corridors of Ioville and the area outside.

A line of doors waited on either side of the wide corridor. Brigid halted, watching them for a moment. A Magistrate came striding down the corridor past her, making his way to his room, removing his helmet as he walked. The helmet was painted a dull gray that seemed to suck in all available light and it featured a shaded visor, which entirely hid an individual's eyes, reaching all the way down to the very base of the nose, leaving only the mouth and chin visible. The effect of that helmet was terrifying, striking dread into any citizen who faced it.

Brigid watched the Magistrate walk the corridor and push the door open into his private sleeping quarters.

Brigid smiled inwardly. Now all she had to do was check the sleeping quarters, hope that Kane was here or, if he wasn't, that there was some sign, some clue, as to which unit he inhabited.

Be bold, Brigid Baptiste, she told herself. Act like you belong.

She began to walk down the corridor, moving toward the first of forty doors behind which lay the private sleeping quarters of the Magistrates. She pushed open the first door—unlocked—and confirmed that the room was unoccupied. She took a moment to look around the room, seeing the basic bed with gray blanket and wall screen above, single chair and countertop beside which was a lockup box set into the wall where weapons would be held.

There were two doors within the room, standing next

to one another at the end of the bed. Brigid walked over to these and tried the first. It slid aside on runners. Inside was a short rail and three fixed hangers on which clothes could be hung. It was a wardrobe.

The second door also slid back, this one revealing a trash unit with a faucet and one single half-pint glass. Brigid drew the door closed again, closing the wardrobe, as well.

Then she made her way to the door, her heart beating a little faster. The thought occurred to her that she might have been observed, that she may have triggered a silent alarm or that there could be a camera watching her.

Doesn't matter, she told herself. Just find Kane.

Brigid stepped from the sleeping unit and back into the main corridor. Thirty-nine rooms to go.

As she stepped out, two more Magistrates appeared from behind her, striding down the corridor purposefully, their expressions fixed and grim. Brigid turned, her heart racing faster, worried that perhaps they had come for her. Perhaps her paranoia about triggering an alarm had been well-placed after all.

Brigid stepped back, pushing into the nearest open doorway, pulling the gray peak of her cap down self-consciously. The two Magistrates walked straight past her, neither acknowledging her nor failing to see her.

They simply don't see me as a risk, Brigid confirmed. To them I'm just another obedient citizen, and my being up here must have a rational explanation.

She was barely able to contain her smile as she stepped out from the doorway and strode along the corridor. She moved quickly but tried not to look too hurried.

Please be here, Brigid thought. Please be in one of these rooms.

Most of the doors were wide-open. Brigid trotted

along the corridor, peering into each one. The rooms were bland and characterless, gray walls and neatly made beds, sparse furniture and zero decoration. To Brigid they seemed like prison cells, but as she thought that she realized what a bad analogy it was—even prisoners, especially prisoners, personalize their cells, try to make the blandness somehow their own, somehow special. The people of Ioville, however, had lost all of that; that wonderful uniqueness that made them human.

Three doors of the corridor were closed, one after another. Brigid walked more slowly past them, wondering what to do.

She would try a door, but what if someone inside wanted to know why? She needed a reason, an excuse.

"Then use the truth," she told herself in a whisper.

Brigid knocked on the first door, painted a kind of oatmeal gray, then opened it. It was a bunk room like the others, a single cubicle where a Magistrate would sleep while off duty. No one was inside and the bed was neatly made. She wanted to stop, look around, hoping she might see a clue that it was maybe Kane's room, but she knew how ridiculous that was—Kane was a part of the system now, and he had lost his individuality just like everyone else.

She exited the room, then tried the same knock-open pattern on the next door. A voice spoke up even as she swung the door open, and Brigid saw a man lying on the bed, holding his hand up before his eyes. The man was in his twenties, dark-skinned with black hair and a muscular torso, naked but covered by a rough blanket.

"Is it shift?" he asked groggily.

"No," Brigid said, and she began to step from the cubicle. She stopped herself, eyes still on the half-asleep Mag, and something occurred to her. "I have the wrong instructions," she explained, taking a single step back into the room. "I was told to meet a Magistrate called—" she thought back, remembering the number Kane had given her when he'd told her to report her behaviour "—620M. He's new."

The man in the bed looked mystified, then pointed vaguely in the direction that Brigid had been headed. "Six doors down. 620M should be about to start shift, I think, but you may catch him," the man explained, his words slurred.

"Thank—" Brigid stopped herself, swallowing the word. "Acknowledged," she said, stepping from the apartment and closing the door.

She hurried up the corridor, counting six doors farther along until she was faced with her next dilemma. There were two doors there, one on either side of the bland corridor. Which one? Which one?

Brigid tried the one to her right, entering with a single knock.

Kane stood before her, dark Magistrate uniform on, the top not yet zipped up. Brigid gasped, seeing him look up as he reached for his helmet. She had seen him like this before, years ago when she had first met him in Cobaltville. He had come to her apartment there and challenged her, alcohol on his breath, fear and disarray clouding his mind. He glared at her now, the cruel armor of the Magistrate Division making him into as much a symbol as a man.

"Do you require something, citizen?" Kane asked.

Chapter 25

"Kane, it's me," Brigid said, suddenly finding it hard to swallow. "It's Brigid."

The man in the Magistrate armor glared at her, challenge in his steely blue-gray eyes. "Citizen, what is your purpose?"

Brigid stepped into the tiny, single-room apartment, pushing the door closed behind her. "Kane, it's me. Snap out of it."

Kane looked at her, a hint of confusion furrowing his brow. "Citizen…?"

"Kane!" Brigid blurted, striding across the room and grabbing Kane by both biceps, the same way he had grabbed her just a few weeks ago when she, too, had been lost in the miasma of Terminal White. "You need to listen to me and really try hard to hear what I'm saying—"

Kane flexed his muscles and shoved Brigid away, dropping the Mag helmet he had been holding so that it rolled across the nightstand.

"Take your hands from me, citizen," Kane snarled, as she stumbled back into the nearest wall.

Brigid saw Kane turn, reaching for something on the side table next to his cot. It was a gun, long and needle-thin at its end, like the ones that she had encountered out in the snows, outside the ville.

"Kane, don't," Brigid commanded. "Just think for a minute, let it—"

Kane raised the tranquilizer gun in a rapid sweep, bringing it up to target Brigid, his face fixed in a cruel sneer. Brigid leaped, springing from her place against the wall to the opposite wall, even as Kane squeezed the trigger and fired a tranquilizer dart at her.

"Cease and desist, citizen," Kane snarled.

The dart cut through the air past Brigid's retreating form before burying itself in the plasterboard wall behind her.

Kane was already shifting his aim, drawing the long-nosed blaster around to shoot at this red-haired intruder a second time. With nowhere else to go, Brigid leaped at him, arms outstretched, head low as the blaster fired again. A second dart zipped past her, cleaving a web of strands from her gray overalls as it went wide before colliding with the sliding door of the refresher station.

By then Brigid was in Kane's face, driving one knee up into his groin even as she reached for the outthrust blaster. Kane grunted as her blow struck, and in that moment of pain Brigid tugged the tranquilizer gun out of his hand and tossed it across the room. The blaster landed with a clatter in the corner.

Kane shoved forward, an automatic reaction, pushing Brigid away. She recovered instantly, coming at him again, delivering a brutal leg sweep that forced Kane to struggle to retain his balance as he went dancing back into the cot.

Brigid followed through, kicking out at the room's sole chair, using it to push herself up and forward, propelling her lithe body at Kane's stumbling, uncoordinated form. Brigid's left leg fired out toward Kane's face but there was not enough space—instead, she caught the side of his head with her calf, but it was enough to send Kane reeling against the wall.

Brigid landed in a tumble on the freshly made bed, bounded against its paltry springs and flipped herself around to face Kane, poised in a crouch like a jungle cat. "Listen to me, Kane," she hissed. "Get this through your thick skull before you get us both killed."

Kane had recovered also, muscle memory kicking in as he struck the wall, reaching out for the discarded Magistrate helmet and throwing it in his attacker's direction as he fell.

Brigid batted the flying helmet aside, pounced from the bed toward Kane once more, launching herself like a projectile from a catapult.

Brigid was not stronger than Kane, nor was she faster. He was an expert in all forms of combat, trained from birth to be a Magistrate, master of a dozen deadly forms of unarmed combat. But she had something that he did not in that moment—free will, the ability to think, to process, to react.

Kane crossed one leg over the other, trying to flip Brigid, but she danced out of his reach, then drove a fist into his gut in a rapid rabbit punch. She followed this with another, forcing the man she knew as Kane to suck heavily to get his breath, doubling over in surprise and agony.

"Slow down," Brigid snarled at him. "Think! You are Kane of the Cerberus organization. You've been tricked into serving the Magistrate Division here in a ville you never chose. Think!"

Still doubled over to catch his breath, Kane charged forward, drilling his head into Brigid's chest and driving her back until she slammed against the wall behind her. The wall shook, plaster breaking loose, and Brigid grunted in pain.

"Think, dammit," Brigid growled, slumping down against the wall. "Try to remember."

They were *anam-charas*, these two, soul friends throughout eternity, linked by some deep, impossible-to-define bond that promised they would always be tied together, looking out for each other no matter what the turn of destiny's wheel. They had lived a thousand lives, as friends, as lovers and as something more, their bond never explicit but always drawing them together, magnetic poles finding each other in the darkness. Now Brigid needed that link they had, that tie—and yes, that love—to draw Kane back to her, to bring his brain back to life and away from Terminal White. "Try to remember," Brigid muttered again, struggling for breath.

"Remember this," Kane spit, lunging for her. He snatched Brigid up in his arms, dragging her to a standing position. As he raised Brigid, his head came rushing toward her face, striking her in a vicious head butt that knocked her back against the wall with a loud thump.

Brigid sagged back, seeing swirling black dots cloud her vision, pain running through her forehead. She felt herself slide down the wall, a mixture of dizziness and nausea threatening to overwhelm her. She was defeated, had no hope of recovering before Kane came at her with another attack.

But he didn't.

Instead, through the haze of dark smears that occluded her racing vision, Brigid saw Kane just standing there, confusion contorting his features, looking down at Brigid where she was sprawled at the juncture where wall met floor.

"Baptiste…?" Kane muttered, shaking his head.

"Kane? You remember me," Brigid said, her voice suddenly loud in her ears, the sensation of air against her vocal cords making her choke back bile. She coughed, tried again. "Kane, it's me. Yes—Baptiste."

But Kane was barely listening. Instead he seemed to be transfixed, caught in the mire of his own terrible confusion, a man waking from a nightmare but still reliving the horror of it. "Baptiste," he said uncertainly. "I know you."

"Kane…"

"Who am I?" Kane asked, staring at Brigid. "I can remember you. My partner Grant. Something about a… three-headed dog—"

"Cerberus," Brigid said, watching Kane's befuddled features. He looked like a little boy in those moments, one who had lost his parents. "Kane, we've been tricked. Somehow, the regime here has us wired into it, hooked into something that's stopping us from thinking, that's making us forget."

"Cerberus," Kane repeated, barely listening to Brigid's words. "What's going on?"

Brigid fixed Kane with her lustrous emerald eyes. "Kane, please try to concentrate. This is so important."

He looked at her, rubbing at his forehead with his left hand.

"Your head hurts, doesn't it?" Brigid said.

"Yeah," Kane confirmed.

"Let it," Brigid told him. "The hurt may be the only thing keeping you *you*.

"We're warriors, Kane, working for an organization called Cerberus that tries to protect the world from all the…the nastiness out there."

"So I'm a Magistrate," Kane said, bewildered.

"No," Brigid told him, pushing herself slowly up the

wall until she stood. "You're something better than that. The Magistrates were a lie. *This* is a lie, all of it. We came out here to find something but we got trapped inside it."

"To find something?" Kane repeated slowly.

"Don't ask me what because I don't know," Brigid told him. "They trapped us somehow, locked up our minds so we couldn't think. Took away our free will."

She looked up at him. "Stop rubbing your head! Let it hurt, because that may be the only thing making you think straight," she snapped.

Kane drew his hand away from his forehead. "They took away our free will," he said slowly.

"Yes," said Brigid.

"Our lives…"

"Our memories," Brigid said. "They have some way to jam our memories, and they keep us so busy that we never question, never think to challenge what we're doing or how we got here."

The trace of a smile crossed Kane's grim face as he gave Brigid an up-from-under look. "But you challenged it, Baptiste," he said.

"I did. My memory works differently to that of most people," Brigid said. "I remember detail, fix on to it and hold it with a clarity most people will never know. It's called an eidetic memory."

"And that's how you came to be here," Kane said, "searching for me."

"I saw you," Brigid told him. "First, on the day I arrived, I think. You tried to warn me, but you didn't know what it was that you were warning me about—"

"Terminal White," Kane said, speaking the words like a curse.

"Is that what they call it?" Brigid asked.

"There's a guy at the top—Webb, Supreme Magistrate Webb," Kane told her. "He talked me through it all before they…I dunno…inducted me into it. He had information about me, knew I was a Magistrate from way back. I think maybe he thought I might side with him."

Tired now, her adrenaline levels dropping after the fight, Brigid took a seat on the bed, removed her cap and brushed a hand through her flame-red hair. "What does it do?" she asked. "Do you remember?"

"It's a project dating back to the barons," Kane recalled. "It saps people of their free will, makes them… docile, I guess. Malleable."

Brigid nodded. "That's what I thought," she said. "There's something in the air. I don't quite know what, but they guard the air and the ventilation system here like it's sacred. I think maybe it distributes whatever this Terminal White stuff is."

"No," Kane said with a firm shake of his head. As he shook his head, he winced, the ache from his head butt still nagging at him. "It's not what's in the air, it's the way it's delivered. It plays with the inner ear, at least that's how I think Webb explained it."

"The inner ear creates the sense of balance in mammals," Brigid said, nodding now. "If it's disrupted then potentially—"

"A person would fall over?" Kane proposed.

"More than that," Brigid told him, visualizing ancient biological drawings she had seen. "Forced to constantly compensate for failing balance, a person would be unable to concentrate on anything else. They could become susceptible to hypnotic suggestion."

"Hypnotic suggestion through air flow," Kane said, shaking his head. Then he opened his eyes wide and looked at Brigid. "Baptiste, I'm starting to…forget, I think. Even this conversation is becoming muggy, like wherever it began is lost behind a dense wall of fog."

"Automatic forgetfulness," Brigid said, nodding. "That happens. You have to fight it."

"*That* I figured," Kane growled. "You have any idea how? Assuming I don't have your whatchamacallit memory."

"Disrupt the signal, disrupt the signal," Brigid muttered, thinking aloud. "There has to be a way."

"No. If you built this, would you create a way to break it?" Kane asked.

"Point," Brigid accepted. "But it wasn't designed with us in mind. You, me, Grant—we're different. We're not the local bumpkins who've wandered into this hellhole and been press-ganged into staying."

"'Bumpkins'?" Kane asked with an amused smile.

"Shorthand," Brigid dismissed his query. "A voice spoke to me in my ear. The Commtacts," she snapped her fingers. "The Commtacts!"

Kane looked at her, his brows furrowed. "You're not making a lot of sense to me…Baptiste," he said. Her name was becoming more difficult to recall.

Brigid lifted one hand to her ear, manipulating its shell. "We have Commtacts, communications devices hidden beneath the skin, running along the mastoid bone," Brigid said. Her words were rushing out in a tumble now, as if she couldn't get the information across to Kane fast enough. "These Commtacts allowed us to communicate with Cerberus. But they're not working, the signal is blocked here in Ioville."

"Then that's a great big bust," Kane said dourly.

"No, it isn't," Brigid told him. "The storm outside is blocking the satellite bounce—"

"It's artificial," Kane said, remembering his encounter with the snow wagon.

"Yes, of course it is," Brigid said excitedly. "And it's been going on so long that this ville must have a way to send a message through it, so that the—what did you call him?—Supreme Magistrate running the show can communicate with the—"

"Barons," Kane finished for her.

Brigid's eyes widened as he said it. "I was going to say 'outside world,'" she explained. "Are you trying to tell me that this Supreme Magistrate Webb believes he's still talking to the barons? But they're dead, Kane. They're all dead."

"I told him that, and he didn't like it," Kane said. "I could tell. So, going back to the comms— What's your plan?"

"The ville must have a booster or a wavelength that can penetrate the storm," Brigid theorized. "If we can somehow tap into that, piggyback our signal onto theirs—"

"We could get a message out," Kane agreed uncertainly, "but how does that help us if we're in danger of losing our minds?"

"Memories," Brigid corrected, "not minds. We can still think, we've just forgotten how to string thoughts together and what it's like to think for ourselves."

"So?" Kane prompted.

"So we contact Cerberus and get them to blast off a signal to us that—" she waved her hands dramatically in the air "—keeps us from slipping back into the walking coma."

Kane looked dubious. "That's one heck of a signal," he said.

"Not really, no," Brigid assured him. "We just need

something that will block the effect of this Terminal White programming. Without that, everything else should be how it always was in our heads—shouldn't it?"

Kane nodded real slow. "Maybe," he said, "just maybe."

"But I don't know how we're going to do that," Brigid admitted. "Things are kind of a jumble in my head just now."

"I think I know how," Kane said.

Chapter 26

Kane had replaced his Magistrate helmet and finished dressing. His dark uniform now looked neat and smart, its dull fabric absorbing the light rather than reflecting it. Dressed, Kane led the way through the corridors of Cappa Level with Brigid following a pace behind. "Stay close," he said out of the corner of his mouth, watching the various crisscrossing corridors for potential danger. There were Magistrates everywhere, some just coming on shift, others returning from shift, and others using the corridors as they went about their business.

"For a place with no free will, there's a heck of a lot of law enforcement," Brigid observed as they reached the end of the corridor unchallenged.

"More than you think," Kane said. "Everyone in the ville is trained for enforcement. I know—I've been training them."

"Including me," Brigid realized with evident surprise. "Designated Task #015. Fitness."

Kane glanced back at her for a moment as he led the way through the main area of Magistrate Division. "You think... What do you think?" he asked.

"I think we're in trouble," Brigid said dourly. "A whole ville of trained Mags, or at least people with Magistrate training—even just six hundred or so—would pose a credible threat to another community."

Kane strode past the tidy, uniform desks where Magistrates were working at computer terminals. No one looked up. "So you think Webb is what? Building up an army?"

Brigid nodded. "Distinctly possible," she stated.

"Not good," Kane muttered as he pushed open the door and stepped into the Magistrate comms area. "No sir, not good at all."

A few steps behind Kane, Brigid halted as she entered the room. It was a large area, twenty square feet at least, with communications equipment lining every wall. Two dull-eyed Mags were operating the equipment from high-backed swivel chairs, their eyes set on the bank of monitor screens and waveform registers, radio mics at their throats.

Kane turned back to Brigid and mouthed for her to close the door, which she did.

As the door clicked shut, Kane pulled his tranq gun from its holster and stepped between the two occupied swivel chairs. The Mags turned to face him, a look of consternation on their previously blank faces. Without a word, Kane turned the pistol on the Magistrate to his left and blasted him with a tranquilizer dart, which embedded itself in his chest before he could even say a word.

The second Mag moved fast, responding to the sudden danger within this operations sanctuary. He leaped from his seat and reached for Kane, who drove a sharp elbow at the man's face.

The Mag stumbled back with a cry of pain. Kane turned in the same instant and brought the tranquilizer gun up in a swift movement, targeting the Mag, front and center of the chest, before launching another tranq dart from his weapon. The dart fired with a *pfft* of expelled air, drilling its nonlethal discharge into the flailing Magistrate.

It had taken four seconds in total.

A little longer, Brigid recalled, and the drug would kick in, putting both men to sleep.

Kane reloaded his tranq gun while Brigid gazed around the vast, equipment-filled room. The equipment featured many monitoring devices, including live camera feeds from both inside and outside Ioville. Brigid glanced across the bank of split-screen televisions, each one showing four different viewpoints at once from varying locations. Several showed banks of snow and she wondered if this was how the Mags had caught her and Grant all those weeks ago.

"Somebody certainly likes to keep watch," Brigid observed.

"Magistrates are linked by helmet radio," Kane told her, gesturing to the helmet he wore. "We get orders from Central Command instructing us where we are needed. Each order is sent to a specific Mag or group or Mags, strictly referred to by citizen number."

Brigid smiled without humour. "Of course."

Kane rolled the sleeping Magistrate from the console and let him drop gently to the floor. Then he studied the console readouts before turning back to Brigid. "You have any idea how this stuff works, Baptiste?"

Brigid's brow furrowed in thought as she examined the wall of controls. "They remain in touch with Magistrates outside the ville walls," she reasoned, "which means—you're right—they have a booster signal that can penetrate the storm. Let's see—"

She flipped a switch, bringing up a wire-frame representation of the comms system on one of the computer screens. Tapping a few keys, Brigid brought up a diagnostic and followed the pattern of the broadcast signal.

"Got it," Brigid said after a few moments. "If we tap

into this signal, we can piggyback the Commtact broadcast and—hopefully—speak to Cerberus."

Kane fixed Brigid with his steely stare. "So what are we waiting for?"

Brigid nodded, pulling the empty swivel chair over before sitting down and working at the keyboard. A series of rapid images flashed across the screens, showing the signal strength, tapping into the broadcast wavelength and running a hidden layer into the established signal, buried deep within the pattern itself.

As Brigid typed, Kane watched her, his eyes slowly narrowing. "Who...are you?" he asked. "What are we doing here?"

Brigid turned to him, her hands still working the keyboard. "Kane, it's me, it's Baptiste. Try to remember. Say it, say your name and mine."

"Kane...?" Kane said. "Yeah, Kane. And you're... Baptiste. What is—?"

"Keep focused," Brigid instructed. "Don't lose yourself to Terminal White again."

Kane nodded reluctantly. "I'll try."

Brigid's hands continued to operate the keyboard, altering the broadcast system's protocols so that it would carry a Commtact frequency.

MEANWHILE, SUPREME MAGISTRATE WEBB was pacing through Alpha Level with a six-strong squadron of Magistrate guards, having just exited the private elevator that opened onto the highest level of the Administrative Monolith. He had a broadcast to make, one that required Alpha jurisdiction to engage. As such, it was one he could not make from the comms suite on Cappa, nor even from his own private suite—no, he needed to be here, a baron in everything but title.

He had tried to contact the barons forty times over, ever since Kane had sown that seed of doubt in his mind three weeks before, when he had inferred that the barons were all dead. Webb followed the barons' orders, and he had been entrusted to run Ioville and the mind experiment known as Terminal White away from their direct supervision. He was trusted to make decisions, to smooth the day-to-day running of the ville. A truly obedient administrator does not need to be spoon-fed orders; he is able to operate under his own initiative and do so in perfect accord with the wishes of his superiors. As such, Supreme Magistrate Webb had reached the decision days ago and wrestled with how best to implement it. He would launch the assault on the rest of the country, taking control of each ville—first Ragnar, Snakefish and Cobaltville—to reinstate order under the miraculous protocols of Terminal White. To do less was to fail in his duty.

Ioville had been an experiment in ultimate order, in instilling full obedience in its subjects, the human race. But it had a deeper purpose than that—instilling order was merely an offshoot. In fact, Ioville was a spoke in the grand war machine of the barons, both factory and training camp for the construction of weapons and soldiers to fight in the name of baronial rule. Now it was time to set things in motion, to wipe out the Outlanders and protect the Program of Unification, to save mankind from itself.

After posting the six-man guard outside in the lobby of the baronial suites, Webb entered the comms room and sat down at the communications array. His gray eyes—eyes the color of a snow wolf's fur—searched the console displays, hoping that maybe Kane had been wrong and that, after all these weeks of waiting, one of the barons might finally have responded to his request. But no, there was no indication that his coded broadcast had been received, let alone acknowledged.

Webb sat back, plucking up the microphone that rested on a stand, feeding into the baron's comms unit via a thick, dark wire.

"Protocol Zero-zero-zero," Webb stated into the mic. All around, speakers set within the walls of Ioville carried his summons, echoing it across the rooms and corridors, the factories and living quarters. The words echoed in the mind of every citizen of Ioville, and every citizen knew instinctively just what they were expected to do next. As one, the citizens left their designated tasks to obey.

"COME IN, CERBERUS, this is Brigid Baptiste," Brigid said, watching the trail of her own signal register in a tiny oscillating wave on the computer display before her. She was using her Commtact, its subdermal mechanism hidden from human eyes, and she had managed to bolster the signal now through the Ioville Magistrate Division's comms array. "Repeat, this is Brigid Baptiste. Please acknowledge."

Kane stood across the room, close to the closed doorway that led out into the workroom, where over a dozen Magistrates were oblivious at their designated tasks. "Anything?" he asked.

Brigid rubbed her hand over her face and let out a heavy sigh. "Come on, Cerberus," she muttered, "hear my plea."

The comms array remained silent for what seemed a very long duration. Brigid and Kane waited, holding their breath, listening to the nothingness stretching out before them, the silence that promised to lose them forever to the hypnotic thrall of Terminal White.

"Hello, Brigid." The words came through over their Commtacts. They were cracked and laced with static hiss, but there was no missing the joy and surprise in the voice. "Is that really you?"

Brigid closed her eyes in relief. "Brewster? It's me, all right. I'm here with Kane. He's able to hear you, so don't split the signal just yet."

"Gotcha," Brewster Philboyd responded from several hundred miles away over the medium of the linked Commtacts. "We've been looking all over for you. Where are you? And how is it you're contacting—?"

"Brew— I'll explain as we go along," Brigid promised. "Right now I need you to do something. Lock on to this signal—"

"Already doing so," Brewster assured her, speaking over Brigid's words.

"—and send a continual stream of chatter to me, Kane and Grant."

"Do what?" Brewster asked, clearly surprised.

THE CERBERUS OPERATIONS room in Montana was abuzz with nervous energy. Brewster Philboyd had been manning the comms console when Brigid's message had come through—in fact he had been in the middle of a negotiation with Domi, who was out in the field in the Florida Everglades following up what was evidently a false lead on the disappearance of the CAT Alpha team. When Brigid's signal came through, Philboyd had excitedly called over Lakesh from his supervisor's desk at the back of the room.

Now, Lakesh stood behind Philboyd's desk. Philboyd himself was standing also, a headset over his ears, fingers rushing over the keyboard of his computer terminal to try to get a fix on Brigid's signal. Brigid's voice came over the terminal's speakers, accompanied by hiss.

"I need you to send chatter," Brigid repeated.

"What kind of chatter?" Brewster asked, confused.

"Anything, doesn't matter," Brigid said with a hint of strain in her voice. "We're currently in a location called Ioville—"

"A ville?" Lakesh said in shock. There were nine villes—to discover a tenth was such a shift in paradigm it felt like fiction.

"—but the place uses something called Terminal White to brainwash its inhabitants," Brigid continued, unaware of Lakesh's interjection. "I figure that if we can run something to disrupt that signal then we might just be able to hold on to our sanity. Or regain it. Whichever."

Philboyd nodded uncertainly. "I'm hearing the words, Brigid, but I'm not sure I'm following. You say you're—?"

Lakesh tapped urgently on Brewster's desk and the younger man stopped talking. "Let me speak to her," Lakesh said gently. A moment later he was linked up to the Commtact via a portable headset with built-in microphone.

"Brigid dear, this is Lakesh," he began. "I cannot begin to express how relieved we all are to hear that you are safe."

"Well, I wouldn't exactly—" Brigid began.

"Hush, my dear," Lakesh interrupted. "Let us get this signal you have requested up and running, then we may discuss the whys and wherefores at our leisure."

"Good idea."

"Now, what precisely did you have in mind?"

"From what I can discern," Brigid explained, "Terminal White is a constantly evolving hypnotic suggestion which pumps into the brain, bypassing and overriding all other thoughts. I haven't worked out a way to stop that, but I figure that we can use the Commtacts to at least disrupt it."

"I see," Lakesh acknowledged, gesturing over for physician Reba DeFore to come join him from her monitoring desk close to the ops room's large doors. "And what would this signal entail?"

"Anything really," Brigid reasoned. "Just something that would keep us grounded and stop us getting drawn into the hypnotic miasma."

Lakesh thought for a few seconds. "So, 'Mary Had a Little Lamb,' say?"

"Yes," Brigid said. "Exactly that. On a loop to break the conditioning that's trying to get inside our brains."

As he spoke, Lakesh looked at Philboyd, who had retaken his seat before the comms desk. "'Mary Had a Little Lamb,' on loop, repeating every—what?—four minutes, Brigid?"

"Four minutes is good," Brigid agreed. "We still want to be able to hear what's going on around us. But you need to pipe it through to Grant and Kane, too. We cannot find Grant."

"Cannot or *haven't*?" Lakesh mused.

"Good point," Brigid agreed.

Philboyd took over then while Lakesh recruited computer expert Donald Bry to set up his voice on loop reciting the nursery rhyme that he had discussed with Brigid.

Brigid explained how they had hijacked the broadcast signal of Ioville, using that to penetrate the artificial storm and contact Cerberus. The signal would run through the Commtacts, but it had to be set at the one frequency and it was awash with static.

"We're still not picking up your transponders," Philboyd told Brigid, running a diagnostics check on the relevant equipment in parallel with the discussion. "Where are you?"

There was a brief pause, then Kane's voice came over the Commtact broadcast. "Kane here. Ioville is located within that damned snowstorm we came to investigate. Storm's blocking all signals, I guess."

DeFore had joined Brewster Philboyd at his desk and she took up the headset and mic that Lakesh had vacated. "Are you well, Kane? What is the status of your team?"

"Well, yeah," Kane assured her. "Just a little confused. Can't speak for Grant, though. Like Baptiste says, we've not had a chance to locate him yet."

"Kane, do you need anyth—?" Reba began but Kane's next words cut her off.

"You hear that? What the hell is that? Baptiste?" He evidently was not speaking to Cerberus now.

"What is it?" Brewster asked urgently over the Commtact. "What's going on there?"

No one responded.

IN THE MAGISTRATE comms room, Kane turned to face Brigid, his brow furrowing in confusion and anger. "You hear that?" he asked.

Brigid nodded. She heard it, too, although it was not like hearing, more like sensing, the way an animal senses the territory or presence of another animal.

"What the hell is that?" Kane asked. "Baptiste?"

Brigid closed her eyes and "listened" to the message playing inside her head. "Protocol Zero-zero-zero," she said. "Core command, superseding any and all designated tasks with immediate effect. We are to gather in the Zeta Level garages where we will—"

"—be armed," Kane picked up, "and then sent forth—"

"—in the name of the baron." Both of them were speaking now, hearing the words in time.

Kane looked at Brigid, wide-eyed. "Well, we should go."

"No, Kane, no," Brigid said, shaking her head vigorously until her red tresses broke free from beneath her cap. "Remember who you are."

"Magistrate 620M," Kane announced automatically.

"No," Brigid told him, grabbing him by the tops of his arms and pulling her face close to his. "Listen to me. You are Kane—you are a warrior in the Cerberus organisation. What you're experiencing right now is a trick to stop you thinking."

In the corridor outside, Brigid could hear the sounds of marching feet as the Magistrates on Cappa Level followed the order, making their way toward the elevators and from there down to Zeta Level.

"I need to go," Kane said in confusion. "We need to be at Zeta—"

"No, we don't," Brigid told him. "You are Kane."

"I'm…" Kane screwed his eyes closed as he tried to get a fix on Brigid's words. He kept hearing the command in his skull, compelling him to join the rest of the ville in Zeta Level where the Sandcats awaited, ready to start a grand push into the Outlands. "…needed," Kane finished, turning to walk out of the room.

Brigid reached for him, pulling him back, but he shrugged her away. He was in the thrall of the Supreme Magistrate now, under the command of Protocol Zero-zero-zero.

Chapter 27

In the Cerberus operations room, Mohandas Lakesh Singh was questioning Brewster Philboyd from two desks over, where Singh had been working with Donald Bry on the looped transmission that Brigid had proposed.

"What do you mean, you've lost them?" Lakesh demanded. "We were speaking to them just moments ago."

Brewster indicated his computer screen where the sine wave of the comms system showed as a luminescent line on a black background. "I've tried hailing them but they're not responding," Philboyd said. "It's like they were called away mid-discussion."

Lakesh scratched his jaw thoughtfully, wondering what was best to do next. He turned back to Donald Bry, who was sitting at another computer terminal where he had been working with Lakesh. "Donald, is the Mary track ready?"

Bry nodded, his mop of copper curls flopping over his eyes. "It is."

"Play it," Lakesh instructed. "Pipe it through the Commtact frequency at four-minute intervals, as Brigid suggested."

Bry tapped in a string of commands on his computer keyboard, linking the prerecorded message to the comms system. Then he pressed Execute.

GRANT, OR Citizen 618M as he had been rebranded three weeks before, had heard the command run in his head, as had the other mechanics on Level Zeta. The transmission was carried via the unique air flow system of Ioville, sending the message into the mind of every citizen. Each blindly adhered to the instruction, and each had their own role in the activation of Protocol Zero-zero-zero.

Grant marched with the colleagues, moving in absolute silence toward the main garage area. A set of quadruple doors towered before them, four times the height of a man, hinged in such a way that they folded in on themselves as they were drawn back into slots in the walls. Grant and the other mechanics worked the heavy doors, drawing them back toward their niches in the walls.

Behind the doors, a cavernous room was revealed. Automated lights began to wink on as the doors were drawn back, bathing the room in blue-white brilliance. There, within the vast room, stood over three hundred Sandcats, painted white and factory-new, along with one hundred Deathbird helicopters lined up in a grand strip down the center of the room. Each vehicle was armed and fueled; each was ready to be activated.

The Sandcats were arranged to face away from the gigantic doors, creating a neat line of back plates facing out toward Grant and his colleagues. The turret guns were all facing forward, the armaglass blisters glinting beneath the powerful illumination of the room, white streaks like crescent moons painting each lethal bubble.

Grant and his crewmates marched through the vast lines of Sandcats and Deathbirds, eyes forward, splitting up as they made their way toward the distant doors that opened out onto the wilderness beyond the walls of

Ioville, out into the world. Around them, the Sandcats and the Deathbirds powered up automatically, artificial positronic brains bringing them to life. Ioville had only approximately nine hundred citizens in total, and fully one-third of those were children. Each had been trained in the ways of the Magistrates, but they alone would not be enough to wage an assault on the moral decline of the outside world. Webb had foreseen this and had instructed that each vehicle have an automated system that could be applied as required, much as the snow wagons could function unmanned.

Grant continued to pace toward the distant doors that would unleash this new assault on the world.

BRIGID WATCHED KANE reach for the door handle to the Magistrate comms room, following the instruction that surged into his mind like an injected drug.

"Mary had a little lamb, its fleece was white as snow. And everywhere that Mary went, the lamb was sure to go."

Both of them heard the words, spoken in Lakesh's soft voice with a pleasant, lilting accent. The voice was playing in their heads, through the medium of their subdermal Commtacts.

Kane halted, brows furrowing in confusion, his hand clenching the door handle.

"Kane," Brigid said, her voice barely a whisper.

Kane turned to look at her, his brows still furrowed. After a moment he smiled. "Baptiste," he said. "I'm me. I'm me."

Brigid smiled then, too. "You heard the song," she confirmed.

"Yup, inside my skull," Kane explained with a nod of his head.

"That means Lakesh got it working," Brigid said. "Think it'll be enough to bring you back to reality?"

Kane looked wary, his hand finally receding from the doorknob. "Let's hope so."

Outside, the sounds of marching feet continued to echo down the corridor, Magistrates obeying the call to arms. The two Cerberus warriors knew they needed a plan then, and they needed one quickly.

Brigid turned back to the comms desk, her eyes searching frantically across the board of lights and dials and buttons.

"MARY HAD A little lamb, its fleece was white as snow. And everywhere that Mary went, the lamb was sure to go."

Striding between two Deathbirds, Grant's step suddenly wavered and he stopped in place.

"What the hell—?" he muttered, shaking his head. He had heard the voice in his head, the children's nursery rhyme playing through his skull.

Around him, Grant could hear his fellow mechanics marching through the ranks of vehicles, keeping step as they made their way toward the external doors of the enormous garage level. He stepped back beneath the tail strut of the nearest Deathbird, ducking beneath it to hide himself as he tried to make sense of the words in his head.

"Hello?" Grant said, muttering the word.

Around him, something in the atmosphere, the very air itself, seemed to be telling him to get back to work, to get the vehicles prepped and ready to launch, to draw back the external doors and begin the assault on the broken world waiting beyond Ioville's walls. But the other voice, the other words, rang in his ears like a taunt, filling him with doubt.

"THERE!" BRIGID SAID, jabbing her finger at a display panel on the vast control board of the Mag comms desk.

Kane looked at the panel for a moment, then, realising he really had no idea what he was looking at, turned to question her. "What is it?" he asked.

"Alpha Level," Brigid said, translating the data stream that ran across one of the computer screens, "baronial suite. That's where the broadcast is coming from—the one that's instructing everyone to go to Zeta Level."

Kane huffed angrily. "Makes sense," he said. "Damn baron had to be at the heart of this mess."

"Protocol Zero-zero-zero is a command to begin an assault on all enemies," Brigid said, listening to the instructions running through her head in a solicitous whisper. "We have to stop this somehow, Kane."

Kane smiled grimly. "So we go to Alpha Level, block the broadcast, kill the baron…" He trailed off at Brigid's look.

"The command's already in action," she said. "Someone needs to get down there, to Zeta Level, and stop the assault from launching."

Kane nodded. "I'll go find the baron on Alpha," he said. "You think you can handle the war machine on Zeta?"

"No," Brigid said, a tremor of incredulity in her voice.

Kane smiled grimly, clamping Brigid by the shoulders. "You'll think of something, Baptiste," he assured her.

Then Kane reached for the door handle once again, pulling the door toward him and exiting the comms room. As he stood in the doorway he turned back to Brigid. "But think quick," he said.

Brigid nodded solemnly as Kane disappeared from

sight. "Think quick," she muttered to herself. "I guess that's as good a plan as any."

With that, Brigid plucked up one of the fallen tranquilizer guns and exited the room, hurrying along the deserted corridor toward the bank of elevators that would take her down to Zeta Level.

Chapter 28

The metal doors slid closed as Kane entered, and then he stood surrounded by the gray walls of the elevator. He checked his blaster—just a tranq gun, no sign of his old Sin Eater, but then he had had no time to search for it. The ville must have weapons—the whole place was geared for war, Kane realized now, Sandcats and Deathbirds all armed and ready for some grand assault that only the Supreme Magistrate truly understood. Was there a baron up there, in Alpha Level? Kane wondered. The barons were all dead. Whoever was sending that signal to follow Protocol Zero-zero-zero was someone new, not a hybrid baron like the inhuman monsters he had spent so much of the past decade rebelling against.

Kane waited as the elevator ascended, a grid of lights on the wall plate beside the door indicating his passage through the levels, from Cappa to Beta, then Beta to Alpha. There was no specific security protocol in place, but the elevator only went as far as Alpha Level, not right up into the towering suites assigned to the baron him or herself. To reach that area, Kane needed another elevator or he would walk.

The elevator halted with a graceful hush of hydraulics. Alpha Level. Kane stepped to the side as the doors slid back, revealing a gray-walled corridor beyond. He had his blaster in his hand now, up and ready to fire. There were eight shots in the blaster, eight thick needles of tranquilizer that could be used to drop a foe without killing them. Kane hoped that would be enough.

The corridor was empty. Kane ducked his head out, glancing along both directions to be certain no one was waiting to ambush him. There was nothing.

He paced out into the corridor, scanned swiftly for the other elevator that would take him up higher into the restricted area. It was not obvious, nothing stood out. But there were stairs running up the side of the bank of elevators, going all the way through this central tower with its white cyclops-like eye that stared out across the ville like a sentry. Kane pushed the door open gently, making sure not to make too much noise. Then he stepped into the stairwell—white-walled with pockmarks in the concrete—and hurried up the steps, keeping his knees bent, his movements light and fluid.

Two turns of the staircase and he was at the next level, a closed door waiting before him, white like the bland walls of the stairwell itself. Kane pushed against it, placing his ear to the door and listening. *Nothing.*

He took the handle in his left hand, the blaster poised in his right, and pulled the door slowly back toward him, holding his breath. Nothing happened. The door pulled back with just a whisper of noise from its heavy hinges like a breath, and then Kane could see what lay beyond. It was a service corridor, with access to ventilation ducts and removable wall panels for wiring and pipe work. The walls were painted gray.

Kane stepped out into the corridor and decided on a direction, pacing away from the stairwell door, alert to any danger. His pointman sense was on high alert now, that fabled, almost Zen-like ability to sense possible threats that remained unseen.

And then—

"Mary had a little lamb," his Commtact blared, "its fleece was white as snow. And everywhere that Mary went, the lamb was sure to go."

Kane stopped, almost stumbling, such was the surprise that the silly tune had engendered within him. He waited for the music to pass, refocusing his mind on the situation at hand, reaching out with honed senses for any hint of movement that could spell ambush.

A moment later he was at the end of the service corridor, a blind corner that turned out into the lobby of the baronial suite. Kane tensed, preparing to reveal himself to whoever waited beyond.

As KANE ASCENDED through the ville, Brigid caught her own elevator car down into its very depths. She, too, was armed, having taken one of the discarded tranq guns from the unconscious Magistrates in the communications room. Having assured herself that the blaster was armed, she slipped it down into the large pocket of her gray overalls, pushing it back behind where her right arm fell. However, it would hardly stand up to scrutiny, as what pockets she had were not designed to hold a full-length blaster like this.

Brigid watched as the white lights on the wall plate moved, indicating her descent through the ville. Cappa, Delta, Epsilon. At Epsilon, the elevator car stopped and the doors drew back after a moment's hesitation. Brigid stepped back to the farthest wall of the car, from where she could best see who entered and what lay beyond. Two people were waiting there, clad in gray uniforms with peaked caps drawn down over their hair. One was a man, taller than Brigid—taller than Kane, in fact—but lanky and undernourished, his thin wrists showing where his overalls were just too short in the arm.

The other figure was a woman, gray haired with a face defined by its wrinkles, the puckering around her lips like the crags of a cliff face. They were nothing special, Brigid knew, just workers from the factories here, probably on a rest break when the alert had come through to follow Protocol Zero-zero-zero. Neither spoke to Brigid, nor did anything to really acknowledge her.

They have been turned into dead people, Brigid told herself with disgust. Living dead, going through the motions of life, breathing and eating and moving, but with nothing else to their lives but the instructions laid out by the regime.

Each regime throughout history had done this, in its own way, Brigid knew. Each regime had tricked and cajoled and forced people to behave in a certain way, filling their minds with dull buffers that weighed down their individualism, their real thoughts. Because thoughts were dangerous, Brigid knew. Thoughts were what brought the system to revolution, changed the structures of power.

Brigid smiled as the nursery rhyme refrain began to trill through her ear canal via the Commtact. Today, her thoughts would be the most dangerous ones of all, and they would bring this whole sick project to its knees.

She waited as the elevator descended farther, plummeting down to Zeta Level.

His back flush against the wall of the service corridor, Kane peeked very carefully out into the lobby beyond. It was a wide area, walls painted white with two couches on opposing walls along with a desk between them, behind which an empty chair stood. Behind the desk there waited a tinted-glass wall containing a set of double doors.

The lobby area was empty and the doors were closed. Kane could see two uniformed Magistrates where they waited through the tinted glass, inside the baronial suite itself.

Kane ducked back, considering his options. There was no way to shoot the Mags from here, not with a tranq gun through the glass, and certainly not without drawing attention to himself with the noise—attention that would most likely involve more Magistrates swarming on the scene.

But to step out there and reveal himself was suicide—there was nowhere to hide with that great glass wall between himself and the Mags on guard. He considered for a moment longer, wondering if there was some other way into the baronial suite from which the message was being broadcast. The service corridor—that was it!

Kane rushed back along the corridor, retracing his steps.

THE DESCENDING ELEVATOR HALTED. Brigid and the two nameless citizens of Ioville—literally nameless, their old names long excised from their rewritten minds—waited as the doors drew open on their hidden tracks to reveal Zeta Level.

Brigid gasped, her heart skipping a beat at what she saw. The other occupants of the elevator filed out without comment, but Brigid simply stood there, gazing at the spectacle before her. The elevator had opened onto a gigantic underground room, covering at least half the area of the ville above it. The room was filled with Sandcats and Deathbirds, hundreds of them, arranged in neat, perfectly straight lines, their profiles facing Brigid, and each one poised for launch through the distant doors at the far end of the room. The ceiling was high—high enough to allow those Deathbird helicopters space to take off, Brigid realized with dread.

All around, gray-clad citizens were marching in step, making their way toward the waiting vehicles, guided by Magistrates in their dark uniforms and grim helmets. Brigid estimated there must be over four hundred people in the room, with more filing in from arriving elevators even as she watched. The Mags were handing out weapons to all the citizens as they passed, like adding components to a production line. Each took a weapon, checked that it was loaded before holding it pointed at the floor in a loose grip, never once slowing their step.

The elevator doors began to close and Brigid stepped forward, pushing them back as she entered the garage space with a dwarfing sense of incredulity.

"Mary had a little lamb," her Commtact chimed, reminding her to remain sane, remain Brigid Baptiste.

The two residents who had arrived in the elevator with her were already in one of the orderly queues, waiting to be handed their weapon before joining the disciplined assault force who were waiting to leave the ville.

Brigid felt it, too, in that moment as hundreds of gray-clad, almost identical citizens prepared for invasion. She felt the pull of Protocol Zero-zero-zero, deeply programmed into her subconscious via the Terminal White system that dictated every human being's behaviour who had ever lived within Ioville's walls.

Brigid's attention was drawn to a great flash of light, brighter than the overheads that hung from the high ceiling. She turned to look, saw two great, rollback doors drawing apart like a nut being cracked, and beyond them the vista of falling snow.

Brigid realized something horrific then—something so obvious that she could hardly believe she had not realized it before. Terminal White had been perfected—it no longer required citizens to remain in the ville to be affected by its subliminal commands. The program would continue to dictate to Ioville's citizens outside of the walls.

And not just Ioville's citizens. They in turn would take Terminal White out to the other villes and to the Outlanders who lived beyond them, reprogramming the whole human race into mindless slaves who functioned only for the pleasure of the dead barons, following the protocols of a project that should have died with its instigators years ago.

Brigid stood there, stunned by the awareness that it was up to her to stop this whole terrible nightmare.

Chapter 29

Grant was beginning to remember things. The nursery rhyme had played through his Commtact four times now, each time disrupting the mind-dulling effects of Terminal White.

He staggered between the waiting vehicles on Zeta Level, ducking under the tail rotors of Deathbirds, out of step with his fellow mechanics who had been tasked with opening the great doors to the outside. When the doors began pulling back, Grant stood away from them, hidden in the shadows between two white-painted Sandcats, eyeing the brightness of the falling snow beyond the garage doors. Zeta Level was set beneath the ville, in the place where the Tartarus Pits were located in Cobaltville and others, serving to provide a ready stream of cheap labor to the ville above. But here, that space had been turned over to storage, service and repair of the mighty vehicles that made up Ioville's war machine. When the rollback doors drew back, they revealed a snow-covered slope that led upward and out of the ville, beyond the high walls, out into the wilderness of British Columbia.

Grant realized as he saw that snow falling, that hint of a world beyond the one he had become trapped within over the past three weeks, that something was very, very wrong.

"Mary had a little lamb," the voice in his ear cooed,

and Grant looked behind him, wondering just where it was coming from.

"I had a name once," he muttered as he staggered bewildered between the waiting vehicles. "A name and something else—a mission."

He continued walking, making his way toward the open doors to the outside.

BRIGID WAS STRUGGLING with the enormity of the task ahead. She had the pistol, eight shots of tranquilizer fluid that could drop a man without killing him. Facing her were four hundred personnel with Magistrate combat training, armed with handblasters and backed by three hundred Sandcats and one hundred Deathbirds. Her only viable option was to stop this invasion before it started.

Brigid marched swiftly through the queuing ranks who were waiting to be issued with their blasters, past the two people who had accompanied her in the elevator from Epsilon Level. She pushed the person who was second in the queue aside, taking the docile woman's place without a word of complaint. The Magistrate handing out the weapons to the waiting citizens took no notice of Brigid's disruptive actions, and in a moment he was facing Brigid with a handblaster held out for her.

"Let me get two," Brigid said with a smile.

The Magistrate looked at her emotionlessly, the majority of his face hidden behind the hard lines and tinted visor of his uniform helmet. "Move on to your position."

"My position requires two blasters," Brigid insisted.

Beneath his helmet, the Mag seemed to cock his head in confusion. Beside him, another Magistrate was handing out weapons to his own orderly queue of citizens, and he took no notice of what his partner was doing.

"Two," Brigid said, holding up two fingers. "Baron's orders."

The Mag seemed almost to shut down at this, standing before Brigid perfectly still as he tried to process her request. Behind her, the queue of gray overalls waited without complaint, ready to serve, to perform this last designated task, the one that ended in the annexing of the world in the name of the dead barons.

Finally, Brigid stepped forward and took a second pistol from the Magistrate's hands, the one he had picked up to hand to the next citizen. He seemed unable to respond, unable to react with this subtle change in routine. So long as it did not threaten him, it seemed he would let it pass.

In a few moments, Kane had reached a turn in the service corridor on Alpha Level. To his left side there lay a removable wall panel behind which wiring and pipe work would be located, access to which was necessary during the construction and maintenance of the ville. To his right there was a similar panel, this one located low to the floor, an access hatch leading into the guts of the building itself.

Kane checked behind him before slipping the tranquilizer pistol into his holster. He worked the catch on the right-hand panel, pulling it away from the wall. Then, ducking down onto his knees, he crawled inside.

Within it was dark, and it took a few seconds for Kane's eyes to adjust. The space behind the hatch was high, tall enough for Kane to stand without touching the ceiling. Pipes ran along the walls here, but there was still enough room for a man to work his way along the space walking sideways. Kane hurried along the space, making his way around the outside wall of the

Administrative Monolith, squaring the circle to reach the baronial suite.

Kane moved through that darkened space for three minutes, making slow progress because of the tightness of the gap, the only light coming from the distant wall plate that he had removed. Then he hit a snag. A jumble of crisscrossing pipes stood in his way, the gap between them not wide enough for him to move through. Brigid maybe, Domi certainly, but not him.

He looked around, narrowing his eyes against the darkness, trying to find another route. There was something glinting in the dark, he noticed after a moment, and as Kane focused on it he saw it was one of four matching circles of metal, each one about as large as the pad of his thumb.

Screws.

Kane reached forward and felt his way around the area marked out by the screws. It was some kind of wall plate with a grille over it, the surface rough to the touch. The plate was two feet square.

Kane reached for the screws, pushed his thumbnail into one and began to turn it. It took a moment to get it to move, but once it started moving the unwinding proved easy, if laborious.

Inside of a minute, Kane had all four screws off the wall. He pulled the wall plate away—held now by nothing but habit and dirt—and placed it gently at his feet without making any more sound than was absolutely necessary.

Once the plate was on the floor, Kane pressed his hands to the top of the opening and poked his head inside. It was a large space, big enough for a man to crawl through, with a tiny beam of light glowing against the side of the wall closest to Kane just five feet from where his head was. Kane reached inside with both arms and pulled himself up and into the hidden shaft.

It was tight in there, claustrophobic, and it smelled of dust and grease and oil. Kane was forced to crawl, his head held down so that it did not brush the top of the shaft. He moved artlessly toward the shaft of light, flailing like a beached fish as he dragged himself down the metal-walled shaft.

In a moment, Kane was at the beam of light. It was three inches wide and seemed to be emanating from a position to his right and a little way above him. Kane struck the wall with his hand, listening to the echoes and wincing as the sound carried down the metal shaft. The dull thud of a solid wall came back.

Bringing his legs forward, Kane maneuvered himself into a sitting position then reached up for the source of the beam of light, tracking it with his outstretched palm. It was hard to make out in the darkness, but after a moment he detected another shaft, the same proportions as the one he was sitting in, this one stretching vertically upward to a second grille.

Kane floundered in place for a moment until he could bring himself up into the vertical shaft. Once there, he stood, his feet close together in the cramped space beneath them, his head level with the grille.

Kane pressed his face to the grille, felt the rush of ice-cold wind against his skin. A brightness of light flickered against his eyes, but all he could see was whiteness, as bland as any corridor in Ioville.

Efficiently, Kane reached around the grille, locating the same four screws as he had removed from the preceding grille to gain access to this area. They took a little effort, especially with the cramped conditions within which he was called upon to work, but after a few minutes Kane had all four screws off the wall and was holding the grille in place by the pressure of his arm against it.

Carefully, Kane pulled back the grille with his right hand, holding it in place until he could get his fingers around it. Then he pulled it back with both hands, drawing it down so that he could let it slide very gently to the floor without making too much noise. As he pulled the grille away he saw what the whiteness was that he had peeked at through its open slats—it was snow, falling from above and covering everything in sight. He was looking outside the tower.

NOW BRIGID WAS armed at least. Slipping one of the two blasters into her waistband and retaining the other in her grip, she hurried through the milling ranks of citizens who had massed between the waiting lines of Sandcats and Deathbirds. Many were already inside the Sandcats, Brigid saw, both in the driver's seats and in the gun turrets that stuck out from the rooftops. Those guns could be automated, Brigid remembered suddenly, recalling the systems she had helped screw into place on the factory production line.

Brigid kept moving, making her way toward the open doors to the outside that loomed in the distance, snow billowing beyond their threshold. If she could maybe close those doors, prevent this invasion force from leaving the ville—maybe then she might just stop this madness.

Brigid was twenty feet from the doors when her hopes were dashed. The first Sandcats surged out of the open doors, five vehicles exiting in unison, crossing the snow-blanketed slope in a rumble of roaring engines.

Brigid cursed, running faster toward the doors, hoping to spot a mechanism with which to close them. Instead she saw something better—a man she recognized from countless adventures together. A man who had become bewildered and almost lost to the curse of Terminal White. A man called—

"Grant!"

KANE PULLED HIMSELF through the gap in the vent, drawing himself up until he could gain purchase. He was four hundred feet up, almost as high as the tallest structure in the ville. Snow billowed about him, landing on his dark gray uniform and helmet, the air cold against his skin. The wind howled in his ears like a wounded animal.

He hung there for a moment, dangling half-outside the removed vent panel, taking in the view. He was on the outside of the Administrative Monolith, the central and tallest building in Ioville. Everything was covered in a thick layer of snow, ice crystals glistening in the morning sunlight that filtered reluctantly through the silvery-gray cover of the clouds. Kane took it all in, recognizing the design as identical to Cobaltville, where he had grown up and served as a Mag for so many years.

Besides the falling snow, Kane could see a line of movement from one of the gates, gray shadows against whiteness as a line of vehicles emerged from the garage area beneath the ville—white-painted Sandcats moving out to the horizon, distributing the new regime to the rest of America. For a moment he wondered if he should be with them, join in their quest to bring order to the chaos…

"Mary had a little lamb," his Commtact blurted in his ear, reminding him to stay focused on the mission and to remember who he was.

Kane watched the line of Sandcats—five in total—

their white exteriors almost invisible against the blanket of snow. "Go get 'em, Baptiste," he whispered. "If anyone can figure a way to stop this it's you."

With those words, Kane hefted himself out of the little vent and pulled himself out onto the wall of the tower. It sloped gently, narrowing as it rose above Kane toward the building's summit, while the white eyelike circle was located ten feet below.

He scrambled for a moment, searching for a way to stay outside the building without falling off. There was a ledge there, running close to the top of the "eye," almost hidden by the settled snow. Kane got his feet on it and, pressing his hands against the wall and clinging there as best as he could, began to work his way around the building's exterior.

"GRANT!" BRIGID CALLED.

Grant looked up at Brigid as she called his name. He was standing by the door mechanism wearing gray overalls that strained at his muscular frame. His eyes were wide with confusion, his expression sour.

He saw the pale-faced woman come running toward him, her lithe form moving with the ease and grace of a natural athlete, the cap falling from her head to reveal a cascade of red-gold curls.

"Grant," Brigid said again as she reached him, her pace slowing to a trot.

Grant looked at her cockeyed. "Do I know you?" he asked. "I think I do…"

Around them, the mounting roar of engines was growing louder as the second wave of Sandcats was despatched through the open doors to the Zeta Level garage.

Brigid smiled tentatively.

"I feel like I know you," Grant said, "but things are so muddled."

"Grant, it's me," Brigid said. "It's Brigid. We work together for Cerberus—"

"Cerberus," he repeated tentatively.

"You, me and Kane. We were investigating something and somehow became caught up in it," Brigid hurriedly explained. "We've been tricked. We don't belong here."

Grant looked around him as the second wave of Sandcats trundled away up the slope. "Where are we?" he said. "Ioville?"

"Yes, but we don't belong here," Brigid told him. "They brainwashed us but I broke the programming. I got Cerberus to stream a cue through our Commtacts—"

"Commtacts…" Grant muttered, his brows furrowed. Gradually a smile began to tug at the corners of his mouth. "Brigid Baptiste, am I glad to see you! I thought I was going—no, *had gone*—mad. All that damn music in my head."

"No, that's just the cue," Brigid said. "It disrupts the signal that tells us to obey."

Grant nodded uncertainly. "So, just what the hell is going on here?"

"Kane's here," Brigid explained quickly. "He says there's a guy at the top who has ultimate authority over this ville. He's the one who's ordered all this—" she gestured to the garage where gray-clad citizens were climbing into the waiting Sandcats, ready to launch the next wave "—and Kane's going to find him and stop the instruction being broadcast."

Grant looked at the garage, its assault vehicles and its milling army of citizens turned soldiers. "And what about us?"

"Take this," Brigid said, handing him the spare hand-blaster she carried, "and help me find a way to stop this army from starting a war."

Grant nodded, his expression fixed in grim determination as the next wave of five Sandcats started their engines and began to accelerate toward the open doors of the garage.

THE WIND WAS picking up.

Clinging to the outside of the Administrative Monolith, Kane moved cautiously around a sharp corner and straight into a gust of wind.

"Dammit!" Kane cursed.

He hung on, his feet shifting on the narrow ledge as he struggled to keep his balance while the icy wind drummed into his face, throwing snow and flecks of ice at him like stones. The wind howled with all the passion of a wolf howling at the full moon, a deep moaning that seemed to press against Kane's bones beneath the protective layers of his uniform.

Finally, the gust passed.

Kane was holding his breath, clinging on for dear life, hundreds of feet up from the ground. He scrambled, moving quickly but carefully, shifting his weight and balance as he swung around the corner of the towering building and onto the next ledge. He moved like a spider, finding the tiniest of grips, the narrowest of ledges as he clambered across the building's facade.

A moment later, Kane spotted what he had been looking for. Up ahead, almost hidden by the reflection of the silver-gray clouds, was a bank of windows, stretching almost the full length of the wall, taller than a man. This would be the baron's suite, from which he or she might look out to survey Ioville.

Kane scrambled along the edge of the building, crab-walking along the ledge until he was close to the window. Inside was what appeared to be a conference room, with a long formal table about which over a dozen straight-backed seats had been arranged. A more forgiving couch had been placed against one wall. There were five figures in the room—four Magistrates standing guard and facing away from the windows, and the fifth sitting on the couch looking out at the majestic vista of the snow-clad ville. The man wore a variation of the Magistrate uniform and had iron-gray hair tied back in a ponytail. Kane looked at the man for a few seconds, recognition dawning. It was Supreme Magistrate Webb, the man who had shown him around the ville all those weeks ago.

Kane stepped back for a moment, securing his footing on the narrow ledge he stood on before reaching slowly for his holster and pulling loose the pistol. Darts against a window—not ideal, but if he could get the angle right…?

"Mary had a little lamb," his Commtact chimed in the background.

Clinging on to the exterior wall with his left hand, Kane swung himself out as far as he dared and targeted the very center of the closest pane of glass, where the glass was weakest.

Kane sighted down the barrel of the blaster then fired, sending one of the tranquilizer darts rocketing toward the giant glass pane from just a few feet away. The projectile struck the window dead center and embedded there, fixed halfway through the glass. Around the dart, a spiderweb of cracks seemed to materialize from nowhere, spreading outward in a crazed pattern that emanated from the center.

The man on the couch looked up in surprise, and two of the Magistrates turned at the whisper of noise that the striking dart had made, sounding like a flint striking stone. Then Kane came into view, leaping across the gap and striking against the window with full force, causing the fractured glass to shatter inward as he smashed against it, feetfirst.

"What th—?" Supreme Magistrate Webb bellowed. "Stop him!"

As one, four gray-clad Magistrates spun, turning their weapons on the rolling form of Kane as he came thundering through the window and into the room.

Chapter 30

On Zeta Level, Brigid and Grant watched as the third wave of Sandcats shot up the snowy slope and out into the world. Already there were fifteen Sandcats outside now, fifteen that the Cerberus warriors would have to stop or capture.

Grant was already running back into the garage area, leading the way through a wide aisle toward the massing vehicles. "Come on, this way!" he shouted, and Brigid hurried to follow.

"I thought you were going to close the door," Brigid called to him.

"Yeah, me, too, but that won't stop those 'cats that already got out, will it?" Grant said as he reached the first of the waiting vehicles. He shoved a citizen aside with a forceful blow.

"Then what did you have in mind?" Brigid asked as she pushed her way into the crowd after Grant.

Grant pointed. "Deathbird," he said. "I'll pilot, you play percussion."

Brigid smiled at his turn of phrase—it was the kind of silly off-the-cuff remark that only Grant could offer in such a fraught situation. The kind of remark no one in the thrall of Terminal White would ever make.

Together, the two Cerberus warriors clambered up into the cockpit of the Deathbird, with Grant adopting his familiar position in the pilot's seat.

"Just hope I can still remember how to pilot one of these," he muttered.

Brigid showed him her bright smile. "Kane always says you're the second-best pilot Cerberus will ever have," she assured him.

Grant raised an eyebrow as he ran through the pre-flight checks. "Second, huh? Let's see if we can shoot for first."

With that, he powered up the engine and the grass-hopper-like form of the modified Apache helicopter took off from the deck, its powerful rotors swooping around with a low thrum that echoed through the cavernous garage. The mystified crowd of citizens and Magistrates ran out of the vehicle's path as it began to surge forward, making its way at a thirty-degree angle toward the open doors to the ville.

SNOW FLURRIES BILLOWED in through the shattered window, icy winds turning the whole of the baronial suites cold in just a few seconds.

Kane had arrived in the baronial suite in a shower of shattering glass and snow. He rolled as he landed, bringing his blaster up to target the Magistrate at the center of the group of four. The blaster fired with a *pfft* of expelled air, sending a dart into the Mag's chest and causing him to sink to his knees even as he squeezed the trigger of his own weapon.

Kane didn't like to fight Magistrates—no matter the terms he had left the service under, he still respected these men for doing their jobs to protect the masses, still considered it a noble pursuit. So using the tranq gun on them eased his conscience at least. He knew, however, that being struck by one himself meant he would be sent back to Processing, reprogrammed as a mindless machine, albeit one born of man and woman. It was a terrible fate, he knew now, and one he intended to do his utmost to avoid.

Kane moved, mentally dismissing the tranquilizer dart that rocketed past over his head.

The other Mags in the room were targeting him with their own weapons. Highly trained, highly skilled and three against one—Kane's only hope was to keep moving and use their numbers against them.

"Stop him!" yelled Webb, getting up from the couch with a look of horror on his face. He had never expected anything like this, not after nine years of Ioville's strict, orderly lifestyle. It was almost too hard for him to process that it was happening.

Kane dived under the long conference table as the Mags blasted, sending a triple assault of tranquilizer darts at him. Two darts struck the table while the third embedded itself in the far wall.

Kane slid on his haunches, rolling under the long table as the Magistrates tried to get a bead on him. He could hear Webb calling for backup—presumably the other two Magistrates he had spotted waiting by the glass wall beside the designated elevator.

Kane peeked out from under the table, lined up a shot and blasted, sending a tranquilizer dart into the fleshy part of an unsuspecting Magistrate's leg as he scrambled past in his search for Kane. The man seemed to tumble in on himself, crashing to the deck in a jumble of splayed limbs.

Mags turned, two shots firing across the room at the space where Kane had briefly emerged. But Kane had already retreated, scrambling on elbows and knees beneath the conference table, heading back toward the broken window through which he had entered the room.

He halted at the far end, still hidden by the table and temporarily protected from an assault from above. He eyed the room from beneath the table, listened to the strange—almost eerie—lack of discussion from the Magistrates. Like everyone else in the ville, they had been reprogrammed by Terminal White. They functioned on orders now, not instinct, cared nothing for discussion.

Kane could see two sets of feet pacing around opposite sides of the table, three more pairs of legs at the end of the room dressed in uniform gray. He could not confirm a clean shot—there were chair legs in the way and he didn't want to waste his limited ammunition in case there were even more Mags up here waiting to challenge him.

Kane moved swiftly, scrambling out from under the table even as the two Magistrates to either side of him lunged down with their weapons thrust before them. Twin tranquilizer darts zipped across the space between the table, passing out into the room before disappearing from view—one embedding itself in a far wall while the other sailed off through the open window behind Kane.

Kane was still moving, leaping atop the table and running along it at full pelt. Both Mags looked up with surprise, realising that their victim had already left his hiding place. A blur of motion, Kane kicked out at the one to his left, striking the man's exposed jaw with the heel of his boot and sending him flying backward.

The Mag to Kane's right drew his weapon up to blast Kane but Kane ducked, dropping beneath the shot like a limbo dancer, then skidding on his knees along the table as the launched dart cut through the space where he had been a fraction of a second earlier. The dart zipped across the room and embedded itself in the Mag to the left, who was still tumbling backward, trying to regain his balance after being kicked in the jaw.

"Mary had a little lamb," Kane's Commtact chipped in, but he was too focused to pay it any attention.

THE DEATHBIRD POWERED through the garage area toward the open doors. Below, the fourth wave of Sandcats was just beginning to launch, picking up speed as the five white-painted vehicles accelerated toward the open doors to the ville.

"See that switch?" Grant shouted to Brigid, raising his voice over the deep thrum of the cycling rotor blades.

Brigid looked to where Grant indicated, high in the rooftop where the door frame met empty space.

"Door mechanism," Grant said.

Brigid nodded. "On it," she confirmed, powering up the Deathbird's weapons. The Deathbird featured a turret-mounted chain gun, as well as missile armaments, and Brigid brought these to life with a few flicked switches, keeping one eye on the moving Sandcats below them. "Things are about to get messy," she warned as she jabbed the switch to prime the chopper's Sidewinder missiles.

An instant later, the long shaft of a Sidewinder missile went spiraling away from the Deathbird, rocketing toward the target that Brigid had selected—the high-placed mechanism which worked the rollback doors. The missile struck a second later, exploding in a burst of brilliant flames and noise.

The explosion was followed by an automatic alarm, spinning red lights bursting into life and a low *arooga* noise echoing through the garage on a repeat cycle.

Grant fed speed to the Deathbird, driving it for the opening up ahead where the Sandcats had disappeared.

He knew what was going to happen next, goosed all the speed he could from the chopper's powerful engines as he hurried to exit the ville.

The ville's central computer responded immediately to Brigid's assault on the doors. Along with the alert, there came a loud creaking sound, and the mighty roll-back doors began to shudder and move, drawing inward to close the opening and seal the ville from the perceived attack. Of course, no assault had ever been imagined from inside the ville, so sealing the doors would only serve to lock the army inside the garage, where they could do no further harm. The doors would seal in ten seconds, powered by mighty motors located in the roof and floor.

Grant ducked his head as he maneuvered the Death-bird past the flames that licked the ceiling and out through the closing doors, navigating the rapidly clos-ing space. A moment later, his Deathbird came shoot-ing out of the ville as behind it the doors sealed closed on almost three hundred Sandcats, ninety-nine Death-birds and a whole army of willing, brainwashed soldiers.

"Now, let's see if we can put a stop to this mess," Grant growled as the Deathbird ascended past the sloped ramp and up into the air.

SLIDING TOWARD THE END of the conference table in the baronial suite on Alpha Level, Kane rolled, bringing one leg out to halt his course. Ahead of him, two Magistrates had joined Supreme Mag Webb at the double doors to the room, and Kane saw Webb himself duck out of the conference area to safety.

Not yet, you don't, Kane promised.

The Mag to Kane's right was taking aim again, strid-ing forward to get closer to his fast-moving jack-in-the-box of a target. Kane ducked his head as the tranq gun fired, and he growled as something struck the hard surface of his Magistrate helmet—it was a dart, impacting but not penetrating the protective headgear.

Then Kane was barreling forward again, his head still down, feet scrambling on the table and lifting his body up with finesse. He slammed headfirst into the Magistrate who had just fired, with a sound like a crack of thunder. The Mag went flying back under the impact, Kane's helmet having struck him high in the chest, knocking the breath out of him.

Kane could not stop his momentum in time and he went sailing off the edge of the table and out beyond, tumbling onto the glass-strewn floor of the conference space. The Mag he had knocked down began to get back up woozily while the other two came charging into the room, their own tranq guns raised.

OUTSIDE, THE SANDCATS were well camouflaged in the snow. Hurtling away from the ville, Grant brought up an infrared display on the Deathbird's console, homing in on the heat generated by their engines as he navigated through the falling snow. There were fifteen out here, each one showing up as a tiny blip of red on the target grid. The burning door of the Ioville garage showed as a smudge of red behind them on the display.

"We won't have enough missiles to stop all of them," Grant warned Brigid.

"Missiles versus Sandcats is the obvious choice," she lamented, "but I guess we'll improvise after we run out. Any ideas?"

"I've seen a well-placed rifle shot take out a Sandcat once," Grant suggested.

Brigid's eyes flicked to the storage space of the Deathbird, searching all around. "We don't have any rifles," she told him. "Anything else?"

"I'll get ahead of them and do what I can," Grant said, driving more power to the whining engines. "After that, we'll just have to see how the cards get dealt."

The Deathbird whipped through the air, following the course of the Sandcats a hundred feet above them. Any moment now, the 'bird would be showing on their sensor equipment. The Cerberus teammates could only hope that the crews assumed that the helicopter was a part of the assault force until it was too late to matter.

A moment later, the Deathbird overtook the second wave of Sandcats and powered on through the masking curtain of snow to pass the first. Grant urged more speed to the engines, bringing the mechanical death machine farther ahead of the speeding Sandcats before bringing it around in a fast-moving loop.

A moment later, the Deathbird was set to hover as Brigid primed the missile ports again, launching the first of the Sidewinder missiles at the Sandcat leading the charge. The missile left the Deathbird with a cough of propellant, cutting through the air with a whoosh. Even as it left its housing, Brigid launched a second missile at the next Sandcat, a third at the vehicle to that one's left.

Grant watched grimly as the Sidewinders hurtled away from the windshield and were lost in the curtain of falling snow. A moment later, three explosions showed like fireworks launched in the whiteness where the first Sandcats were destroyed.

At the gunner's panel, Brigid flicked switches and prepared the next cluster of missiles for launch.

KANE LEAPED TO his feet and grabbed for a chair, lifting it by its high back as two of the Magistrates fired their long-nosed pistols. The familiar sound of the expulsion of compressed air cut through the whistling winds that came through the broken window. Kane used the chair to deflect one of the tranquilizer darts while the other went a foot wide of his right shoulder, thudding into the far wall with a thump.

Still hoisting the chair, Kane ran across the room as the Mags prepared to fire again, launching it at them both with a grunt of effort. The makeshift projectile spun through the air, crossing five feet before striking the Mag to the left hard in the chest, knocking him from his feet. The second Mag fired again, but the speeding dart missed Kane by the merest fraction of an inch.

The third Mag had recovered and stood now, taking aim at Kane from the distant end of the room where the window had been shattered. Kane spun as the man fired, dipping his head just in time as the dart hurtled toward him. Kane was perfectly in line with the other Magistrate and, as he ducked, the dart missed him and embedded instead in his foe's right shoulder, ruining his aim even as it loosed its drug into the man's system.

Kane watched as the struck Mag fell to his knees, a line of drool appearing almost instantly down his chin where it could be seen beneath the grim visage of the Magistrate helmet.

Webb was watching from the doorway and he seemed to realize how things might turn. He had received the report on Kane after his DNA had been flagged on entry to Ioville, knew the man was a spectacular fighter and survivor. His eyes widened as Kane drew a bead on him through the door, ducked back as Kane stroked the trigger, launching his latest tranq dart at him. The dart embedded into the wooden door, striking so hard that it split the wood and prevented the door from slamming closed.

OUTSIDE IOVILLE, GRANT was juking and weaving as the Sandcats began to fight back, running the turret-mounted chain gun hot as he sent stream after stream of bullets at his camouflaged targets, turning another Sandcat into an angry ball of flame. Brigid set another Sidewinder missile away, sending it into the heart of the battle where it ripped another Sandcat in two with a roar of splitting metal.

But the Sandcats were fighting back now. Perfectly camouflaged against the white backdrop, their blister cannons functioning via computer program—a positronic brain linking the guidance system to the drive shaft—the seven remaining Sandcats had turned their powerful USMG-73 heavy machine guns to the air, tracking their attacker as Grant dipped in and out of range. Great swarms of bullets propelled from the roof-mounted turrets, tracking the grim shadow of the Deathbird as it was momentarily revealed through the falling snow.

"I can't keep us from getting hit for much longer," Grant spat, lifting the joystick and raising the Deathbird thirty feet in a violent swoop.

Brigid felt her stomach rush up into her throat, tamped it down with a gulp, her hands never leaving the fire control panel. She tapped out another command sequence, watching on the targeting screen as the heat trail of a Sandcat glowed amid the chill ground.

"We're all out of missiles," she told Grant as she tapped the controls, launching the last remaining sidewinder missiles and tracking their path on her display panel. A moment later, she received confirmation that the two missiles had struck their intended targets, cutting the remaining Sandcats down to just five.

Grant brought the Deathbird around again, strafing low over the fast-moving Sandcats as they weaved past the smoldering shells of their ruined comrades, trails of thick black smoke billowing into the sky. His turret gun blasted again, sending a stream of bullets across the ground as they sought their target, kicking up plumes of snow before meeting with the windshield of a Sandcat and peppering it with holes, continuing up across the roof and destroying the turret blister in a sudden burst of flames.

Another Sandcat spied the Deathbird swooping past to attack its teammate and sent a thick stream of bullets at the fast-moving aircraft. The Deathbird wavered in the air as the line of bullets struck its belly and flank, rattling against it like rain on a tin roof even as Grant tried to lift out of harm's way.

"We've got to stay low if we're going to finish this," Brigid shouted as Grant fought with the controls, turning in a tight spiral as he ascended higher through the falling snow.

"How many targets do we have left?" Grant asked, shaking his head at the prospect.

"Four showing," Brigid told him, "assuming there aren't any armed survivors out there looking for revenge."

"And assuming they haven't got the doors back open," Grant growled with another shake of his head.

"Grant," Brigid said in a reasonable tone, "we've faced worse odds than this. Get me down there and I'll keep those Sandcats distracted while you set them up for the killing blow."

Grant pulled on the joystick, bringing the Deathbird around in a roar of straining engines. "You're nuts, Brigid—you know that, right?" he yelled as they dipped through another storm of bullets.

A moment later the Deathbird was racing toward the ground. Brigid was out of her seat and working the controls of the door, disabling the catch and holding it in place with a tight grip as alarms went off through the cabin.

"Just get me down there and make sure you're there to back me up, okay?" she bellowed over the roar of the rotor blades.

An instant later, Grant brought the Deathbird down to the ground with a rough bump. Brigid Baptiste leaped from the chopper, slamming the door behind her before racing away. In a moment she was lost to the obscuring curtain of falling snow.

Chapter 31

Brigid felt the chill of the atmosphere straight away, inwardly cursed the loss of her shadow suit from when she had been inducted into the Ioville population.

Behind her, the Deathbird ascended into the skies, disappearing behind the thick curtain of snow in a few moments, the drone of its rotors lost almost as quickly. She tuned that noise out, listening instead for the rumbling engines of the Sandcats. There were four heavily armed war machines moving on high alert and ready to shoot down anything they distrusted—anything or anyone.

Brigid ducked her head to make a smaller target, ran for the nearest engine noise. It came from her right, muffled by the snow but still audible here on the ground. It sounded like a distant beehive, the angry buzz of the bees as they toiled at their honey-making.

Brigid spotted it a moment later, as the snow fell all around her. Painted white, the Sandcat was well camouflaged in the snow, but its tracks were black rubber and its guns poking out of the blister bubble were black, too. The guns were firing, away from Brigid, up into the atmosphere where Grant had taken the Deathbird chopper.

Brigid ran, pushing herself on against the drag of the snow beneath her, closing the distance between herself and the Sandcat as it held position, blasting into the skies. As she neared, she drew the blaster that she had shoved into her overalls.

Brigid came at the Sandcat from behind, leaping onto the back armor plate—the very plates she had been responsible for securing in the factories of Ioville—clambering up the side. A moment later she was on the roof, running across it toward the protruding blister where the cannons blasted their continuous stream of bullets into the sky.

The blister was empty, Brigid saw; the whole operation was automated. The heavy machine guns kept firing, steam billowing from the hot metal of the muzzles, unaware of Brigid's presence just a few feet behind them. Brigid took her blaster and slammed it down against the protective glass of the turret, searching for the spot where the guns met the inner workings. She ducked beneath the stream of bullets and pulled the trigger on her blaster, sending a stream of her own into the gun's housings. The mount shuddered as Brigid's 9 mm bullets struck it, and one of the twin pair of guns ceased firing with a cough of straining metal. The blister turned, aware now of Brigid's presence, the remaining USMG-73 still sending that near-ceaseless stream of bullets from its nose as it spun.

Brigid dropped from the Sandcat roof, falling in a swan dive, arms outstretched and handblaster still clenched in her right hand while the Sandcat's bullets cut the air above her. As she fell, a dark shape appeared through the falling snow, Grant's Deathbird come to deliver the killing blow. As the Sandcat tried to track Brigid with its lone operational blaster, Grant zeroed in on his target and unleashed a stream of bullets across its armor plating, ripping through it and into the guts of the engine.

In an instant, the Sandcat's engine erupted in a fireball, ripping through the metal beast in less than five seconds. Brigid hit the ground in those same seconds, landing on her back against the forgiving snow, allowing it to absorb her impact.

As the flames caught the turret gun, the bullets were set alight, and for a moment a stream of flaming bullets spit across the land before the whole vehicle was lost behind a curtain of flame. A moment later, the turret stopped firing.

"One," Brigid said to herself as the Sandcat melted before her eyes. That still left three more to track and destroy. She only hoped that Kane was having more success wherever he was.

STILL MOVING, KANE brought his tranq gun around and behind him, running backward and blasting over his shoulder to take out the Magistrate by the window. The man fired at almost the same moment, and Kane was forced to roll out of the dart's path as it hurtled toward him, his own shot missing.

Kane fired again and the man fell back as the dart hit him in the gut, flipping him almost over himself as he crashed to the ground amid the shards of window.

The last of the Mags steadied his aim with his free hand and shot at the moving target Kane presented, firing off two more tranquilizer darts even as the Cerberus warrior weaved and leaped his way across the length of the room.

Kane blasted again, sending the last of the Magistrates slamming against the back wall in a blur of ruined armor. He had just one shot left.

He ran for the wooden door at the end of the room,

his dart still poking from its cracked face. He saw Webb running ahead, glancing over his shoulder at his pursuer.

"It's all over, Supreme Magistrate," Kane bellowed. "I'm shutting this whole place down."

"Never!" Webb barked.

Kane watched as Webb slipped through a gray service door ahead, accompanied by a momentary roar of rushing air. Kane's boots slapped against the floor as he chased after the retreating gray form.

BRIGID STRUGGLED BACK to her feet amid the burning wreckage of the Sandcat. Around her, she could hear the growl of engines as the other Sandcats—three in all—came to investigate, circling to find the attacker from the skies. They didn't know that she was here—that was the one advantage she had just now and she had to use it.

She hurried through the snow, arms pumping, legs driving, booted feet dragging into the snow. Up ahead, scarcely visible through the falling flurries of white, she saw the familiar black snouts of a Sandcat's turret guns. The guns were moving, circling as they tried to locate the Deathbird that had attacked them.

Brigid ran as fast as she could, eyes fixed on that swiveling cannon and the man silhouetted in the blister bubble behind it. It would have been so much easier if they had all been automated, but Brigid knew that only a fool wished for a different enemy in the heat of battle. The vehicle was still moving, trying to locate Grant and to present a moving target at the same time.

Brigid ran straight for the sloping windshield, weapon in hand, arms pumping as she clambered over the front fender and ran up the windshield itself.

The driver watched her, his jaw dropping with surprise. Brigid pointed her blaster down and squeezed the trigger as she ran, sending a shot from the Sin Eater into the windshield, at barely twelve inches from its surface. The bullet struck, creating a spiderweb of fractured glass across the windshield, but the glass held.

The gunner had been alerted to Brigid's presence by then, but she continued scaling up the vehicle, getting off another shot as she targeted the figure inside the gun blister. The protective glass there cracked but held, even as the USMG heavy machine guns powered up and began coughing out their stream of death at the redheaded Cerberus warrior.

Brigid sprang across the roof, moving swiftly, firing again, blasting shot after 9 mm shot into the blister as a stream of bullets cut the air to either side of her.

The blister gave off a loud crack of noise, like thunder in the night, and then the whole bubble-like structure collapsed in a shower of shattering safety glass.

In the air above, the Deathbird seemed to come swooping out of nowhere as Grant arrived to provide backup to Brigid's fearless assault. The gunner in the turret swiveled his guns again, targeting not the woman who had now sprung behind him, but the mighty helicopter that was stealthily picking off his colleagues, using the snow for cover. The machine guns rattled loudly as they spit their deadly cargo, drilling a flurry of slugs across the front pane of the Deathbird even as it brought its own turret gun to bear.

Brigid kicked the gunner in the face, knocking out a tooth in a brutal twist of his jaw. Before the gunner could say a word, Brigid brought her blaster down and fired, delivering 9 mm death to the man in a instant, skull and brain matter exploding in a sudden burst of blood.

Brigid leaped from the Sandcat as bullets came battering against its front end from the guns of the helicopter. There was a brief clattering of bullets on metal, and then the whole front of the Sandcat seemed to rise up before catching light and exploding in a shower of metal splinters. Its driver had the sense to leap from the ruined vehicle just before the bullets made their mark, and he was buried in a cloud of snow, glass and metal as the vehicle went up in flames.

By that time, however, Brigid was already running, searching for her next target in the masking field of whiteness.

KANE HESITATED AS the service door drew closed. He was walking into an ambush and he knew it. Whatever was through there, it would give Webb ample time to coldcock him.

Unless Kane moved faster.

"Mary had a little lamb, its fleece was white as snow," the Commtact bleated, reminding Kane to stay sane, remain in control of himself. "And everywhere that Mary went, the lamb was sure to go."

The door was sealed. Kane tried the handle, discovered it was locked.

"Dammit," he cursed, taking a step back from the door. He was trying to figure out where the door led, trying to piece together the muzzy, broken map he had for Ioville in his head. He was in the Administrative Monolith on Alpha Level, a level where, strictly speaking, only barons and their most trusted advisors and guards could access. Of course there were no barons left. So what would be through the door?

Steadying himself, Kane kicked out at the lock. His booted foot slammed against it with a crash, shaking the door in its frame. The door withstood the assault, and Kane kicked it again—three times in total, until his final kick was met with the sound of splintering wood as the door, lock and frame all gave.

The door lurched lopsidedly in the frame. Raising the tranq gun in his right hand, Kane pushed against the door with his free hand, thrusting it firmly away from him, into whatever room lay beyond. He was greeted by the roar of rushing air, impossibly loud to his ears.

IN THE COCKPIT of the Deathbird, Grant looked at the readouts with disdain. The vehicle had taken some serious hits, and it was barely holding together after that last assault.

He scanned the snow below, searching for Brigid and the remaining Sandcats. By his reckoning there were still two of the assault vehicles out there somewhere, and all it would take is a lucky shot to finish the Deathbird.

He circled around, searching the ground for Brigid, using the infrared to find the last of the running engines amid the heat sources of the burning Sandcats.

BRIGID HAD FOUND another Sandcat, this one creeping beside a high snowdrift that partly shaded it to disguise its silhouette, its turret whirring around as it sought its sky-bound enemy. She hurried toward it, moving in a semicrouch better to not be seen.

Brigid hunkered down, running toward the vehicle, keeping to its left flank. The gun turret circled again, searching the skies and ignoring her on the ground. As it swept past, Brigid straightened up and began to run faster, powering through the snowdrifts until she was at the side of the Sandcat. Switching weapons, she grabbed the handle of the gull-wing passenger door and pulled, hoping it would open for her. It did, recognizing her fingerprints as a citizen of Ioville's.

Brigid swung inside even as the driver turned to face her, a look of surprise on his face. Brigid brought the tranq gun up and fired, sending a single tranquilizer dart slug into the driver's chest before he could issue a challenge. The driver slumped in the seat, crashing against the steering column accompanied by a loud honk from the horn and a sudden swerve of the front wheels.

Above her, Brigid heard a second man cry out in surprise. "What is going on down there, Citizen 014M? My aim is being compromised."

Brigid poked the nose of her blaster through the gap between the seats, targeting the foot of the man operating the turret and sending another dart into the man's ankle. The ankle blurted out a spray of blood and the man shrieked in pain.

Brigid hurried through the rear of the Sandcat and fired again, this time directing her shot straight up into the gun turret. The gunner had no time to react, and he took the tranq to the gut, openmouthed in surprise.

Brigid took just an instant to catch her breath before reaching for the gunner and dragging him out of his seat. A moment later she had taken the gunner's place—dangerous in light of her inability to contact Grant to warn him of the manoeuvre—slipping behind the triggers of the turret gun.

Brigid spun the gun, searching for the last Sandcat.

It appeared without warning on the targeting scope, blasting shot after shot at a familiar silhouette that the scope had detected in the sky above—Grant's Deathbird.

As Brigid watched, the Deathbird seemed to circle on the spot and began to drop from the sky, the roar of its failing engine suddenly loud even inside the Sandcat's cabin. A moment later the insectile frame of the chopper appeared above her, cutting through the snow like a scythe before slamming into the front end of the Sandcat within which she was seated. The Sandcat shuddered, an alarm sounding as its structural integrity was shattered.

Chapter 32

Air rushed around Kane in a deafening wall of noise.

He was standing on a metal catwalk in a towering cylinder like a turbine, a gigantic fan dominating the tower thirty feet below. The fan's huge rotor blades were a blur of rushing movement as they sucked air into the ville from outside, delivering it to the ventilation system that fed the Terminal White program to every citizen in Ioville. It was the air processing plant, located inside the tallest building in the ville.

The realization took less than a second. In that time, Webb pounced on Kane, appearing from his hiding place just behind the door and driving one bladelike hand down on Kane's extended right arm in a karate chop.

Kane huffed in pain and surprise, kept hold of his grip on the blaster, but his aim was lost.

Webb followed up his attack with a whirring punch to the side of Kane's head, the blow ringing in Kane's ear even as he staggered forward.

"You're on the losing side, son," Webb snarled as Kane stumbled on the rail-less catwalk, teetering close to the edge and that deadly drop into the whirling blades of the fan. "Terminal White is the future for mankind. Petty squabbles like this one are to be relegated to history forever."

Regaining his balance, Kane dipped low and swung out with his left fist, swiping for the gray-haired Webb.

The older man stepped aside, bounding on his feet like a prize fighter, impossibly nimble.

"People need to choose," Kane snarled. "Free will—"

"Free will is a concept as outdated as the dinosaurs," Webb hissed, leaping at Kane and delivering a vicious kick to the Cerberus warrior's gut.

BRIGID LEAPED FROM the gunner's seat as the Deathbird struck the front end of the Sandcat, scrambling into the cabin as the vehicle shuddered and began rolling backward with the impact. The words "Mary had a little lamb" played in her ears again, too close and too loud even over the sound of the explosion. The front of the Sandcat burst into sudden flame and the windshield was turned into a pane of searing heat.

Brigid looked around, searching for the side exit, away from the burning front of the vehicle. She pulled the door back only to be greeted by the *ratatat* of bullets that ricocheted around, narrowly missing her.

"Shit," Brigid muttered, pulling the door shut again. It was armored, and that armor should hold off the attack for a few seconds at least. Outside, the remaining Sandcat must be targeting this one because of its proximity to the fallen Deathbird, making sure of the kill.

Grant, Brigid thought with a pang of regret. He might just have survived—the Deathbirds were well armored and designed to protect the pilot. But he wouldn't last long—not unless she did something—and nor would she.

Brigid looked all around her, searching for an option. Bullets rattled against the side of the Sandcat, flames licked at the front. Brigid's eyes fixed on the rear, where the armored back panel protected the interior from any assault. She remembered the work she had been assigned in the factory, Designated Task #004—Manufacturing. Brigid had worked these back panels dozens of times, secured them, removed them, checked them and attached them all over again, all part of her routine as a productive citizen of Ioville. She reached for the cabin repair kit without even looking, snatched the box from its housing against the port-side wall above the fire extinguisher. In a second, she had the tool kit open and had removed the screwdriver, tossing the rest of the contents and the box aside with a clatter.

Crouching down, Brigid worked at the screws with practiced haste as the sound of gunfire rattled all around her. She glanced back just once to eye the grounded chopper, saw its dark lines peering through the flames that had taken hold of the front of the Sandcat.

In moments, she had the panel unscrewed, discarding the screwdriver and pulling the heavy metal plate toward her in the same swift movement. The panel fell toward her with ease, and Brigid shuffled back on her haunches, letting it drop to the deck with a clang.

A moment later Brigid wriggled out from the open back of the Sandcat, ducking down as bullets flew all around her. She scrambled away from the burning vehicle, creating as much space as she could before the fire hit the fuel tanks and it went up in flames. It did so just five seconds after Brigid exited, the shockwave sending her crashing into the snow.

With the explosion, the sound of gunfire came to an abrupt halt.

KANE STUMBLED BACK, once again too close to the guardless edge of the catwalk, the spinning fan roaring beneath him.

"A few decision makers," Webb spit. "That's all that mankind needs. Everyone else will follow."

"Because you force them to," Kane growled, circling a few steps away from the drop, keeping his eyes on Webb.

The Supreme Magistrate looked almost amused at Kane's words, amused and angry. "That's man's history, Kane," he retorted. "The leaders who make their decisions by force, ensuring everyone follows for their own good."

"Not me," Kane muttered, shaking his head. He raised the tranq gun, pointing it at Webb. "I'm closing this hellhole down and taking you in."

Webb smiled then, an ugly show of teeth on his drained face. "Taking me in?" Webb said with evident delight. "Listen to yourself, Kane—you're a Magistrate through and through. You can never escape that."

Kane glared at Webb, sighting down the barrel of his blaster. "Hands where I can see them, asshole."

Webb raised his arms slowly, hands open to show that they were empty. "You have such potential, Kane," he said. "You broke away from the baron's regime, broke my conditioning here with Terminal White. The future needs good men to lead the masses. You could be one, if only you can set aside this insanity and let me show you."

Kane heard the words and for a moment he wanted to trust Webb. He felt the wave of sympathy, of obedience, something inside him that said to trust the man who stood before him. It was Terminal White, he knew—that hidden program that sapped his free will, that sapped everyone's free will.

"Put down the blaster, son," Webb was saying. "There's

plenty for us to talk about, and a whole world waiting for good men to pull it back from the abyss."

He knew it was a trick but still Kane lowered the tranq gun, the calming effect of the Supreme Mag's words and his own sense of obligation setting in. He tried to remember why he shouldn't trust this man, why he should not trust his words.

"Put the blaster down," Webb said again, and Kane lowered the weapon and loosened his grip, dropping it to the catwalk. It landed there with a clang of metal on metal.

"That's it, son," Webb said gently. "Now, why don't you and I get out of here and start figuring out how to fix the mess that you and your old friends have caused."

Citizen 620M nodded, a Magistrate and a citizen of Ioville once more. Webb strode across the catwalk, closing the brief distance between them.

BRIGID LAY IN the snow, ears ringing with the aftereffects of the explosion. After a few moments—she could not tell how long it had been—she became aware of a figure moving toward her, trudging through the snow and standing over her.

She looked up, groggy, her head pounding, and saw the gray-clad legs of a Magistrate.

"Are you okay, citizen?" the Mag asked. To Brigid's ringing ears, the Mag's words sounded like they were coming from the far end of a very long tube.

She could fake it, maybe, get drawn back to Ioville and potentially get sucked back into the whole Terminal White program that would destroy her identity. No, never that.

Brigid drew the blaster up from beneath her belly and fired, sending a 9 mm bullet up in the direction of the wavering silhouette of the Magistrate. The man leaped back in surprise, the bullet going far wide of his position.

Brigid watched as the Mag pointed his right arm at her, a gesture accompanied by the familiar sound of a Sin Eater powering from its hidden wrist holster.

WEBB WALKED ACROSS the catwalk to Citizen 620M.

Then Kane's Commtact chirped to life, trilling the familiar refrain in his ear: "Mary had a little lamb, its fleece was white as snow. And everywhere that Mary went, the lamb was sure to go."

"Dammit," Kane spit, realising what was happening and where—and *who*—he was.

Webb saw the change in Kane's demeanor and had the presence of mind to step back even as Kane swung for him. He was quick but not quite quick enough.

The knuckles of Kane's right fist cuffed Webb across the jaw, and Kane was already turning around to target the older man again, drawing his left fist around for a vicious second blow. Kane's follow-through slammed into Webb's jaw, sending the man back on unsteady feet, his head reeling.

Kane came at him again, driving his right fist in a cross that powered into Webb's torso like a pile driver, striking the man hard in the gut so that his feet almost left the deck.

Webb staggered backward, his left heel slipping over the edge of the catwalk. "You're a fool, Citizen 620M," Webb snarled, "and you will obey me. It's all just a matter of time." He took a step forward, away from the edge.

Kane stood before Supreme Magistrate Webb, and his eyes narrowed in anger. "People aren't machines, Webb," he said. "They have faults and foibles and sometimes, yes, they make wrong decisions and they fight."

"Pah," Webb spat. "We almost lost the world once. Man tried to kill himself in one grand nuclear suicide that almost aced every living creature on the planet. And you and your ilk want to go back to that?"

Kane stepped back, eyes searching the metal catwalk for his dropped blaster. He spied it lying a few feet away, strode across the catwalk toward it. "I'm taking you in," Kane stated grimly, bending down to pluck the weapon from the deck.

Webb lunged at him then, leaping across the scant five steps to where Kane was plucking up the tranq gun, screaming in sheer frustration over the sounds of the whirring rotor blades. Kane turned and blasted, sending a projectile with flared fins and a pointed end at his attacker. The tranquilizer dart drilled through Webb's dress uniform just below his breastbone, burying its nib into the inferior vena cava vein that ran up the center of his chest.

Webb staggered back at the impact of the dart, the momentum of his attack drained to nothingness. "Kane, you bloody fool," he muttered, even as he stumbled back two short steps.

A split second later and Webb was falling, dropping over the edge of the guardless catwalk toward the fiercely spinning rotor blades of the air intake fan. Kane watched him drop, moved to grab him but already knew he was too late, the effect of Terminal White just slowing his reactions that infinitesimal amount so that he would never quite reach the plummeting man.

Webb dropped thirty feet until his fragile human body met with the spinning metal blades of the fan. It was over a moment later, blood and tattered clothing and hunks of bone and gristle flying in all directions as Supreme Magistrate Webb was diced into so much offal by the whirring blades.

Kane watched over the side of the balcony, disgusted by what he saw. The fan ground to a halt with a groan of straining mechanics, something jammed in its center stopping the ceaseless spin of the rotor blades. And where a man had been mere moments before, now there was just a bloody smear splashed up the circular walls, a red tribute to a pitiless idea called Terminal White.

Free will or no, all men die the same, Kane thought grimly, when they meet with destiny.

In his ear, the words of the familiar refrain began playing once again: "Mary had a little lamb, its fleece was white as snow..."

BRIGID WATCHED AS the Magistrate drew his Sin Eater, powering it into his hand with a practiced flinch of the wrist tendons. Then his helmet and head exploded in a burst of blood and bone, and the Mag crashed to his knees in the snow.

"What th—?" Brigid asked, pulling herself up from the ground.

As the words left her mouth, Grant came trudging toward her, his broad shoulders and hulking form familiar, even obscured as they were by the falling snow. "One man in the last Sandcat," he explained. "Saw him exit and followed. Guess he wanted to see whether any of his partners had survived after the Deathbird struck the other 'cat, and that's how he found you."

Brigid looked at Grant in confusion, the sense of relief welling inside her. "You saved me," she said.

"From what I understand, you saved me from something worse," he replied. "The whole brainwash thing," he added when he saw the confusion on her soot-smeared face.

"I thought you'd died with the Deathbird," she said.

"Almost did," Grant told her. "Bailed out at the last second. Kicked the door open and just jumped."

"Pretty risky," Brigid said, struggling to process it all. "You could have died."

"Figured 'could have' was better than 'almost certain' anyway," Grant told her. He held out the blaster in his hand. "Lucky you gave me this."

"Yeah," Brigid said. "Lucky." What else could she say?

Chapter 33

The fans had stopped turning. Ventilation was at a standstill and the whole of Ioville seemed suffused with a choking thinness of air. When Webb had plunged into the fan's blades he had stopped the rotors and the intake had trailed off. Terminal White needed the constant intake of air to feed it and so feed the system. Without that, it began to stagnate fast.

Kane looked around the lifeless, empty corridors of Zeta Level, where he, Brigid and Grant were helping gather the remaining citizens of the ville before letting them back out into the wild and freedom. The snow machines had been halted, and enough Sandcats remained that the people would have transport over the icy plains until the snow began to thaw. The Sandcats would need to be disarmed, of course, but that could be done.

It would all take time, Kane knew. For the next few months, this area would remain a winter wonderland created by one deluded man in service to masters who had long since died.

Kane thought of Webb and how he had died, destroying the very system he had brought to life for all these years. The man had been doing his duty, however wrongheaded that duty may have been. Falling into the fan like that was a rotten way to die.

"Hey, Kane? You okay?" Grant asked as he helped usher another group of bemused citizens toward the waiting transports. Their mental programming was a mess now, but at least they were docile and open to taking orders.

Kane looked at Grant and grimaced. "Just thinking," he said, before correcting himself: "Hoping."

"Hoping for what?" Grant asked. "A better tomorrow?"

Kane shook his head. "That could have been any of us," he said. "What Webb was doing here—could just as easily have been me or you recruited out of the Mag Division to head up this ghastly project to turn people into obedient drones."

Grant nodded somberly. "It's a sobering thought," he agreed.

"Webb bought into it," Kane continued, "did his duty, believed what he was doing was for the common good. He wasn't a madman—he was just fed the wrong lies and got too caught up in his obligations to ever question them."

"The evil of the barons seems to reach further than we ever imagined," Brigid said as she joined her partners, overhearing the last of Kane's speech.

"So what were you hoping?" Grant asked Kane after a moment.

"I shot Webb with a tranq," Kane recalled. "I'd hoped to bring him in, close this place down, maybe rehabilitate the man behind it. But he slipped and he fell into the fan before I could..." His voice trailed off. "I just hope that that tranq had kicked in by the time he struck the blades. Because, whatever all this was, however easy it is for us to step back and say we stopped a great evil, no man deserves that death. No Magistrate—not one just doing his duty."

Grant bowed his head, his expression fixed and grim. "Amen, brother," he said. "Amen."

CAT ALPHA RETURNED to the Cerberus redoubt shortly after, exhausted mentally and physically, the whole experience under the thrall of Terminal White hanging over them like a heavy cloud. Back home, Kane assured his companions that he intended to sleep for a week, and nothing short of the end of the world was going to wake him.

"Time for a drink before you turn in?" Grant asked as they trudged through the cave-like corridors of the redoubt. "Maybe a bite to eat, too?"

Kane looked from Grant to Brigid and nodded. "Yeah," he announced. "Feels like I've been eating day-old leftovers for the past few weeks."

"Nutritious goop," Brigid said. "Trust me, I know. I was the one preparing it."

The three of them entered the Cerberus canteen, a vast room of plastic-covered tables and fixed seats, and halted. There, over a dozen personnel were enjoying a respite from their shift, including Lakesh, Brewster Philboyd, Donald Bry and Reba DeFore. Each of them was dressed in the plain white jumpsuit that was the uniform of the Cerberus facility, with the blue vertical zipper running up its center. Despite their physical differences, it made everyone look the same.

"My dearest friends," Lakesh called, spying Kane and his team standing at the open door to the canteen. "Come over, join us. We were just discussing your mission report."

Kane turned to his companions, his face the picture of doubt. "I think maybe we've all had enough of hanging around matching suits for one day, huh?"

Brigid and Grant laughed in agreement before pushing Kane ahead of them and into the throng of their trusted—and occasionally uniform—colleagues.

* * * * *

JAMES AXLER

DEATHLANDS®

END DAY

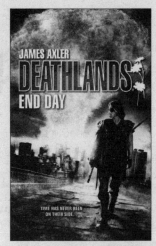

Time has never been on their side...

On the heels of Magus, a Deathlands nemesis, Ryan and his companions find themselves in a place more foreign than any they've encountered before. After unwittingly slipping through a time hole, the group lands in twentieth-century New York City, getting their first glimpse of predark civilization—and they're not sure they like it. Only Mildred and Doc can appreciate this strange metropolis, but time for reminiscing is cut short. Armageddon is just seventy-two hours away, and Magus will stop at nothing to ensure Ryan and his team are destroyed on Nuke Day. As the clock ticks down, the city becomes a deadly maze. The companions are desperate to find their way back to Deathlands...but not before they trap Magus in New York forever.

Available March 2015 wherever books and ebooks are sold.